THE WOMAN IN WARD 9

Naomi Williams grew up in Yorkshire and now lives in London with her family. She studied English at university and started her career teaching English and Drama, before becoming a full-time writer. *The Woman in Ward 9* is her first psychological suspense novel.

THE WOMAN IN WARD 9

Naomi Williams

HEADLINE

First published in Great Britain in 2025 by
Headline Publishing Group Limited

1

Cataloguing in Publication Data is available from the British Library

Paperback ISBN 978 1 0354 1113 9

Typeset in Sabon by CC Book Production

Printed and bound in Great Britain by Clays Ltd, Elcograf S.p.A.

Headline's policy is to use papers that are natural, renewable and
recyclable products and made from wood grown in well-managed forests
and other controlled sources. The logging and manufacturing processes
are expected to conform to the environmental regulations
of the country of origin.

The authorized representative in the EEA is Hachette Ireland,
8 Castlecourt Centre, Dublin 15, D15 XTP3, Ireland
(email: info@hbgi.ie)

HEADLINE PUBLISHING GROUP
An Hachette UK Company
Carmelite House
50 Victoria Embankment
London EC4Y 0DZ

www.headline.co.uk
www.hachette.co.uk

For Emma Warburton
With love and thanks for decades
of inappropriate laughter

Prologue

The police sirens woke me, or perhaps it was the splintering of wood as they smashed down my front door. 'Woke' is the wrong word. *Brought me around.*

Blinking into semi-consciousness, I raised my head. Sticky hair clung to my face and lips. I swiped the strands from my cheek and lifted on to my elbows, confused about why I was lying on cold, wet tiles.

Still disoriented, I shifted on to my knees. Then, head spinning, I dropped my chin to my chest. Cold dread flooded my veins when I saw the front of my white shirt was drenched red. My stomach heaved. I retched but felt no pain. I tapped at my body under the shirt. No pain. This was not my blood.

My breath halted. I couldn't bear the wet cotton next to my skin. I tugged at the material with trembling fingers while my thoughts floundered, searching my memory for what the hell had happened. But I found nothing but a petrifying void.

I tried to stand, but my legs shook too much to bear

my weight. There were shouts behind me. I turned to see people moving, then stopping, standing still, all eyes on me.

Again, everything went black.

Chapter One

Monday

I fanned out the folders of psychiatric case notes on the desk in the therapy room, checking the labels for my new client's name: Laura Winters. I pictured the skeletal information inside: the patient's age, marital status and close family connections, profession, pre-existing conditions and why they'd been detained. It was my job to add flesh to the bones of Laura's file in our sessions, the first of which was due to begin in a few minutes' time.

A small, square photograph of a dark-haired woman was stapled to the front of the file. She was around my age, and appeared unassuming enough, but I knew from experience that having an innocent-looking face meant very little. The true self lived behind that mask of skin and muscle. I examined her eyes, wondering exactly what secrets lay beyond her blank gaze. Was this the face of a witness, a victim or a killer? I had less than a week to find out. With that amount of pressure, it was no surprise a tension headache was building in my skull.

Lifting the file, I questioned again why she'd asked for me

specifically, insisting I was the only psychologist she would speak to. Since she was a practising psychologist herself before being detained here, I presumed it was because of my reputation – the good part at least, the name I'd made for myself for improving support in women's shelters. She clearly hadn't heard about the mistake I made last year. Shoving the thought to one side, I glanced at the clock above the door and saw time was ticking down to our first meeting.

I turned to look at the small room allocated for the daily therapy sessions. I'd been disappointed by the unwelcoming atmosphere – its naked walls and one high window enclosed by a wire panel. Natural light was more conducive to helping a patient relax. The strip light buzzing quietly in the centre of the ceiling, throwing out a harsh fluorescent light, was about as far away from natural as it was possible to get.

Two squat sofas sat at right angles, one against the far wall and another to the left, taking up too much space. On a pine coffee table, a box of tissues was open, one tissue lifted like a white flag. I found the room stuffy, claustrophobic almost, so God knows how someone suffering from a mental health condition would feel – especially since I'd been told the door must remain locked at all times, even when I was in there alone.

I thought of the spacious office I rented back in London, decorated in calming greens. My clients sat in the comfortable armchair and would invariably stroke the teal velvet as they talked, the soothing movement of the pile soft under their fingers. If anyone rubbed the synthetic pink fabric covering the sofas in this room, they'd probably cause enough static to burst into flames.

Picturing my office made me yearn to be back home. My back ached from sleeping on the shallow mattress in the room Heaton Place had provided for the duration of Laura's treatment. When I shifted in the chair, the soles of my shoes rasped on the same carpet tiles that lay on every floor of the facility, including the staff quarters in the adjacent building where I'd been given a room. It was an old barracks, and I'd spent sleepless hours shivering with cold under a flimsy duvet. The contrasting heat in this modern treatment facility was stultifying. I turned to the slim radiator behind the desk and put my hand on the metal, snatching it back when it burned my palm. I kneeled to look for a temperature dial, hoping that wasn't the moment my new patient arrived to be greeted by my rear end. There was nothing but metal pipes tracking into the floor.

Sitting back at the desk, I lifted my hair to allow air to my neck. Sweat gathered at my hairline. This was no way to begin a course of treatment. I was meant to be relaxed and prepared, not a sticky mess. I cursed myself for letting my curiosity about Laura's case draw me in. I could have turned this job down. I could have told them it was too much of a sacrifice to put my life on hold, but there was something alluring about all the secrecy. I had to admit my pride played a part too. It was flattering to be picked out of the crowd; and it was exactly the validation I needed after the inquiry.

A clanking noise outside the window made me start. It was followed by the roaring of some kind of engine. That was all I needed. Heavy machinery moving nearby wasn't the best background noise for a therapy session. I looked again around the sparse room, noting how it affected my emotions. There was a bleakness to the bare walls, a hopelessness to the sagging sofa cushions. The difference to my usual, homely working environment reignited my guilt about the privileged life Connor and I led, especially in comparison to the experiences of some of the women I worked with in shelters. It would be good for me to spend some time in an environment like this, I decided. It would remind me to appreciate my freedom and my home comforts. I missed Connor already. Thankfully, in a few days' time, we'd both be back home where we belonged.

The roaring outside stopped, leaving the room unnaturally silent. I closed my eyes and tried to ignore my nagging sciatic nerve. I needed to remember why I was here. After what happened to my sister, I'd trained as a psychologist specifically to help women who'd suffered trauma. This incident was undeniably traumatic. However uncomfortable I was in this room, accepting this strange case was the right thing to do, and the sooner I helped Laura to remember what happened that night, the sooner I could go home. Assuming I could help her in the six days of intensive treatment we'd been allocated.

I opened the file with 'Laura Winters' printed on a white label stuck next to the photograph. I would do what I could to help Laura reach into her subconscious for the memories she'd locked away. Since there was no one else at the scene and no body, the police urgently needed to know whose blood it was, and where that person was now; especially if there was any chance they might still be alive.

Laura Winters. I said her name out loud in the quiet room. I repeated it until my mouth knew the pattern and the word sounded peculiar to my ears, just a sequence of sounds with no meaning. That's all language was, I mused, a jumble of sounds to communicate what goes on in our heads.

Or what we want people to think goes on in our heads.

We also use language to lie. That's why I had been called away from my cosy office and my comfortable home; why I'd left behind my lovely husband and my lovely life to stay in this soulless facility until Laura Winters could tell me what really happened on that terrible night.

She says she doesn't know why she has lost her memory, or why she was found alone, soaked in someone else's blood. The only thing she seems absolutely sure about is that I am the only psychologist she can – or will – talk to.

Chapter Two

I looked up from the file at the sound of the door unlocking. A woman wearing a suit smiled as she took a tentative step into the room. 'Emma?' She walked towards me, and two more people followed, a muscular man with slicked-back hair and a thick-set woman, both in blue scrubs. They had lanyards hanging around their necks printed with the words 'Heaton Place' attached to rectangular laminated identification cards. I needed to remember to ask for my ID. I hadn't been given my key fob yet and didn't like the feeling of being trapped in locked rooms, even if it was for my own safety.

I closed the file and walked around the desk, holding out my hand. 'Yes, Emma Best. Good to meet you.'

'Melanie,' she said. Her cold hand shook mine then disappeared behind her back. 'Melanie Coldwell. I'm the supervising psychologist at Heaton Place. Nice to meet you.'

She looked very young to be a supervisor. Her brown eyes were large in her slim, elfin face and the dark pixie-cut of her hair made her look like a pretty young girl rather than a senior member of a psychiatric team. I supposed she must've had adequate training for the advisory position. I did peer supervision with the two other psychologists I shared space with in London but, despite multiple requests since my work gained recognition, had never taken on the role with someone outside my professional circle. I didn't like saying no, but I'd never felt I had the extra capacity. One day I planned to, when I had more time.

I glanced behind Melanie at the two people in scrubs. She turned. 'This is Aidan and that's Julie, they're our orderlies.' They lifted their hands in greeting and nodded. I noticed a skull tattoo on the inside of Aidan's forearm, with an old-fashioned key between the jaws instead of teeth. It seemed in bad taste, bearing in mind where he worked.

'I'll be sitting in with you in the sessions with Laura,' said Melanie.

'Oh.' My hands clenched at my sides. It was a long time since I'd been observed. 'I didn't know I'd be supervised during the sessions,' I said, attempting to keep the annoyance out of my voice. I wasn't a probationer and could do without being marked out of ten for performance. Harvey had been my supervisor for years. Our relationship had been built up over the last decade and I planned to FaceTime him to discuss any issues which arose. Being watched by this woman would make me uncomfortable.

Melanie lifted a hand to stop me. 'Don't worry about that. I'm only here to support you. Think of me as your wing woman. We thought, since you've been generous enough to give up your time, you deserved a minion to help out.'

'A minion?' I raised my eyebrows. That was an interesting word for a senior practitioner to choose. She probably wanted to ingratiate herself because, if I walked away, the Heaton Place management would be in a difficult position. I sighed inwardly. That was the problem with working with mental health professionals: you ended up second-guessing every word they said, mining for motivations.

I gestured to the sofas. 'Shall we sit?' Melanie moved to the seats, but the orderlies stood awkwardly in the centre of the room, hands grasped behind their backs. The space wasn't big enough for so many people. 'Do you two need to get on with . . .'

'Every patient in Ward 9 is allocated two orderlies.' Melanie interjected as they walked towards the door. 'They'll be with us every time we meet, outside the room.' The door clicked closed behind them.

'That's unusual,' I said, aware of the lumpy sofa under me and the threadbare fabric of the cushions. Even a private secure mental health unit like Heaton Place didn't have money to waste on staff just standing around.

'The thing is' – Melanie glanced up at the door, then back at me, her eyes serious – 'we have to keep this quiet until we have some answers, so there's a small team designated solely to this case. Nobody in the unit other than the management, myself, Aidan and Julie know about what happened or why Laura is here. To anyone else, she's known as Patient X. The police and lawyers have taken the unusual step of agreeing to stay silent for six days, in the hope Laura will disclose who was injured and where they are now. There was so much blood at the scene it's unlikely anyone could survive ... but while there's even a slim chance, we have to do everything we can to get Laura to remember what happened that night.'

'And that six days is set in stone, is it?'

Melanie nodded. 'Yes, I'm afraid so. Until Saturday. After that, if we don't have what we need, she'll be moved to a prison hospital and the police will have no choice but to take her in for formal questioning. Because her mental state is precarious, that's our worst-case scenario, and I really hope it doesn't come to that. Then there's the potential media circus waiting to happen if we don't handle this well. Everyone likes a mystery, don't they? We don't want it getting into the press for the world to make their judgement before we've had a chance to uncover the truth.'

'I understand.' Images of Connor yelling at journalists and photographers who waited for me on the street outside our house last year flicked across my mind.

Melanie's eyes flitted to the door, then back to me. She picked at a thumbnail.

'I take it you think Laura might be dangerous?' I said, attempting to manage my rising sense of unease.

Her hands stilled. 'Why do you say that?'

'Two orderlies, your bitten nails.' I nodded to her thumb. She separated her hands and made them into fists in her lap. 'Me being brought here so quickly and all the secrecy.' I looked at the camera to the left above the door, round and black like the pupil of an eye. 'The constant surveillance.'

'That's the thing,' said Melanie. 'We still have no idea. She could be a witness, or a victim. Or, she could be a murderer. Until she can remember what happened that night, we don't know what she is, or whose blood she was soaked in. That's why we have to take reasonable precautions.'

'Okay, I understand,' I said. 'I've read the file, but I'd like to get your take on Laura Winters. What do you know at this stage?'

Melanie's fingers unfurled and she laid her palms flat on her tailored trousers. 'She was discovered alone, in her own home, by the police after a neighbour reported hearing someone screaming. She was catatonic and covered in blood that wasn't hers. It was all over her hands and the front of her clothes, but when they got her to hospital, she had no injuries.'

'None at all?'

Melanie lifted her hands then let them slap back on her knees. 'None. Physically, she was fine, but she was in a stupor, completely unresponsive.'

I stood and walked back to the desk to retrieve the file and my pad and pen. 'Was she given any stimulants to bring her around?'

'No, she became responsive before the doctors made a decision on what to do, but she appears to have no memory of what happened.'

'Nothing, not even fragmented?'

'Nothing.'

I scanned the typed report, checking that all this information was there. Sitting, then turning back to Melanie, I said, 'And how is she now, would you say?'

She looked up to the left and I imagined her visualising the patient and searching for the right words to describe her. 'Lucid.'

I wrote 'lucid' on the first page of the pad.

'And anxious.'

I scribbled that down too. 'Anxious. Right.' I tapped the end of the pen against my teeth. 'I think we'd all be anxious in her situation, wouldn't we?' I read the report's last paragraph again. 'So, she's insisting that she'll only speak to me.' I looked up. 'Why do you think that is?' Melanie's cheeks coloured and hot blood rushed to my face. She must've thought I was fishing for compliments. If only she knew how unsure I'd become of my own abilities of late.

Even before my professionalism was brought into question, years of working with women who'd been in abusive relationships had impacted my worldview. I'd spent a decade treating people suffering trauma and PTSD and, in that time, I'd seen the filthy, damaged underbelly of humanity. Despite my best efforts, what I saw at work had bled into all areas of my life, leaving me feeling helpless, sometimes even despairing.

Melanie leaned forward, balancing bony elbows on her thighs and steepling her fingers. 'We wondered if it was something to do with your specialism.' She tapped her index fingers together. 'As you know, she's a psychologist too, and she must've been aware of your work. She asked for you by name, but wouldn't say why.'

That was another reason I'd been hesitant about taking the case. Whether she was suffering a psychotic episode or not, we had similar professional backgrounds. That knowledge added to the tension thrumming in my head.

Melanie smiled. 'I've read all your papers. I really admire the work you've done to improve support at women's shelters. I'd be surprised if Laura hasn't read everything too.'

'Thank you.' The word 'everything' chimed in my head. I wasn't named in the press last year, at least. I was keen to get the conversation back to the case. 'Do we know if Laura has a partner?'

'We know she lives alone but she won't tell us whether she was seeing anyone. Her neighbour reported seeing the same man coming and going, but when the doctors, the police and her lawyer questioned her, she refused to say anything about this man. Obviously, they're looking into it, but it takes time and resources, the system works slowly and they're desperate for answers. That's why everyone is so relieved you're here.'

'No pressure, then.' I gave a short laugh. 'Do they know I'm not a criminal psychologist? If they really do think she's a potential murderer, maybe they should . . .'

'She was very specific. She'll only be treated by you.'

I sat back and closed the file. 'Okay.' Even if she had committed a crime, I reasoned, that didn't preclude her from being a victim too. I would help her if I could. I ignored a sensation like tiny, prickling electric shocks just under the surface of my skin. 'We'd better get started then.'

Melanie nodded and stood. 'I'll go and get her.'

Chapter Three

Alone in the room again, I did a mental checklist of my body, trying to relax the muscles clamped tight in my lower back and neck. I breathed in for four, held for seven, out for eight. I'd met many victims of crime in my career – too many – but I'd never been face to face with someone who might have ended a life.

I exhaled, giving up any attempt to steady my breath, and wondered if I could formulate a reason why I had to get back to London. I patted my pocket for my phone, forgetting for a moment that I'd accidentally left it on the reception desk when I was filling out the endless forms when I came into Heaton Place. I would pop down and get it after the session. I noted how vulnerable I felt without it. Like most people I knew, I'd become reliant on the device, and not having it to hand left me feeling strangely naked. Added to that, now I couldn't pretend I'd been urgently called away even if I wanted to.

I lifted the hem of my top and pulled it away from my body, flapping it, grateful for some movement of air on my overheated torso. It was perfectly normal to feel nervous in this situation, I reminded myself. I forced myself to remember why I'd gone into this job. I brought Sarah's face to mind, remembering her bright smile, her zest for life, her determination to always think the best of people. She would want me to do everything I could to help someone traumatised.

The rise and fall of women's voices reached me from the corridor. The electricity under my skin gave a jolt.

The lock clicked and Melanie stepped over the threshold, followed by a woman with dark hair. The woman's shoulders were rounded and there was fear in her eyes. I knew then that I would not go back to London that day.

I stood and approached her, holding out my hand. 'Hi, Laura.' I wished I'd wiped my clammy palm on my jeans before offering it to her. 'Is it okay if I call you Laura? I'm Emma Best, I believe you asked to see me?'

She shook my hand. 'Hi, yes, erm, Laura's fine,' she said, her voice quiet.

'Please take a seat.' I directed her to the sofa against the left wall. I sat on the one facing the desk, angling myself towards her. Julie and Aidan left the room quietly, the door catch clicking into place behind them. Glancing through the glass, I could see Aidan's ear in the corner of the pane. They hadn't gone far, then.

Melanie hovered by the desk. When I turned to her, she was looking from me to Laura, like a child arriving late to a tea party, wondering where to sit at the table. I spoke to Laura. 'Melanie is Ward 9's supervising psychologist. Are you happy for her to stay during our session?' I avoided Melanie's eyes. I wanted to hear Laura give her consent. It was the ethical thing to do.

In the pause when Laura glanced over at Melanie, I noticed how similar Laura's colouring was to Sarah's. Her dark brown hair, tied back in a low ponytail, had a kink, like the unruly waves that had fallen over my sister's shoulders. Her eyes were blue, lighter and without the hint of green that had changed Sarah's eye colour depending on what shade she wore.

When Laura turned back to me, I had to work hard not to superimpose Sarah's face on hers. I blinked to dispel the image. This was not my sister. This was not our story. This was a different tragedy altogether.

'She explained she'd be sitting in on the way down here,' said Laura. 'It's okay with me.' Her lips twitched at the edges in a nervous smile. Her anxiety calmed me. Watching her eyes flit around the bleak room, I recognised she felt trapped and was surprised to find I felt protective towards her. I stored that away in my head to make a note of later.

'Thank you.' I opened the file on my knee, as Melanie shook off her jacket and hung it over the back of the chair. I waited for her to sit, not envying her position next to the radiator. She took a pen from the inside pocket of her jacket and clicked the top. I turned back to Laura. 'In this first session, I'd like to start by getting to know a little about you, if that's okay?' I imagined she'd be prepared for the soft questions. She probably started her sessions with new clients in the same way. The problem was, I had to get a picture of what she knew about the night she was brought here first.

She nodded.

'Before we begin, can you tell me your understanding of why you are at Heaton Place?'

Her eyes flicked to Melanie, then down at her hands, clamped together in her lap. 'I don't remember.'

'I know this is hard for you, Laura' – I kept my voice soft – 'but could you tell me the last thing you do remember before . . .' I stalled clumsily. I hadn't thought about what to call the horrific scene I'd read about in her notes. '. . . The incident.'

Her hands pressed together in slow pulses. 'I remember driving home from work and putting my key in the lock. That's it. I don't remember anything after that; not until I woke up here.'

I could easily imagine how terrifying that must have been. 'You're doing really well,' I said. Did that sound patronising? It's something I often said to patients, but they weren't usually my peers. 'And what have you been told about the period of time you can't remember?'

Her hands released and she turned her palms up; a supplicating gesture, like she was giving herself up to the therapy. I took it as a good sign. 'They said that when the police found me I was covered in blood' – her voice wavered – 'but I don't remember. Police and doctors kept asking me whose blood it was – and if I knew, I'd tell them.' She looked at me with wet eyes. 'Honestly, I would, but I don't know.'

'I understand,' I said. 'And you know we'll be working

together to try to discover where the blood came from and if there's someone who needs medical attention?'

Her eyes closed tight and she nodded. I was satisfied she knew why she was here, and was about to ask my next question when a shriek made us all turn towards the corridor. Another scream rang out, followed by a violent banging which made me jolt, dropping my pad from my lap on to the floor.

The door opened, and Julie and Aidan stepped inside, closing it quickly behind them.

'What's happening?' My question was almost drowned out by a strangled howling which seemed to come from directly outside the room. I strained to see past Julie's blonde, undercut hair to the window in the door. Dark figures rushed past, accompanied by shouts from multiple voices.

'Nothing for us to worry about,' said Melanie.

My nerves jangled as a deep voice bellowed over the shrieking of a woman who sounded like she was in terrible distress. 'Shouldn't we do something?' I said, watching Aidan. Snake tattoos slithered up his muscular forearm from the skull's eye sockets, then disappeared under the blue sleeve of his scrubs at the elbow. He stood motionless behind the door while a sickening crack, like a head being smashed against a wall, sounded less than a metre away.

'I'm afraid this kind of disturbance isn't unusual,' said Melanie. A bout of howling turned to sobs, then quietened to distraught gasps. The deep voice rumbled more quietly, then faded away. 'This is a secure mental health unit,'

Melanie continued, 'and we treat people with very complex conditions. Some of our patients are extremely dangerous. Every patient has a team allocated according to need and we have to follow guidance to the letter. That's how we keep our patients and ourselves safe. We follow protocol and no team interferes with another. We are all well trained to manage in situations like the one you just heard.'

I was suddenly very grateful to have Aidan and Julie with me everywhere I went inside Heaton Place. I'd thought having two orderlies like bodyguards was overkill. Clearly, it wasn't. I turned to look at Laura. Her hands clutched the bottom of her sweatshirt, the pads of her thumbs turning white with the pressure of her grip. I couldn't imagine how it must feel for her to be captive here, with people who would be termed criminally insane, to be considered potentially as dangerous as them. 'Are you all right?' I asked her.

She nodded and looked up with a nervous smile. There was no way the scared woman across from me could be as threatening as whoever had made the noise in the corridor. She was suffering from trauma, that was all. In that moment, I felt certain of that.

Chapter Four

I picked up my pad from the floor, hoping Laura wouldn't notice my hands were trembling. The events in the corridor had shaken me. This was a far cry from my calm therapy room in London. Aidan opened the door and he and Julie stepped back outside. I turned towards the brief flow of cooler air, and before the door closed my gaze landed on a streak of red on the wall outside.

I turned away and smiled at Laura in a way I hoped belied my palpitating heart. 'Right,' I said. 'Sorry about that.' As soon as it came out of my mouth it seemed like a stupid thing to say. Why was I apologising for someone else's violent outburst? 'I read you're a psychologist too?' I said, smiling.

'Yes. I've been practising for ten years.'

What would you ask, if you were me? I thought but stopped myself from saying. I felt unprepared. When I met a new client at a women's shelter, I usually had a file overflowing with police and social workers' reports, or at least their own detailed notes. I thought back to Laura's flimsy file, wishing I had more to go on. I was afraid she'd sense my hesitancy and think this supposedly eminent woman she had asked for by name, who specialised in trauma and PTSD, who wrote papers on how to best help women who'd suffered at the hands of abusive partners, didn't know how to start a therapy session.

'And you grew up in Suffolk? That's a beautiful part of the country.'

'Yes. It's a lovely place.'

Her eyes flicked up to meet mine, then back to her jeans. We were both wearing jeans and sweatshirts. I wouldn't normally dress so casually for a session, but I'd been called in with such urgency that I hadn't given much thought to packing. I hoped it suggested a lack of hierarchy to Laura, rather than a lack of professionalism.

'Then you studied in Liverpool? That must've been a change.'

She crossed her ankles. Her toes moved under the thin fabric of her regulation slippers, curling and uncurling. 'A bit different to Suffolk, yes. But I loved Liverpool. It was . . . eye-opening.'

'I bet.' I imagined a teenage Laura moving from a rural village with thatched cottages and hedgerows to the throaty roar of Liverpool's bustling streets.

The first time my husband had taken me to the city where he was born, I was amazed at the unadulterated energy pumping through the place. I grew up in a quiet London suburb, so thought I knew about city life. But where London encourages you to go privately about your business, Liverpool embraces strangers, sometimes literally, and demands intimacy through probing questions and professions of allegiance.

'I've been a few times,' I said. 'It must've been a great place to study psychology. Everyone I met there wanted to know my entire life story and couldn't wait to tell me theirs.'

'Born psychologists,' said Laura, smiling nervously again. 'Always looking for a narrative.'

Perhaps that's why Connor moved away, I found myself thinking. He preferred to keep his cards close to his chest. He'd been in London so long that his accent, which had never been pronounced, had faded away altogether. These days, people presumed he came from the Home Counties. I loved that there were things I knew about him that other people didn't. The intimacy of a close marriage like ours meant we knew each other's layers, from the shiny top veneer we allowed the outside world to see to the foundation levels at our core that were just between us.

'Why did you move to London after you graduated?'

'More people, more problems. I hoped I could do more good in a bigger city.' She shrugged. 'I wanted to make a difference.' Her eyes clouded. 'We all want that, don't we? We start out naïve and enthusiastic, sure we're going to make a mark ...' She trailed off.

I nodded, feeling a strong connection to this woman. That's exactly how I'd felt after what happened to Sarah. I'd wanted to make a difference too. I reminded myself not to over-identify with this new patient. Psychology 101.

There was vulnerability in the way Laura was sitting,

23

hands tucked between her thighs. Her shoulders rounded in towards her chest, protecting the softest part of her. I knew it was foolish, unprofessional even, to make a judgement so quickly, or at all, but if this intelligent, nervous woman in front of me had been involved in a murder, it struck me that the provocation would have had to be extreme.

'You still live in London?'

'Yes. I bought a Victorian end-of-terrace house, not far from the hospital where I work.' She reached back and tightened her ponytail, dividing the hair into two and tugging the halves apart to move the black band higher. She ran a shaky hand from her forehead over her skull to smooth the rest of her hair.

Her eyes were moist when she glanced at me. The sadness I saw there reminded me of my mother's eyes after Sarah died. I dug my fingernails into the palms of my hands. I reminded myself about the focus of this therapy: to unlock Laura's memories of the night she was found covered in blood. Someone else had been there, that much was indisputable. But who, and where were they now? 'Do you live alone?'

'Yes.' Her hands went back between her thighs and her gaze dropped to the floor. I could see the question made her uncomfortable. That was notable.

'Tell me about your home.'

She raised her eyes to mine. 'It's my sanctuary. I imagine that sounds like a strange word to use, but when you do the kind of work we do, it's good to have somewhere that feels completely safe to go back to, isn't it?'

I found myself nodding. It occurred to me that was the second time she'd used the word 'we' and wondered if this alignment was strategic; a way of reminding me that we're not so different. If it was, I should be on my guard. However true it was, I must not allow a patient to lead me. 'Which is your favourite room?'

'My kitchen.'

I watched her closely, keeping my face impassive while I searched hers for any indication that she remembered what happened when she was last in that room. She blinked down at her hands, her expression unchanged. 'Do you like to cook?' I said.

'I don't bother much for myself. But when . . .'

'When . . .' I prompted. I waited, hoping she'd offer more, but the moment stretched. Aidan's voice rumbled something indistinguishable outside the door and Julie replied in a flat tone, but inside the room the silence thickened. I caved, 'You like cooking for other people?'

'Yes.'

'Anyone in particular?'

Laura straightened and, when she raised her head, her bright eyes caught the reflection of sun shining through the window opposite. 'Yes. Daniel.' There was a lightness to the way she said his name, like it was something precious she was sharing. A gift. The word seemed transformative. All traces of anxiety and meekness disappeared, replaced by a grin which illuminated her face.

'Who's Daniel?' I kept my voice level, not wanting to give away how keen I was to hear about the man the neighbour had seen coming and going from her house. In my peripheral vision I was aware of Melanie shifting position.

'My partner.'

So, she did have a partner, but she hadn't asked for him since she was brought to the facility. She wouldn't speak to the police or her lawyer about him, but it looked like she might be about to share more with me. The question of why tapped at the back of my brain, but I ignored it. I kept my face neutral. 'How did you meet?'

She uncrossed her ankles and relaxed back into the sofa. 'At an event. The old-fashioned way. I'd tried internet dating, but it's hard to meet someone you couldn't easily diagnose with something on the first date that strikes them off the list, don't you think? The downside of the job. You don't want your relationship to be one long busman's holiday.'

She was looking at me with a playful smile. Another attempt at alignment. That was interesting. I smiled back, feeling more than a little relieved that I was securely married. I'd tell Connor that when I spoke to him. Any irritation I'd felt since our argument a couple of nights ago had since faded and I longed to be able to put my arms around him, let him know how glad I was to be married to him. And not only because I never wanted to have to do the dating thing again. The scene must be hard enough these days, without the knowledge Laura and I shared of red flags.

'He offered to buy me a drink, and . . . I don't know . . .' Her expression turned wistful. This was good. Memories were what we needed to mine, especially if this man was significant in this mysterious case, and I had a gut feeling he was.

'I wasn't looking for a relationship. I really wasn't,' she said. 'But he was charmingly persistent, and I gave in. Thank God I did. Honestly, I know it sounds a bit Disney, but he really is the best thing to have ever happened to me.'

'Tell me more about Daniel.'

'Well, physically, he's tall, about six two.' She grinned. 'He's going to sound like a walking cliché – tall, dark and handsome – but he is. He's traditionally good-looking. He's even got a square jaw, like a cartoon hero.'

She touched her index finger to her chin, and I watched, spellbound, keen to hear more. Keen not to appear too keen.

'And his personality? What's he like?'

'Kind. Thoughtful. He'll remember if I've mentioned a restaurant I liked the look of and book a table. He's attentive, calls and texts to see how my day's going. He does that a lot, actually. And he's funny. Not in a tell-a-joke way, more like funny observations – witty, you know?'

She looked at me and I nodded. 'He sounds perfect,' I said, despite the unease creeping in. I'd heard this story before: men who are too good to be true. Men who call and message, under the guise of attentiveness, until it becomes something far more sinister. My instincts for recognising potentially disturbing traits were honed, but I could be jumping to conclusions. I heard Connor's voice in my head, gently reminding me to be wary of developing a jaundiced view of men because of my work. He was right. I couldn't afford to let any bias colour my sessions with Laura. I needed to keep an open mind. I needed to find out more about this Daniel.

'He is perfect,' she replied, holding my gaze.

'Tell me more about when you first met.'

She began her story. I let her talk, holding back the question which quivered on the end of my tongue: *Where is Daniel now?*

Chapter Five

The Past

I'd failed at giving up smoking. Again. I rolled my eyes at myself as I ground the stub of my cigarette into the wet tarmac with my boot. That was partly why I'd taken a course on managing habitual behaviour, to give up for good; and to exorcise some of my own demons. Turned out, my demons weren't so easily expunged. They were tenacious little bastards, refusing to leave me whatever clever new therapy methods I tried.

Maybe it was because they weren't just my demons. I shared them with my whole family. 'Sharing is caring,' I muttered under my breath, then laughed bitterly. Maybe I shouldn't have had that third pint of lager.

I rested my back against the hotel's wall, breathing in the scent of the recent summer rain, trying to remember the word for that smell. It began with a 'p', but I kept returning to 'pterodactyl', and it wasn't that. I definitely should have stopped at two drinks. Shallow puddles reflected the street-lights on the car park's perimeter, dappling the ground with yellow patches which shimmered as the breeze skimmed across the water. I tried to summon the energy to go back inside. These networking events were exhausting. Early in my psychology training I'd labelled myself as an introverted extrovert. Looking back, I saw how self-indulgent myself and my cohort were when we started our degrees; always finding ourselves in our research, looking at everything through the lens of the self-obsessed.

Despite that, I still believed the introverted extrovert label. I loved social situations, but there was a point where my social battery became so depleted I just wanted to go home. That point was now. I picked up the dog-end and looked around the hotel's frontage for a bin.

'There's a bin over here,' said a man's voice.

Startled, I looked into the shadows where the voice came from, glad to have the hotel's illuminated entrance at my back. If whoever spoke was a threat, I could be inside in seconds.

A figure stepped away from the shadow of the building and moved towards me. As the light crept on to his features, his face came into view. If he was a threat, he was one with a very appealing square jaw.

'Want me to take that?' He held out a large hand and I was confused for a moment. 'The cigarette stub?' he said. 'I'll put it in the bin for you.'

I extended my arm as he got closer, but then, breaking out of the trance I'd fallen into watching this man's fluid walk, his self-assured grin, I pulled my hand back. 'No, thanks, but ... you don't want to touch this. I'll ...' I moved past him in the direction he'd appeared from, skipping over a puddle, and was relieved to see a slim aluminium bin for spent cigarettes. I dropped the stub in and rubbed my hand on my skirt.

He watched, his lips curling into a lopsided smile. 'I would have done that.'

'What are you?' I said, returning his smile. 'Some kind of knight in shining armour, relieving maidens of their filth?' Where had that come from? It took all my strength not to lower my eyes and mutter an apology. I didn't, though, and was rewarded with a deep chuckle.

'Do you always use such questionable innuendos?' he said.

'Nope,' I grinned, feeling empowered, sexy even. 'That one was especially for you.'

'I'm honoured.' He dipped his head in a bow. 'You at the networking event?' He stood, his shadow stretching long and slender on the wall behind him, and nodded in the direction of the hotel.

'I was, but I'm not sure the corporate world is for me,' I said.

'What are you peddling?' His lips pursed, as if trying to control laughter.

'I'm not peddling anything.' I used an indignant tone. 'I was networking. Just dipping my toe in the water.'

'And corporate water isn't for you?'

'Too murky,' I said.

'So, back to . . .'

He left a pause which I didn't know how to fill. I couldn't quite decide whether to carry on with my NHS work or try

31

to open a private practice. I'd been hoping this event might lead to a job as an in-house psychologist, but the people I'd met were mainly small-business owners who looked baffled when I talked about the benefits of psychology in the workplace. 'Not sure.'

'Maybe I could help you work it out,' he said. 'Over an espresso martini?'

I crossed my arms. 'You don't mess about.'

'Faint heart never won . . .'

'You can't be serious?' I laughed. 'Do you climb through women's bedroom windows at night and leave boxes of chocolates on their pillows like some kind of Prince Charming?'

'The opposite, actually,' he said. 'I catch the people who climb through women's bedroom windows at night.'

'You're police? Where's your uniform?'

He dropped his chin to his chest. 'Sorry, no uniform. I'm past all that. Are you disappointed?' He glanced up through dark lashes, a question in his eyes.

'A bit.' I shrugged and huffed out a loud breath, pleased when he laughed.

'Let me make it up to you over a drink.' He stepped closer.

A black cab drew into the car park, orange light glowing on its roof. I raised my hand, not looking at the man as the cab's tyres splashed through the puddles towards us.

Before opening the door, I delved into my bag and pulled out my business card. I handed it to him. 'I'm heading home now, but you can get me on that number, if you like.'

I opened the taxi's door and climbed in. As it pulled away,

I kept my eyes forward. After seeing my parents' marriage disintegrate, I'd decided on a strict no-relationship rule, and even someone who I'd felt an immediate attraction to, like old Prince Charming back there, wasn't going to make me break that rule. Anyway, I was far too busy deciding what direction to take my career in to think about starting a relationship.

I allowed myself to glance through the rear window of the cab just as the man slipped my card into his wallet. He stood still then, keeping his eyes on the car as it turned on to the main road. From this new perspective, his shadow seemed to elongate, stretching until it appeared huge, almost monstrous. I sat back in the seat, satisfied he hadn't thrown my card away. My stomach swirled, giddy. I might not be looking for a relationship, but that didn't mean I couldn't have a bit of fun.

Chapter Six

I was distracted by movement in my peripheral vision. Through the glass panel in the door, I watched a hand holding a sponge swipe back and forth over the smear of blood on the wall. A few strokes and it was gone, as though the screaming and splitting of skin had never happened. I looked back at Laura, as she finished her story of when she and Daniel met, and wondered if her kitchen had been cleaned of blood so easily, or if it was still there, hardened to a black-brown mess.

Was it his blood soaking her clothes that night? Asking directly would not be appropriate, even though the relaxed way she sat back in her seat suggested she was much more comfortable now than she was at the start of the session. Instead, I planned to try to unlock memories of her and Daniel's relationship chronologically, hoping to trigger fragments of what happened in that kitchen. Daniel seemed to me to be the most likely person involved at this point, so recalling him with as much clarity as possible was my current plan.

'Could you tell me more about the early days of your relationship?' I said, laying my pad and pen on the cushion beside me. I tried not to make too many notes during sessions. I knew the disquieting feeling of wondering what was being written about you all too well from my own therapy with Harvey. He'd made so many notes in my last session I had squirmed in my seat. He suggested I was holding on to what happened last year, then asked if I was facing up to how I was currently feeling, I told him I'd dealt with it, and I was fine. I knew lying to my supervisor was counterproductive, but I deserved to feel guilty. I wasn't ready to let that go. I'd postponed the next scheduled session. And the one after that.

'What exactly do you want to know?'

Fair point. My question was vague and she was telling me to be more specific. I saw I'd have to work for the information I wanted. That was fine.

'Did your relationship develop quickly?'

She smiled and I felt like I'd passed a test. 'Yeah, it did. He was keener than I was, to be honest. When you've been on your own for a long time, it's hard to let the barriers down.'

'Barriers?' I resisted the urge to pick up the pen. Since she was my only patient here, I would have the luxury of writing up my notes afterwards without the pressure of knowing my next patient was impatiently tapping their toes in the waiting room. 'Why do you think you put up barriers?'

She looked down at her fingers. I noticed her nails were

long, filed into a perfect almond shape. The cuticles were smooth, as though she'd recently had a manicure. I wondered how long it would take for those nails to break and peel in here. 'I don't know, you just do, don't you?'

I waited. Despite my years in this job, I still struggled with silence. It was something Harvey and I talked about a lot. I thought about what he would say to me now. *Wait*, he would say, *feel what's being said in the silence*. I wished he was here with me, wished I hadn't cancelled our last two sessions, unable to face the scratch of his pen on paper as he took his notes, a knowing look in his eyes as he peered out at me from behind his glasses.

The trouble with silence was that unwanted thoughts always filled the gaps. I stayed quiet and watched Laura tug at the seam of her jeans, imagining her weighing up whether to engage with me, with the therapy, or not.

'My parents didn't exactly model the perfect relationship,' she said, at last.

She'd decided to open a door, and it was a significant one: an opportunity to talk about her childhood. I thanked Harvey in my head, promising myself I'd go and see him straight after I left Heaton Place. His pen would be flying across the page and I would bear it because that's what good psychologists did. 'Did you experience a lot of conflict when you were growing up?'

Laura let her head drop back on to the sofa cushion. 'Not conflict, exactly. Anyway, we don't need to go into that,' she said. 'I've worked through it with my therapist. It's *integrated*.' She lifted her head and looked me in the eye. The use of the term 'integrated' and the eye contact were clearly a challenge. She'd opened the door, then closed it again, purposefully. Why?

'I appreciate that,' I said. She knew I'd be reading her non-verbal cues as well as hearing what she said. This was like a game of cat and mouse. I hadn't been in a situation where the power dynamic confused my process before. It wasn't that I ever wanted a patient to feel like I was in charge – that in itself could cause negative transference, with them associating me with previous authority figures, muddying the alliance – but, outside of my peer supervision sessions, I was usually the person who best knew how therapy was meant to progress. 'And it's great you've done the work, but since our relationship is new, I'm sure you'll appreciate that some background would be useful.'

'Sorry.' She closed her eyes. 'Of course.'

The capitulation was quicker than I could have hoped. I stayed quiet, and smiled, indicating I'd like her to continue.

'I thought my parents had a traditional marriage when I was growing up' – she moved her head from side to side – 'nothing more unusual than the standard, if imperfect, family structure.' She sighed. 'But therapy made me understand that what I experienced wasn't . . . healthy.'

I nodded, showing her I was listening. Memories from my own childhood tumbled into my consciousness. I heard echoes of Dad shouting at Mum downstairs as Sarah and I cowered together in my bed. I allowed the scene to sit for a moment, feeling the fear, the vulnerability, my sister's protective arms around me, accepting it, then forcing myself back into the present. I reminded myself that this was Laura's session, not mine.

'It was the silence that I know now wasn't ... normal,' Laura continued, 'the way everyone tiptoed around everyone else. The intentional rationing of words, the sulking that could go on for days.'

'Who was doing the sulking?'

Laura rubbed a finger between her eyebrows. 'Who wasn't? Dad would upset Mum and she would stalk off to another room while he huffed and puffed in the kitchen. Then it would be the other way around. My childhood was one silent meal after another, with me trying to cut through the atmosphere of passive aggression with ridiculous attempts to tell stories about my day at school. Until I gave up, and just sat there like the rest of them, eating as quickly as I could so I could go to my room.'

I could see the scene she painted so clearly it was like I was sitting at the table. The empathy I felt for her made the air between us pulse. My fingers itched for my pad and pen, but now wasn't the time to pick it up. 'That sounds like a difficult environment to grow up in.'

She breathed out through her nose. 'Even now, I get the urge to minimise it, you know, say, *Oh, we had everything we needed. We were fed, clothed and warm enough.* But when I learned about Maslow's hierarchy of needs, I understood there was very little in the way of love and belonging, which made everything else harder to achieve.' She tipped her head to the side. 'And we both know that's not ideal, is it? Not in functioning families anyway.'

I nodded, keenly wishing we had met under different circumstances. I wanted to discuss Maslow's hierarchy over a glass of chilled wine. His belief that, if the needs of survival, safety, love and belonging aren't met, it's very hard to satisfy higher needs regarding self-worth and personal growth. It was something I thought about a lot. I kept my face still while my mind skipped forward, shifting away from how I was feeling in that moment to why I was here, in this overheated room, with this woman. Was she introducing her dysfunctional family background as a clue? Was her relationship with Daniel unhealthy? 'I'm sorry you experienced that.'

'Thanks. You know better than most how common it is.'

At first, I was stunned, thinking she knew about my parents, but then I realised she meant my work. That was the first indication she'd given that she knew about my specialisation. I desperately wanted to ask if my work with women who'd been abused was why she'd insisted on seeing me rather than anyone else, but it was too direct, too soon. I didn't want her to think I'd jumped to conclusions about her relationship, partly because I shouldn't have. Not without more information. 'I do.' I picked up the pen and rolled it between my fingers casually. 'What did Daniel do to persuade you he was . . . worth taking a chance on? How did he persuade you to let those barriers down?' I suddenly realised I'd used the word 'persuade' twice. That was a mistake. It implied a deliberate act on his part. Language mattered in therapy. I needed to be more careful.

To my relief, her eyes brightened. 'What didn't he do?'

Her gaze trailed up to the window to my left, a brief smile on her lips. 'He was so lovely. He sent flowers, left messages, sent voice notes.'

'All before you agreed to a date?'

'Before and after. I was concerned he was only interested in the chase. I steeled myself for that, you know, in case he was the kind of man who only pursued women who weren't interested in him, but even after we'd been out a few times' – she lowered her voice – 'even after we slept together, he was still just as attentive.'

'That must have felt good.'

'It should have,' she said, crossing one leg over the other, 'But it made me back off a bit.'

The word 'should' was interesting. 'Why was that?'

'He seemed too keen.' She pulled at her ponytail again, dividing the hair, tugging both sides to push the band higher. I made a mental note to be conscious that she did this when she felt uncomfortable.

'It felt like love-bombing?'

In training we'd been taught to put names to emotions, to validate what patients said by offering it back to them to show we understood, but the second this came out of my mouth I could see it was a mistake. Her back straightened. The brightness in her eyes dulled, replaced by a steely glare. 'That's not what it was.' She looked away, at the camera above the door. I became aware of being observed, of messing up while people were watching. In an attempt to move forward I'd jumped to an unfounded conclusion. Not all attentive men were abusers. I knew that. I was married to a thoughtful, caring man myself, for God's sake.

'I'm sorry,' I said, wishing I could inhale the words back in. I'd thought I was following her lead, but now I could see I was leading her, putting words in her mouth. The atmosphere in the room had altered. I could sense her closing down and I didn't know how to recover. 'I clearly misinterpreted what you meant. Could you clarify?'

She swallowed. The muscles in her jaw tightened. She looked across at Melanie. 'Could I go back to my room now, please?'

I became aware of the hands of the clock on the wall shifting, marking out the already diminishing time I had left to help this woman. 'Laura, I think it would be useful—'

'I'd like to go back, please.' She didn't look at me.

I sensed Melanie come out from behind the desk but kept my eyes on Laura. 'Perhaps we could—'

'No.' Laura's head snapped back towards me as she spoke. Her eyes were wide, frightened. Was she frightened of me, or of what I was making her face up to? I had the sense that we were on the cusp of something important but knew enough not to push any further now.

'I'd like to go back to what you said about your parents.' My words came out rushed.

'I'm tired,' said Laura, her eyes on the ground. All hope of engaging her again seeped away. She needed to process what had happened in this session and reflect. So did I.

'Okay.' I said. 'Thank you for meeting with me today.'

She stood, gaze lowered, and made her way to the door.

I stood too, watching her walk away in those flimsy slippers, feeling impotent and foolish. 'I'd like to schedule another session for tomorrow, if that's all right with you?'

What would I do if she said no? Go home? Before I'd met with Laura, I would have seen this as the perfect solution. One session, then a refusal to carry on. I'd tried – what more could I do?

But, by the time she reached the door, I knew I wanted to help unlock whatever was trapped inside her head. I'd worked with enough women who'd been through hell to believe that Laura Winters had suffered something so traumatic that it had caused dissociative amnesia. Whatever she had or hadn't done as a result of her experiences, I wanted to be the one who released those memories. Of course, I hoped the police could use any information gleaned, but my priority was helping her to heal.

'See you in tomorrow's session?' I coughed, pretending it was phlegm that tightened my voice, not the urgency of the question. She hesitated then gave a brief nod before Melanie let her out of the room. When she was safely outside in the corridor with Aidan and Julie, I called to Melanie to stay behind for a second. 'That camera,' I said, pointing at the black eye above the door. 'Who monitors it?'

Melanie glanced up. 'Erm, it's security.'

'I think it's unnerving Laura.' I didn't add that it made me uncomfortable too. 'Therapy is a personal and private process. I don't think it's right that we're being monitored.'

Melanie looked past me to where Laura was standing. 'Security matters in a place like this.'

'But, surely—'

'You might not think it's necessary now, but what happens if she discloses she has done something so terrible, it makes your skin—'

'Surely they can't monitor her therapy sessions for evidence? That's not ethical.'

'It's not something we do lightly,' Melanie said. 'And please don't think the ethics of our treatments aren't thoroughly considered. They are. We agonise about every decision we make. But in this case, surely the ethical thing is to discover the truth? Especially when we know someone else might be hurt.'

The way her eyes searched mine suggested she truly wanted me to answer. But I didn't know. It just seemed morally wrong to be using treatment in that way. On top of that, I was already convinced Laura wasn't a dangerous criminal. 'I'm sure that even if she has committed a crime, it was most likely self-defence.'

'Are you?' Melanie said. 'I hope that is the case. I wish I had your optimism. But if you'd seen what I've seen in this place . . . if you knew how often the criminally insane seem exactly like everyone else, you'd be glad there're cameras on every wall. Very glad indeed.'

Chapter Seven

I looked up from my pad at the sound of the lock being activated by Melanie's key fob. In the time it had taken for Melanie, Aidan and Julie to take Laura back to her accommodation, I had written notes on the session, ready to give them more thought later in my room.

'Hungry?' asked Melanie from the doorway.

'Yep.' I'd had breakfast in my room that morning, a typical institutional plate of rubbery croissant and coffee with UHT milk, but the croissant had stuck to the roof of my mouth and I gave up after a couple of bites. I hoped I might find something tempting with at least a modicum of nutritional value in the canteen. I closed my pad and slid that and Laura's notes into the tote bag I'd been given for the purpose. Feeling the burn of the radiator at my back, I said, 'Is there any way of turning the heating down in here?'

'Afraid not,' said Melanie. 'There're no individual thermostats in the rooms, so it's on or off, no in between.'

'Ugh, what a pain. And it's freezing in the staff quarters.'

'Is it?' She held the door open wide for me to pass through.

She must have better internal temperature control than I do if she didn't notice the change from the old barracks to this sauna. On our way out of the room, I glanced at the metal panel by the door and remembered what I'd been meaning to ask Melanie. 'When will my ID and key fob be ready?'

'Good point,' said Melanie. 'I'll chase that after lunch.'

'Thanks. I need to go down to reception to pick up my phone, so I could collect them, if that's—'

'Don't worry,' she said. 'I have a quick meeting arranged down there straight after lunch, so I'll get your phone too.'

'Great. Thanks.' I tried not to look into the treatment rooms we passed, but my eyes were always drawn to the people inside. Melanie had explained that the glass panels in the doors were a security measure, so staff could always see if something wasn't right. I thought back to the safety information I'd been told when I first came in and wished I'd listened more carefully. It was slowly sinking in quite how important security was in Heaton Place.

I glanced into the room we were walking by and, in that moment, the woman inside turned her head to the glass. Her swollen face was a vivid canvas of colours: yellow, blue and purple bruises merged together. When her eye caught mine, the blue iris stood out against a completely scarlet eyeball. I turned away and kept my gaze on the seam running up the centre of Melanie's suit jacket as she walked ahead.

We came to another door at the end of the corridor.

Melanie lifted the fob attached to a lanyard around her neck and tapped it against the panel. The door clicked open, leading on to a landing, painted in brilliant white. I followed Melanie down a flight of stairs, Aidan and Julie walking a few steps behind. At the bottom, we went through another set of doors into a room with grey Formica tables and a serving area along the far wall.

The smell of fried food suggested I wasn't going to get the vegetables I'd hoped for, but on closer inspection there was a bank of silver serving trays filled with chopped tomatoes, cucumber, coleslaw and potato salad. I smiled up at a thin woman in a white overall that reminded me of the lab coats we used to have to wear in science lessons at school. I had a sudden flashback to standing, shaking, while my father asked about my results in a science test. I'd come second in the class, not first. I remembered the sting on my upper arm as he pinched my skin between his thumb and finger until I couldn't bear it. Mum had come to my defence, and I could still hear the slap of his hand on her cheek as punishment.

The woman behind the counter caught my eye for a second. My memory must have imprinted itself on my face because she looked away quickly, turning her attention to Melanie. 'What can I get you?'

Melanie turned to me. 'What do you fancy?'

'Salad would be great, with a jacket potato if they've got one.'

Melanie nodded and addressed Aidan. 'Same for me. See you over there.' She put a hand on my elbow and steered me in the direction of a small side room.

'Shouldn't we wait for the food?' I turned back to see Julie pointing at the silver trays as the thin woman tonged lettuce on to a plate.

'No need,' said Melanie. 'Julie and Aidan will bring it over.'

'But don't I need to pay? Does it go on account, or ...' We reached the side room. Two tables had been shoved together with four chairs positioned around it. The space must have doubled as a storeroom because stacks of plastic chairs towered at one end and tables with their folding metal legs flattened were strapped against two walls.

'Heaton Place is covering all your expenses. It's part of the contract.' Melanie sat and picked up the jug sitting in the centre of the table. She poured water into four cups and handed one to me. I was expecting to feel cold glass, but it was moulded plastic. Melanie looked around the room, her lip curling. 'Not the most salubrious of surroundings, is it? We've been allocated this area to eat in so we have some privacy.'

'This is the staff canteen, though, right?' I peered into the main room, viewing the smattering of other people. They all had blue lanyards around their necks. 'So, they'd be discreet, surely?' I caught the eye of a man in a creased white shirt. He looked away and poked at his food in a way that seemed contrived. I got that teams of professionals were allocated to individual patients, but weren't staff allowed to even look at each other at Heaton Place?

Melanie shrugged. 'Just following directives from above. We've been told to keep to ourselves and not to talk about Patient X to anyone outside the four of us.'

It felt faintly ridiculous to not be allowed to mention Laura's name outside the therapy room. We weren't spies. 'I was thinking about that,' I said, turning back to Melanie. 'I know this is all confidential, but I still need to have regular contact with my supervisor, Harvey. You know how important it is to have someone else you can run things by.'

Melanie took a sip of water then placed the glass carefully on the table. 'I'm afraid that's not going to be possible.'

'But he's my supervisor,' I said. 'Anything we discuss would be completely confidential.'

Melanie shook her head. 'He's not on the authorised list. I'm sorry, Emma, but they won't allow it.'

She paused as Julie put a blue tray down in front of me. 'Thank you,' I said. The food on the plate looked limp, the lettuce leaves browning and the red skin of the tomatoes shrivelled like fingertips after too long in the bath. I watched steam rise from the open jacket potato, a leaden feeling settling in my abdomen. I picked up the plastic knife and fork, hovering them over the plate, willing my stomach to unclench.

Aidan put a tray in front of Melanie, his eyes cast down. I got the impression he wasn't thrilled about fetching and carrying for us. He and Julie headed back to the food counter.

'You know how important supervision is,' I said. She was a psychologist. Surely she understood.

Melanie peeled open the rectangular packet of butter and used the small white knife to dislodge it from the wrapper. It dropped on to her potato. I watched it melt, yellow seeping out from underneath and sliding along the hot potato, down the crispy brown skin, eventually pooling on the plate. 'I'll be your supervisor while you're here,' she said, stabbing at the middle of the potato with her fork, mashing the yellow butter into the pulp.

That wouldn't work. 'Thank you, but you know how valuable it can be to discuss things with someone who knows you. Someone aware of your background, your self-structure.' *Your weaknesses*, I didn't add. Harvey was my life raft. He was the one who saw when I was getting too close to a patient. He understood when I talked about my counter-transference, let me know when I was having an emotional response I was at risk of responding to, instead of using those feelings to better understand the patient. I'd lost so much confidence since the inquiry, I needed Harvey to keep my perspective on this case. I'd already avoided telling him too much of what was going on in my life.

'I'm sorry. It's simply not possible. I'll do my best to support you in any way I can.' Melanie's voice was firm. She laid down her knife and fork. 'Is there anything from this morning's session you'd like to discuss?'

I imagined Harvey's warm, intelligent eyes behind his glasses, his brow furrowed as I told him about the moment Laura reminded me of Sarah. I pictured him running his hand over his bald head, taking a second before asking how that made me feel. If I was sitting across from him now in his cosy office, in his worn leather chair, I would tell him that I was concerned I wasn't the right person for this job. What Laura had told me brought up so many memories from my own childhood. I would ask him how I would manage to keep her experiences and mine separate.

But Harvey wasn't here. I wasn't in his snug office in Islington, I was on a hard plastic chair in a canteen side room looking into the face of a woman I barely knew.

'No,' I said. 'I think this morning went as well as we could hope for.'

'I agree,' said Melanie, smiling and attempting to spear a slice of cucumber with the end of the fork. 'I think you're exactly the right therapist for this case.'

You're not, said Harvey's voice in my head. *Follow your instincts and leave. This will not end well.*

Then Harvey's face was replaced in my mind by Laura's. What would happen to her if I walked away now? It was only a few days, then I could go back to my husband and my life. Surely I was experienced enough to be able to manage one case without Harvey.

'I hope so,' I said, slicing through a tomato, stilling my knife when a squirt of red juice made bile rise up my throat.

Chapter Eight

My eyes throbbed with fatigue after lunch. Early therapy was intense. It took significant emotional and mental energy to read a new client and that, coupled with very little sleep, had left me drained.

'What will you do this afternoon?' asked Melanie, as we pushed our chairs back from the table.

'I was planning to make my way through a book on writing non-fiction when I'm not working on the case,' I said, which was true, although what I was actually looking forward to was a post-lunch nap. Connor and I sometimes took a nap after lunch at the weekends, curled up together on top of the covers. 'Look at us having a little nana nap,' he'd said last weekend. 'Does this mean we're old before our time?'

'I don't care if we are,' I said, tucking myself close into his body. When I woke from dozing, he shifted onto his side and leaned in to kiss me, running his hands over my body, then under my clothes. Our naps invariably ended up in leisurely, daytime sex, which felt considerably less like the behaviour of a couple who were past their prime.

'Cool,' said Melanie. 'I'd read a book by you.'

I smiled, trying not to show how flattered I was. 'Thanks, but don't hold your breath. I'm still at the learning how to write stage and, if I'm honest, I don't know if I'll ever actually start it. It will give me something to do when I'm not with Laura or writing up my notes, though.' I didn't add that I felt like I was jumping on the bandwagon. Every other psychologist was writing a book these days, and what made me think I had anything valuable to add?

Melanie grabbed a banana from a wire rack before we left and handed it to me. 'Need to keep your strength up,' she said.

'Thanks.' I took it, embarrassed that she seemed worried about how little I'd eaten. I was meant to be a mental health professional, not a patient. She shouldn't feel like she had to look after me. It occurred to me that she might have preferred to be the lead therapist on Laura's case and could be resentful I'd been brought in over her. A new pressure to prove myself to her bore down on my chest. One more stress to add to the list.

'How do you like working at Heaton Place?' I asked as we left the canteen, followed by Julie and Aidan.

She shrugged. 'It's okay, but I'm keen to move up the ladder.'

I looked across at her, trying to keep the surprise from my face. Her taut, line-free skin made me think she was at least five years younger than me, probably not even thirty yet. To be a supervising psychologist in a place like this at her age was already a pretty high rung to be on. 'You're ambitious – that's great,' I said. 'Any ideas about where you'd like to go next?'

'I've applied for a position at Bethlem,' she said.

'Ah, the city and the NHS. Good move.' I loved living in London and, although Bethlem was on the outskirts, it would offer plenty of professional and social opportunities for a young woman like Melanie. 'I know a consultant psychiatrist there, Marc Greaves. I could give him a call and—'

'No,' said Melanie abruptly. 'That's fine, thank you.'

I was taken aback. 'It's no bother. I'd like to help, if I can.'

'Really, it's fine. I have this thing about getting somewhere on my own merits. I wouldn't feel right about you putting in a good word. It's very kind, though. Thank you.' Her cheeks reddened and I regretted suggesting the call. She was clearly a very principled woman, and I liked her all the more for it.

I smiled and nodded. It was also probably for the best, since I might not still have Marc's number, now I considered it. It was years since I'd seen him or his wife, even though we'd once been close. I was terrible at keeping up with friends. I resolved to look them up when I got home.

As we reached the top of the stairs, my heart thumped against my ribcage, beating more quickly as we approached the glass walkway which connected the staff accommodation and the treatment centre. I'd reluctantly crossed it that morning when I was shown the way to the therapy room, but now I knew it was coming, my brain raced to find an excuse not to have to pass through it again.

Melanie chatted, explaining that the old army barracks

had been converted into bedrooms and the only way to access the modern clinic next door at this level was to use the walkway. I didn't want to disclose my fear of heights, so I casually stopped short, saying, 'I'm happy to use the stairs. I'd prefer to, actually. I need to keep fit.'

'I hear you,' said Melanie. 'But we'd have to open and close endless security doors, take flights and flights of steps to get all the way down, then cross the gravel, get buzzed into the clinic and through reception, then do it all in reverse to get up to the right level at the other side. It would take twenty minutes,' she said, 'instead of two.'

I gritted my teeth and followed her, struggling to keep my breath regular as we came closer. I replayed the cognitive behavioural therapy I'd done to shift my anxiety level from phobic to just intense fear. I reminded myself how far I'd come. A few years ago I wouldn't have been able to get this close to a glass tunnel five floors above the ground. I would be slick with sweat, shaking, crying and hyperventilating to the point of blacking out.

Now, all I had was a dry mouth, an increased pulse and nausea. Winning. Although, as I shifted the banana from one hand to the other to wipe my clammy palms on my jeans, it didn't feel like winning.

A smashing sound like glass breaking came from behind us. We all turned towards the stairwell as shouts bounced off the bare walls.

'Come on,' said Melanie, taking my elbow and steering me away from the noise, which stopped as abruptly as it had started.

I allowed her to move me forward, breathing in through my nose and out through my mouth as I put one foot on to the frosted glass. Thank God whoever designed this hellscape had had the sense to make the floor opaque. I took another step, the blinding brightness of the spring afternoon sun making me squint. Heat trapped in the tunnel made my skin dampen, although that could have been more to do with my body's reaction to the drop beneath me than the sun that glared down over the barracks on the opposite side of the gravel courtyard.

'Aw,' Aidan said, stopping and putting a hand up to shield his eyes. 'Looks like they really are going to demolish that old building. I thought they'd find some use for it, turn it into flats or something. I could have lived there.' He turned to Julie. 'Me and Marnie could have had a nice little place. You could visit.' He winked at Julie, his ice-blue eyes almost translucent in the reflected light. The back of Julie's neck reddened, making me wonder if there was a subtext to his comment.

'Yep, that's definitely a wrecking ball,' said Melanie. 'Time's up for that place.' I forced myself to look across the square courtyard to the old stone barracks. It looked to be similar to the one which housed the staff quarters here, five storeys high, with a majestic bell tower and a blue clock face whose hands stood at twelve thirty. The windows were black against the stone, like sightless eyes.

I wanted to move, to break away and march to the other side of the tunnel, but didn't want to show my weakness. Only when Aidan muttered, 'Bloody shame,' and turned, the others moving along with him, did I pick up my heel, then the ball of my foot, and walk with them. In fifteen more steps, the soles of my shoes rasped on the fuzzy carpet tiles on the other side and I could relax my jaw and breathe freely. Something wet and sticky made me look down at my hand. I found the banana squashed in my fist, pale mush escaping from its bulging skin. I put it behind my back.

My room was the sixth along the corridor. Melanie used her lanyard to open the door.

I turned to her on the threshold. 'Sure you wouldn't prefer me to go down and collect my ID and fob?' I said. 'And my phone?'

'No, I'm on it,' said Melanie. 'But you won't have access to the internet on your phone when you get it.'

'What do you mean?'

'They don't allow smart devices here ... well, they do, but there's a Wi-Fi and data block, like a kind of forcefield around Heaton Place.' She shrugged. 'I don't actually know how it works. All I know is that all the internet here is via ethernet, hard-wired into computers in secure areas. Your phone won't be able to access the internet while you're here, but you can use it to make calls and send texts.'

'Even staff aren't allowed on the internet?' I understood the rule for the patients, but surely the staff should be allowed on the web.

'Not on hand-held devices, I'm afraid. Remember, we treat a lot of sensitive cases here. Some are being assessed before they go on trial. Before the block was enforced, there were leaks of things going on in real time that, realistically, could only have come from staff, so . . .' She pointed at a laminated A4 sheet on top of the desk. 'The security measures are all laid out on that. Have a read through and hopefully it will start to make more sense.' She breathed out through her nose. 'A dangerous criminal can do a lot of harm with internet access. They might do a lot of harm *for* internet access. If no one has a portable device on Wi-Fi, then at least that danger is avoided. Most of the rules are for our safety, Emma. The measures are easier to stomach when you look at them from that perspective.'

'Okay. I'll have a look through now,' I said, defeated. The gluey banana between my fingers made me desperate to get inside the room and wash my hands. A piece dropped from between my fingers to the floor. 'But I do need my phone to call my husband.' I could live without scrolling social media, I might even enjoy having a break from freely available bad news, but I was still feeling guilty about our argument and, since Connor was away for work, I needed to check in with him at the very least.

'No problem. I'll get it now.' She smiled. 'I know a lot of this isn't ideal. We really do appreciate all the sacrifices you're making to help with this case.'

I returned her smile and stepped backwards into the room, hoping she wouldn't think I was a complete weirdo. She must've caught the whiff of banana and decided to help me save face, because she leaned forward and pulled the door. 'Let me get that for you,' she said, smiling indulgently until the door clacked into place between us, leaving me with a need to speak to Connor so urgent it was like a magnetic pull.

Chapter Nine

I was on top of the bed, half asleep, when a knock at the door brought me to full consciousness. I sat upright and ran my fingers through my hair in an attempt to hide the fact I'd been dozing when I should have been reading or working. I wasn't usually this unprofessional. I wasn't usually this tired. 'Come in.'

The door opened and Melanie peeked through the gap. 'I've got your lanyard.'

'Thanks.' On the way over to her, I noticed a brown globule on the carpet tile near the door. I berated myself for forgetting to clean up the dropped banana. Aidan and Julie were standing close together in the corridor, faces inches apart, seemingly deep in an intense conversation. I waved. They nodded and smiled, moving further apart. They began to talk again, but in false-sounding staccato sentences, like actors saying 'Rhubarb, rhubarb' in the background of a scene. 'Come in.' I held the door wide for Melanie.

She followed me into the room, leaving the door ajar.

I could still hear Aidan's rumbling voice. 'What's the deal with those two?' I whispered.

'Aidan and Julie?' Melanie said quietly. 'What do you mean?'

Her furrowed brow made me sure I was imagining things. 'Ignore me,' I said. 'I think being a psychologist can send you a bit bonkers, don't you? I'm always picking up on things, you know, sensing things that make me question . . .' I shook my head. 'There isn't always more going on below the surface, is there? My husband's always reminding me to take things at face value once in a while.'

I moved the chair from where it was tucked under the dressing table which doubled as my desk and gestured for Melanie to take a seat. I sat on the end of the bed facing her, wishing there was another chair. For some reason, speaking to her while perched on my bed made me feel vulnerable. I supposed it was the intimacy of inviting someone into the space I slept in, or the hang-over from knowing we are all at our most defenceless when we're unconscious.

'How's the book?' she said, nodding towards *The Art of Writing Non-Fiction*, which sat unopened on the bedside unit.

'Good, yeah. Interesting,' I said.

'Great.' She fished in the inside pocket of her jacket and drew out a rectangular laminated card attached to a blue lanyard and held it out to me. 'Here you go.'

'Great. Thanks.' I took it from her, and read my name in bold black type, followed by the words: 'Lead Psychologist'. A long ID number was printed underneath. I peered at the photo on the right-hand side. 'God, that picture's awful!' I laughed, but inside I was mortified by the pale, wide-eyed version of myself I saw in the square photograph.

'The camera they use for the IDs on reception isn't flattering, is it?' Melanie said. 'Mine was so hideous, I got this one done and moaned until they replaced it.' She held out an identical laminated ID, but where my picture was grey and unsmiling, hers was full colour, her brown eyes warm, her blue suit jacket looking smart and professional. 'If you were here for longer, I'd definitely advise getting another one done, but there doesn't seem much point for a few days.'

She truly seemed to think Laura's memory could be unlocked in the next five days. I hoped she was right. If the therapy didn't work, then the authorities would have to take the next steps, and I didn't like to think about where that would leave Laura. 'It doesn't matter.' I shrugged and hung the lanyard around my neck, lifting my hair over the ribbon. 'I'm not here for a beauty pageant, am I?' I imagined what Connor would have to say about the ID. He had a vain side he would never admit to. It probably came from always being the most attractive person in the room, although I might be biased about that. Whatever the reason, I doubted he'd ever allow an unflattering picture of himself to hang around his neck. I ran my finger over the circular metal fob that was attached to the top of the ID. 'This is for all the internal and external doors?'

'That's right. Have you read about the process on this?' She picked up the laminated sheet.

'Yeah. I'm surprised, to be honest.' I took the sheet from her and read: '"Please note that there have been some glitches in the new programming system and key fobs activated in the last week may need reprogramming. We are working hard to resolve this issue, but please ensure new fob carriers never travel around the building alone."' I looked up. 'That's not ideal, is it?'

'That's one way of putting it. But I always insist my team travels in a pack, anyway. It's safer that way, and if your fob doesn't work, then one of us can always buzz you in or out. That's one benefit of having a small group of staff on one case. Someone always has your back.'

A laugh came from the corridor. It sounded too girlish to be Julie's, more like someone being flirtatious, but it was followed by Aidan's low voice, then Julie's, so I imagined he'd said something to elicit a giggle from her. I thought about how long it had been since I'd heard laughter. There wasn't much to even smile about at Heaton Place. Melanie tapped her hands on her knees, then stood.

'Before you go,' I said. 'My phone?'

'Ah,' she said. 'About that.'

I gritted my teeth. I knew I should have gone down to reception myself. 'Is there a problem?'

Melanie's lips stretched over her small, even teeth in a grimace. 'I looked everywhere for it, but . . .'

'I left it on the desk in reception. I'm sure I did.' Heat rose up my neck. 'If it's been stolen—'

She put her hand out to stop me. 'It hasn't been stolen. Don't worry . . . When I couldn't find it, I asked everyone in the office, and it turns out Gail accidentally took it home with her.'

'What?'

'Gail. She was on reception when you came in. Apparently, she was going off shift and picked your phone up, thinking it was hers. She didn't realise she had two phones in her bag until she got home. She rang in and left a message about it first thing this morning. She didn't know whose it was, otherwise someone would have come to let you know.'

I pictured the screensaver of Connor smiling on my phone. Unless you knew both of us, there was nothing to indicate the phone was mine. 'Can she drop it back in today?' It was a pain, but at least it hadn't disappeared altogether.

'That's the other problem.'

I didn't want to hear about any more problems. I just wanted to call Connor.

'She's on holiday until Friday.'

I blinked slowly. Friday was the second to last scheduled day of Laura's treatment. 'I'm sorry, but since she made the mistake, I'm afraid she'll have to interrupt her time off and bring it back. I need to ring my husband.'

'I meant actually on holiday. She's gone to the Isle of Wight to visit her in-laws. She physically can't bring it back until Friday.'

'Oh, for Christ's sake,' I said, not caring if it was unprofessional. I was tired, fed up, and I wanted to hear Connor's voice.

'I know. I'm so sorry.' Melanie stood and patted her

jacket pockets. 'It's no consolation, but I found an old phone in the office.' She pulled out a grey device which was definitely not the sleek iPhone I'd arrived with. 'You can use this.'

'What?'

'I know it's an old model, but since you can't use the internet anyway . . . you can call and text on it.' She held it out to me.

The phone looked like the first mobile I'd ever owned. Mum had bought it for me after what had happened to Sarah, so I could always call her if I was in danger, or was having dark thoughts myself. Her paranoia was understandable, but I couldn't help thinking it had made its mark on me. It took a lot for me to trust people, men especially. I took the phone from Melanie, trying not to think of the way Mum had started to ring me almost hourly when her anxiety was at its worst. I turned the device over in my fingers, wondering if all mental health workers join the profession in the hope of learning how to heal those they love, or themselves.

'This thing's ancient.' I pressed the button on the side to turn it on. The small screen at the top lit up in a familiar green and I half expected to see the number for our old landline pop up in black digits. Automatically, I recited the number in my head. Mum didn't have a landline now she'd moved to the new flat. I'd never even tried to memorise her mobile number, or anyone else's except Connor's, for that matter. They were all stored in my phone contacts, usually just a short scroll away.

'It doesn't really solve the problem,' I said. 'I only know my husband's number off by heart.' Connor was the first person I wanted to ring, but I wanted the option of being able to contact anyone I liked.

'If you need to call anyone else, there's always reception. Maybe Sonia in the office could look numbers up for you? Although you'd have to get on her good side first, and if you manage that, let me know how, will you? That woman terrifies me.' Melanie gave an apologetic smile, which made me feel guilty for having a go at her. It wasn't her fault that stupid Gail had picked up my stupid phone and gone to the stupid Isle of Wight. 'To be honest, I like the break from all the WhatsApp group messages and social media notifications when I'm in here,' she said.

'Yeah, there is that,' I said, forcing myself to sound more resigned than I felt. I hadn't considered myself addicted to my phone, but now it wasn't to hand, my fingers itched to scroll the news app or tap on to social media. I couldn't remember a time when I hadn't turned to a screen to fill every spare minute. That wasn't necessarily a healthy habit. It wouldn't hurt me to break it. 'I'll think of it as a digital detox.'

'That's the spirit.' She headed towards the door. 'I'm on lates tonight. Shall I collect you before dinner? We could go down together.'

'Erm . . .' The thought of crossing the glass bridge again made my heart jump in my chest.

'Or I can get someone to bring a tray up if you'd prefer to get on with your reading?' She nodded to the book on the bedside unit.

'I don't want to put anyone out.'

'It's no bother. If I were you, I'd take advantage of whatever time's available.'

'If you're sure, that would be great, thanks. I'll never write that book if I don't learn how. Before you go' – I pointed at the camera in the corner where the ceiling met the wall near the door – 'that thing's not on, is it?'

Melanie looked at the camera. 'No, I'm sure it's not.'

'Phew,' I said, imagining a burly security guard watching me climb out of my greying undies at bedtime. 'Why do you even have cameras in the staff accommodation?'

'We sometimes use this floor as overflow.'

'For patients?' I wasn't proud to feel a shiver of discomfort, but after hearing the screaming and banging outside the therapy room, I wasn't keen to be sleeping in the same corridor as anyone ... in crisis.

'Only those considered safe. Nobody we think would be a danger to either the staff or themselves.'

'All right,' I said, not entirely reassured.

'And Julie and Aidan are in the rooms either side of yours, so you're perfectly safe.'

I stared at her, not quite sure how to reply. Was that just for convenience, or was this place dangerous enough to warrant two orderlies to be stationed either side of my room? 'Good to know. Thanks.' I glanced back at the camera, making a mental note to undress in the bathroom from now on.

When Melanie left, my aching eyes reminded me just how drained I was. Having at least some means of contacting

Connor, and the thought of having the evening to myself without having to go to the canteen and make small talk, made the tight muscles in my shoulders unfurl. The room wasn't set up for relaxing, though. The only furniture was the single bed, the bedside cabinet, a desk and a chair, and a narrow wardrobe to the left of the door. I'd stayed in more salubrious Travelodges.

I opened the cupboard, glad to see a spare pillow in the top section. Plumping it up along with the one already on the bed, I managed to get into a comfortable semi-reclined position, ready to talk to Connor. Since he was away with work, and getting to Heaton Place had been so harried, I'd only sent a quick text to let him know where I was. I hadn't addressed our argument, and as I dialled his number and waited to hear his voice I planned what I was going to say to make things right. I would tell him I understood why he was upset when I took on another client whose family had connections to organised crime. 'Who else is going to support her?' I'd said. 'I can't refuse to treat her because of who's beating her up.'

'You always put the women you work with above us,' he'd said. When I tried to disagree, he said, 'Shannon Bray's husband has connections, you know. He might be locked up for now, but do you think a man capable of kidnapping his own son and attacking police with a machete will forget about the woman who helped his wife take his son away from him?'

'I didn't help her to take him,' I said. In truth, that was what had caused me so many sleepless nights since the kidnap. A woman and child had gone through hell, all because I was so drained after back-to-back sessions I fell asleep on the sofa when I got home. By the time I set the wheels in motion to get Shannon and Kai into a shelter, it was too late. Her abusive husband had taken their son, a manhunt was underway, and my professionalism was rightly called into question. Despite being acquitted of any blame by the inquiry, I couldn't shake off the feeling that their ordeal was my fault. I was determined never to make a mistake like that again.

'As good as,' said Connor. 'That's how he'll see it, anyway – that you were plotting with her to steal his child. And his network will still be active, whether he's in prison or not, especially around here. It's like you're wilfully putting yourself in danger.'

Now I'd calmed down, I could see his point. I hoped my apology wouldn't be negated by my decision to take on this case. He might think I was mad to drop everything and come to Heaton Place. Between putting my foot in it during Laura's first session, that awful glass walkway and my missing phone, I was struggling not to come to that conclusion myself.

Goosebumps rose on my skin. I tugged back the thin duvet and climbed underneath, all the while holding the phone to my ear. The tone rang and rang. I cursed the fact he didn't have an active voicemail box. He hated listening to messages, always saying that, if the call was important, whoever it was would ring back.

I clicked the red cancel button, took the phone away from

my ear and checked the number to make sure I'd pressed the right digits. It was his number. I tried again. Nothing. I sighed. This happened a lot when he was working away. He often had a full day of meetings followed by dinners with important contacts, making it almost impossible to get hold of him. I ended the call, remembering that the phone I was ringing from would show up on his screen as an unknown number. Of course he wouldn't answer. He'd presume it was someone asking about a claim for a fictitious car accident, or selling double-glazing.

I'd better text, to explain it was me. The keys were tiny and difficult to navigate and I got frustrated that I could only see a few words of my text at once on the small screen. I gave up after typing, *Em here. Still away, but will be back on Saturday. Unusual case. Will tell you all when I see you. Hope trip is going well. You can get me on this number. Love you. Xxx*

I tried to read my book, but none of the information penetrated my brain. I closed it and opened Laura's case notes, going over what I'd learned in today's session. My gaze kept drifting over to the phone on the bedside cabinet, willing it to ring. I tried to concentrate on the file, but exhaustion blurred my vision. I gave up and closed my eyes.

I was drifting off to sleep when a metallic tapping noise in the corner of the room made me open my eyes. I sat up, my heart speeding as the sound got faster, then eventually slowed to a quiet tick. I remembered the old iron radiators to the right of the desk and sank back on the mattress, my body feeling weighted down with exhaustion.

I'd once read that when the heart stopped beating, gravity causes blood to collect at the lowest point of the body. Lying on the thin mattress, trying to lose myself to sleep again, my brain conjured the image of thick, coagulated blood leaving my face, dropping to the back of my skull, collecting in my buttocks and the back of my legs. In my half-consciousness, my mind's eyes turned my pale face to Sarah's, and I saw her, with agonising clarity, her blood draining through her broken body to settle against the concrete.

Chapter Ten

Tuesday

When Melanie, Aidan and Julie left to collect Laura for this morning's therapy, I sat in the same place on the sofa as I had in our first session. Consistency was important. That's why I was so frustrated that the sessions were at irregular hours. When I'd asked why we couldn't meet at the same time each day, Melanie told me it was because we had to fit in around the hours the room was already booked. That seemed ridiculous to me. We only had five more days to unlock Laura's memory. Surely Management could have organised things more efficiently?

I wished I'd brought the phone down with me instead of leaving it in my room out of a sense of professionalism. I always made sure it was out of sight during therapy sessions and I didn't want it obviously bulging in my pocket. We all spent enough time being half listened to by people who had one eye on a phone screen. I wanted my clients to be confident they had my full attention. That said, Connor hadn't picked up when I called that morning, and my fingers now itched to send another text, in case the last one hadn't got through.

Ten minutes later, quiet voices came from the corridor. With some effort, I prepared a smile for when Laura came in. Purple circles sat under her eyes, reminding me of the eyeshadow Mum used to wear when we were small. When I was about six, Sarah and I once sneaked her make-up bag into our room and tried to do each other's faces. I remembered giggling at the feel of the soft brush on my eyelids, then the shouting when Dad found us, 'painted like little whores'. We never played with Mum's make-up again.

'Hello,' I said. 'How are you today?'

'I didn't sleep well.' Laura sat on the seat facing me, rubbing at the corner of her eye, leaving it red when she dropped her hand.

In my peripheral vision, I saw the blue of Melanie's suit as she shook off her jacket and took a seat at the desk. I wondered how she didn't melt, so close to that radiator. I was already faint with the heat. My gaze flicked to the glass pane in the door, the sight of Aidan's ear confirming that everyone was in the same position as yesterday.

'Anything in particular keeping you awake?'

'This place is noisy,' she said, dispelling any hope I had of a vivid dream that held a clue to her subconscious. That's what would happen in a film, I mused. I'd had a sequence of disturbing dreams myself last night, all tied up with Laura's case. I woke up with visions of knives and blood imprinted on my brain. There was also a weird filmic image of Connor and my father doing some kind of ritualistic dance that led to them morphing into the same person. That was disturbing. I'd chosen Connor specifically because he was nothing like my dad. It was inevitable, I supposed, that something as mysterious as what happened in Laura's kitchen that day, added to the pressure of getting to the truth of it, would have my own subconscious working overtime. The dreams combined with the uncomfortable bed had left me even more exhausted than I had been the day before.

When planning this session, I'd decided to go back to basics. I was painfully aware that one of our six days was spent, and I couldn't afford to make the same mistake as before. To avoid it, I needed to learn more about Laura, her self-structure, what she believed about herself and the world. That way, I might be able to discover the best way to help her access the memories she'd lost. 'If it's okay with you, I'd like to talk about your childhood.'

She nodded.

In her notes, I'd read she had a sister. 'You have one sibling, is that right?'

Laura smiled. 'Yes, one sister, Nicole.'

'The thought of her makes you smile. Is she older or younger?'

Her smile widened and I became aware of a tinge of envy. I used to brighten when I thought of Sarah. I accepted the feeling then moved it aside, focusing on Laura's blue eyes.

'Younger, by two years.'

'Are you close?'

'Yes, we've always been close.'

I tried to recall what Laura's file said about Nicole. Surely it would have been noted if she'd been to visit her at the facility. Maybe she had information that might help.

'She's been working in Dubai for a few years now, so I haven't seen much of her recently,' Laura said.

Ah. 'You must miss her.' The pain of never being able to see Sarah again stung the back of my eyes. I was over-identifying. I needed to get a grip.

'Yes.'

'And you mentioned your parents had a ... would you say a *difficult* relationship?'

'That's one word for it.'

'What word would best describe it?'

'Passive aggressive.' She tucked her hands between her thighs, her shoulders curling in. She looked like she was making herself smaller. I noted the feeling of protectiveness that rose in me.

'Did you question why your parents stayed together in an unhealthy relationship?' I was invested in her answer. I'd struggled with the fact that my mother had stayed in an abusive marriage. When I understood that my dad's behaviour was actively cruel, I'd become resentful that she made the choice to normalise an abusive relationship by not walking away and taking Sarah and me with her. But that was before I'd learned about the predatory nature of abusive men, about how they carefully chose their prey, assessing the qualities of kindness and generosity before moving in for the kill.

Truly understanding that women who fall prey to abusive men weren't ever responsible in any way for the abuse they suffered, even in repeated cases, had been a turning point in my career. When I discovered that abusers specifically target women who are kind, and often vulnerable, then groom them insidiously until even their thoughts and the language they use become those of the abuser, I made it my mission to help the women see that. It was too late for Sarah by then, so I started with my mother. It helped to mend us. We became very close for a while – before life got in the way.

'I'm not proud of the fact I thought my mum was weak for staying,' Laura said. 'Even though he was the one causing most of the friction, I looked up to my dad, thought he was the strong one.'

I nodded. 'That's understandable.' I noted the word 'strong'. Laura had learned at a young age that there was a power dynamic in a relationship. One person was strong, and one was weak. I couldn't help myself wondering which she had been in her relationship with Daniel? 'And what do you think now?'

She blew out her cheeks. 'Now I know it's not as simple as that. It never is, is it? When two people are together for a long time, patterns of behaviour develop slowly, sometimes imperceptibly. Often, people have no idea they're in a dysfunctional relationship. That's my experience, anyway.'

Her experience was exactly what I wanted to hear. I hoped it might trigger more recent memories. I remained quiet, sensing she had more to say.

'And when they got divorced, for example,' she continued, releasing her hands from between her thighs, the movement seeming significant, 'I should have been pleased for Mum, for both of them. It was the right thing to do.

They were unhappy for as long as I could remember and they had a chance to be happy either on their own or with other people, but ... it impacted me in a way I hadn't anticipated.'

'You felt destabilised by it?'

'Yeah. I suppose it was the end of ... I don't know ... Even though I'd left home by the time they split up, until that point I'd been able to pretend I had a happy upbringing, came from a stable home, you know?'

I nodded.

'We lived in a quaint village, rode ponies, learned piano, that kind of thing. We were like everyone else, even if, behind closed doors, there was an atmosphere.'

'Could you describe the atmosphere?' I remembered the thrum of anxiety in my childhood home. If she described the environment she grew up in, maybe she would recognise similarities in her own relationship, or convince me of the opposite. I had to keep an open mind.

She fixed me with a stare. 'I'm sure you know what I mean.'

I blinked. Had she read my thoughts?

Before I'd gathered a reply she said, 'You've worked with enough victims of abuse to understand what it's like to live in an atmosphere of constant low-level fear of something going wrong.'

I quietly let the air out from my lungs. Of course she was talking about my work. 'I'm sorry you experienced that. I imagine it was difficult for Nicole too.'

'She found it hard, yes.'

'Did you feel you had to make things better for her, since you were the older sister?' How strong were her protective urges?

I sensed a change in Laura. The muscles in her jaw tensed, then released. She didn't answer.

'Did you talk about the atmosphere with her? Have you discussed it since your parents split up?'

She tugged her ponytail higher. I waited.

Eventually she said, 'It's not easy when we can't protect the people we love, is it? I love my sister very much.'

Her voice was quiet, and I sensed a deep sadness. Despite wanting to mine this further, I was concerned she might shut down if the feelings started to overwhelm her. I decided to change direction. 'You spoke about barriers you'd put in place before you met Daniel. Would you say your parents' relationship and divorce were the reason for those barriers?'

Laura looked up at the window behind the wire grille. I wasn't sure if the brightness I saw in her eyes was a reflection of the spring sky or the thought of this man she seemed to worship. 'I guess so. He wanted a deep connection, to know everything about me, and that was intense. It felt too quick. I wasn't used to giving so much of myself. I've never been great at opening up to people.' She dropped her eyes and let out a short laugh. 'Ironic, considering our line of work, isn't it? But if you're brought up in a household where unpleasant things are kept behind closed doors and you're taught to put on a performance for the outside world, you get used to keeping things to yourself.'

I sensed she was loosening up again. 'How did he manage to win you round?'

She smiled and shook her head. 'He knew I was holding back. He has great intuition. It's like he can see inside people, see what makes them tick.' She took up a strand of her ponytail and twirled it around her forefinger in a way that looked self-consciously flirtatious. The gesture could have been in response to the memories she was accessing, but it seemed oddly artificial, as though it was meant to signify something to me. A naïve girlishness, perhaps? 'It wasn't that I didn't have feelings for him from quite early on. I did,' she continued. 'That was the problem, I think. The feelings scared me. I'd told myself I wasn't the relationship type.'

'Do you think that was a defence mechanism?'

'Possibly. But he was persistent. That man does not like to take no for an answer. It wasn't just that, though. He convinced me that he truly cared for me. That everything he did was for me.'

'Convinced' struck me as an odd word to use. I could be reading into it, but to me, it suggested a deliberate act. It suggested deception.

Chapter Eleven

The Past

There was a tarpaulin canopy by the back door to shield the smokers from the autumn drizzle, but the landlord hadn't run to a patio heater. I was freezing cold as I watched fat raindrops shudder at the edge of the tarp then splash on to the crazy paving below. I sucked on my cigarette, enjoying the orange glow and satisfying crackle as the tobacco burned. The gratifying scorch of the last drag burned in my throat, then I stubbed the cigarette out and dropped my dog-end in the bin. I hurried back into the heat of the pub, my cheeks stinging from the bitter air.

He was sitting alone at the table. I felt immediately guilty for leaving my boyfriend with only his phone for company so I could have a fag. I fixed an apologetic smile on my face when he looked up. The term 'boyfriend' sounded funny, even after two months. I leaned in for a kiss when I sat back down. 'All right?'

'I am now you're back.' He gently bumped his body against mine.

'God, sorry, it's so rude to leave you on your own. It's a

filthy habit.' I opened the lid of my cigarette packet. 'Look, only one left.' I glowered at the white circle of the tip, hating the fact I was so dependent on the bloody things. 'So at least I won't be spending all night out there.'

'Want me to get you some more?' he said. He sat up straighter, head turning, scanning the room. 'Do pubs still have cigarette machines? I don't suppose they sell them behind the bar like they used to, do they?'

I flushed, astonished at his kindness. Cigarettes were ridiculously expensive, so the offer was generous. 'I doubt it, I haven't seen a cigarette machine for years. Don't worry, It's fine.'

'I'll pop to the newsagent's if you like?' He reached for his coat and I flushed with affection.

'Don't. Seriously, there's no need.' I put my hand on his arm to stop him. 'It's kind of you, but . . .' I paused, then made a decision, 'I really need to give up. Maybe it's time to give it a proper go.'

He stilled, his eyes searching my face. 'If you want to give up, I'll do whatever I can to support you.' He wrapped his hands around his pint, leaning in towards the scuffed table. 'I do worry about you.'

My heart plummeted. Making someone worry about you was not sexy. Your nan was meant to worry about you, not the hot bloke you're shagging. My mind went back to that morning when I'd woken before him. I'd stared at his gorgeous face for ages, still finding it hard to believe he'd chosen me out of all the women out there. If I was honest, I didn't understand why. I was sure one day soon *he'd wake up and realise I wasn't worth all the effort he put in to make me happy.*

He must've sensed my eyes on him because he'd woken and his mouth had lifted in a languorous smile, then he'd rolled over and pushed me down on to my back. He was already hard and the sex was slow and intense. He'd looked into my eyes when he came, and I could still see his face in my mind's eye, mouth open in a grimace of pleasure.

Now, his jaw was tight, and I hated myself for making him concerned. 'I don't want you to worry about me,' I said.

'It's natural to worry about the people you care about,' he said, running his hand up my thigh, making me imagine it going higher, hidden by the pub table. His hand stopped. 'Don't you worry about me?'

I dropped my gaze. 'You don't have any filthy habits.' I flicked my eyes up to his face. 'That I know about.'

He smirked and his fingers moved a centimetre higher on my thigh. 'Filthy, you say?'

'Filthy.'

He leaned in and kissed me. Then I remembered I stank. I smelled like an ashtray. I was suddenly acutely aware of my rancid breath and my disgusting mouth. I pulled away. 'Got any mints?' I tried a laugh, but it sounded false, even to me.

His brows furrowed. 'What's wrong?'

'I've got fag-breath.'

He grinned. 'That wasn't what I was thinking about in that moment.'

'Oh, yeah. What were you thinking about?' The words

sounded flirtatious, but I wasn't feeling light and coquettish any more. I felt grubby. I lifted my pint and gulped, trying to fill my mouth with another odour.

'You. I find I'm always thinking about you,' he said, shifting on the bench to face me. 'Even when I'm at work.'

'Isn't a counterterrorism officer's mind wandering like that bad for national security?' I smiled at him from under my lashes, hoping the bouncy feeling would return.

'Yeah. Very bad. You're a risk to the welfare of the nation.'

I couldn't think of another smart retort. I turned to look at him, trying not to breathe in his direction. 'I really do want to give up smoking,' I said. 'I keep trying to—'

'I love that you want to stop, because I worry,' he said, an earnest expression replacing his smile, 'that it's harming you – or will, one day. And I couldn't bear it.'

He stared at me, and I was forced to exhale normally, unable to draw my gaze away.

'Because I've fallen in love with you,' he said.

Thrilled as I was at the time, I'd been hiding away in the days since the proclamation of love. I'd diagnosed myself as a commitment-phobe and a coward. I had good reason not to want a committed relationship, I told myself. Growing up in a family like mine would make anyone sceptical about love. Dad always told Mum he loved her, usually over the sound of her crying. Actions speak louder than words.

When my best friend, Gaby, came around and I showed her the massive bouquet of flowers he'd sent, her mouth dropped open. 'Bloody hell, mate. He's well into you.'

She plucked the card from where it nestled against a hyacinth. 'All my love, always.' She blew out her lips. 'He doesn't do things by halves, this one, does he?'

The words 'this one' suggested there had been others, but there hadn't, not for a long time, and certainly not with this intensity. 'Nope,' I said, taking the card from her and placing it back among the purple blooms. Their sweet perfume followed me to the sofa. I fell back on to the cushions. 'He's an all-or-nothing kinda guy.' I said it in an American accent, hoping to add some humour, because I was a little embarrassed by the romance of it. Men my age didn't usually go in for the hearts-and-flowers stuff, not in my experience, anyway. And I was waiting for him to realise he'd made a mistake. Any minute now he'd discover I was just little old me, not the person he'd put on a pedestal too big for someone as ordinary as I am. 'I'm worried that it's all a bit much,' I said. 'It's a lot, isn't it?'

'And you're not feeling it?' She raised an eyebrow. 'Is it because he's a bit of an ug?' She sat next to me, digging my ribs with her elbow and laughing. 'Are you having second thoughts because you don't want to be seen out with someone who looks like Danny DeVito?'

'No. He's gorgeous, actually.' I pictured him and desire flared in my abdomen. 'And he's thoughtful and considerate.' I picked up my glass of wine from the coffee table and took a sip, feeling warm at just the thought of him.

'Crap in bed, then?'

I pretended to make my mouth fall open in shock but couldn't keep it up for laughing. 'He is not crap in bed.' I held my glass in front of my face, hiding as I said, 'Quite the opposite, in fact.'

Gaby squealed. 'I can see why you've taken a step back.' She laughed. 'Nobody needs that shit.'

I rolled my eyes. 'All right, sarky. It's just . . .'

'Your diamond shoes are too tight?'

'Shut up.' I sat back and tried to work out how I really felt about this man who'd seemingly fallen head over heels in love with me. 'Like I said, it's a lot. That's all. I'm scared that . . .' I trailed off. I'd never told anyone about my family background and how it had affected my view of relationships. Not even my closest friends. To the outside world, everything had appeared normal, and I'd gone along with that. Keeping up appearances had become second nature. 'I'm worried he wants more than I can give. I don't do relationships. It's a rule.'

'It's a stupid rule. You've got so much love to give, mate. You're the kindest person I know. You deserve someone who wants to put you first for a change, instead of you always looking after everyone else.' She pursed her lips. Gaby wasn't often serious, and I was moved by her words.

'You know I want to concentrate on my career.' That was the excuse I'd stuck with over the years, and everyone I knew was feminist enough not to challenge it.

'I get that, but you're established now, so you can relax. You might not know which direction you want to take next, but the reason you have choices is because you're bloody good at your job.'

I smiled. It was true, and I wasn't ashamed to admit it.

I was proud of my career. I had a good reputation and, as she said, I had choices. The career excuse wasn't going to stand up for much longer. 'And he's career-minded too, so I suppose he gets it. He's with Counterterrorism, did I tell you?' I raised my eyebrows and my voice, because of course I'd told her. The man who was in love with me was keeping the country safe. There was something important and almost glamorous about that.

Gaby laughed. 'You might have mentioned it once or twice.' She picked up her wine and eyed me over the rim of the glass. 'What's the harm in giving it a go?' she said. 'Obviously, I haven't met him, so if he's a slimy minger . . .'

'He is not slimy or a minger.'

'Then stop being a dick and take a chance on the guy.'

My phone jumped, vibrating on the glass coffee table. I picked it up. 'Speak of the devil,' I said.

'Is he proposing?' She smirked and took a slug of wine. I read the message. 'No, but he's had this mad idea.'

I showed her his message. She bit down on her bottom lip, her eyes bright with excitement. 'Mate, you've got to do it.'

'Have I?' I said.

'Come on.' She pointed at the flowers. 'It's not every day a fit bloke with a reliable job showers you with gifts and invites you on a date like that.' Her face became serious. 'I know you've got your reservations, but you're a psychologist, and a bloody good one. You'd be able to tell if there was something off about him.' She paused. 'And he's in the Met. They've already screened him for you. What's stopping you?'

'He's encouraging me to stop smoking.' It was the only thing I could think of, apart from the fact he was too good to be true, and I couldn't say that without sounding ridiculous.

'Good,' she said. 'You want to stop smoking, don't you?'

She had a point. Much as I was loath to admit it, I'd felt better for cutting down in the last week. I thought back to our dates. He'd been nothing but thoughtful, funny and attentive. The problem really was with me. 'No,' I said. 'No red flags. He's perfect.'

'Then what are you waiting for?' She tapped the side of my phone. 'Answer the man.'

Chapter Twelve

Laura's whole demeanour was transformed by her memories. This was good. The work we were doing on her recall would be easier if she was relaxed. She softened into the sofa and her eyes misted with reminiscences that made the corners of her mouth lift. Her wistfulness made me remember how it felt to fall so completely in love with someone you lost your mind a little.

Most psychologists I know agree that love is what motivates the majority of human actions. I knew from bitter experience that, when what it meant to be loved was presented in as warped a way as it had to Laura, and at such an early age, it was bound to make her hesitant to throw her heart into the ring.

As she continued her story, I gleaned that, when she did love someone, it was with her entire being. The way she spoke about Nicole showed she was capable of enormous love. I suspected she was the kind of person whose affections were hard won, but strong and loyal. Once Daniel was her partner, I imagined she'd do anything for him.

Out of nowhere, I remembered the horrific experiment I'd read about in a novel. It had described how, in a scientific investigation using monkeys and their babies, the floor of the monkey's cage was heated up until it was too hot to bear. Initially the monkey mothers tried to escape by climbing the walls, but, in every single case, when they could no longer sit or stand and there was no escape, all the mothers finally resorted to standing on their babies.

I remembered feeling sick at the images that appeared in my head when I first read the words. I'd searched the internet to see if the experiment had actually taken place, but was presented with more stories of animal cruelty that were even worse than the visions of screaming baby monkeys my brain was playing on repeat and I closed the search down before finding out.

When I discussed it with Connor in bed that night, he said, 'I don't believe the monkeys would do that.'

'Don't you think self-preservation trumps everything, even maternal love?'

He'd looked at me so intently it felt like he was searching my soul. 'No, I don't.' He moved closer, pulling me into his warm body. My head nestled into his neck. His Adam's apple moved against my cheek when he said, 'I'd die for you, Emma.' He kissed the top of my head before adding, 'I'd kill for you too.'

I watched Laura's face, wondering exactly how far she would go for love, but found it increasingly difficult to concentrate because a swelling discomfort in my bladder kept demanding my attention. I ignored it for as long as I could, mortified that I might have to break the flow of the session. Eventually, when the tightness in my pelvis was all I could think about, I knew interrupting our work was my only option. 'Let's take a break for a few minutes,' I said, then turned to Melanie. 'I'm just going to pop to the ladies.'

I stood, averting my eyes from Melanie's as she got to the door before me and pressed her fob against the metal, sure she'd think I was unprofessional for needing the loo in the middle of a session, because it was exactly what I thought. 'Julie, could you escort Emma to the bathroom, please?' she said when the door swung wide.

'It's fine,' I said. 'Just point me in the direction—'

'We travel in packs, remember?' Melanie raised an eyebrow and I felt suitably chastised.

Julie pointed down the corridor, and I led the way. Two men were approaching from the opposite direction, an orderly dressed in scrubs and the other in a tracksuit, the jogging bottoms hanging loosely around his skinny hips. Reminded that teams kept themselves to themselves, I lowered my gaze, my arm brushing against the wall as I kept to the right-hand side.

When the pair came level with us, a fug of body odour filled my nostrils. I glanced up to see the man in the tracksuit's oily hair falling over his face as he looked down at me. His dry, cracked lips lifted in a lopsided smile. I turned away but, as I did, his hand flew out and grabbed the lanyard around my neck. My head jerked forward as he yanked the ID card, dragging me towards him. The stench of his unwashed body grew stronger as my face neared his. A sharp pain speared my neck, then another as Julie grabbed the card from his hand. There was a bang, then a grunted expulsion of air as the orderly shoved the man's body back against the wall.

Julie took me by the shoulders and turned me in the direction of the bathroom. She gave me a small shove in the back and I started to walk. Too shocked to say a word, I moved, trancelike, away from the growled whispering behind me, the sound of footsteps getting fainter as the men walked away.

'You all right?' said Julie, when the corridor was quiet.

'Yes,' I lied. 'I think so.' I saw the sign for the ladies and pushed down the handle with shaking hands. I rushed into the cubicle, pulled down my trousers and knickers and sat, emptying my bladder in a welcome rush. There was a dark patch in my underwear. I was glad it wasn't worse. I'd been so frightened by what happened out there, I could easily have wet myself. I ran over the incident in my head, naming the feelings I'd experienced: shock, terror, revulsion. The man's stench lingered in my nostrils, mixing with the ammonia of my urine. I had the urge to call Connor and cry down the phone line, but since the phone was in my room, that wasn't an option.

Julie greeted me with a sympathetic half-smile when I came out of the cubicle. 'You really okay? That must've been pretty scary.'

The way she said 'must've been' was like she hadn't been there, or, at least, wasn't frightened by it. I couldn't imagine ever not being terrified by an attack like that. It had happened so quickly. I was left with a sense of the speed of it, the unnerving understanding that, in an environment like Heaton Place, things can turn nasty in an instant.

I washed my hands, looking at myself in the reflective metal sheet that was on the wall instead of a mirror. There were danger signals everywhere. Even the wall of the bathroom was a reminder that glass could be broken and used as a weapon. Dents in the shiny surface warped my reflection, making my eyes wider and my mouth curve to one side in a grimace. A red band was blossoming around my neck where the ribbon of the lanyard had cut into my skin. I touched the raised welt with my finger, watching Julie's reflection draw closer behind me.

'Looks sore,' she said.

I turned to face her and took the paper towels she offered. 'Does that kind of thing happen often?' I said, rubbing my hands dry.

'What do you want me to say?'

I walked to the bin and dropped the towels inside. I imagined Connor's face when he saw the marks on my neck when I got home. He was right about the risks I was taking. As soon as this case was over, I would take stock of my practice. Four more days, then I would change my life for good.

Chapter Thirteen

Laura was ushered out of the room while Melanie fussed over me and Julie and I filled in incident reports.

'Are you sure you're okay to carry on with today's session?' Melanie asked, her eyes dark slits of concern.

In truth, I didn't know if I was, but time was slipping away and I really felt like I was getting somewhere with Laura talking openly about her feelings for Daniel. I sensed that was the first step to finding out what had happened the night she was found. I was shaken, but if I went back to my room, I might dwell on the incident in the corridor, and not come out of there again until I could go home. It seemed like a better idea to forge on. 'Yes, let's continue with the session.'

When Laura was sitting opposite me again, her eyes rested on my neck. 'God, what happened?'

'Nothing to worry about,' I said. 'I'd like to carry on where we left off, talking about the early days of your relationship with Daniel.'

'You sure you're okay?'

I resisted the urge to lift my hair away from my neck. Back in the heat of the room, sweat made the grazed skin smart. 'Yes, thank you. So, your friend encouraged you to carry on seeing Daniel, despite your reservations?'

'Yes, but . . .' She shifted in her seat. I waited. Eventually she said, 'It wasn't just that I was reluctant to make myself vulnerable by, you know, committing to a relationship. I was working on a case that made me hyperaware of how badly things can go wrong when a relationship ends.'

I nodded. This line of conversation put me in a tricky situation. I wanted to ask what she meant, but surely patient confidentiality still mattered, even when a psychologist was being detained? 'I know you can't talk about the specifics of a case, but can you tell me why you were affected in the way you were?'

She lifted one slippered foot on to the seat and hooked her hands around her knee, staring up at the window. The position seemed oddly relaxed. 'It was how broken he was,' she said. 'It was a man I was treating. He'd split up with his wife – her choice – and she'd taken his son away from him. He was no angel – he had a criminal record – but he was adamant that he didn't deserve to be separated from his child. The loss he was experiencing was like grief. He could hardly function when he first came to see me.'

'To be clear, it was the loss of contact with his child that negatively impacted him?' The news footage of Kai Bray's tear-streaked face at the window of the caravan, watching his father being disarmed, then dragged away by police, flared behind my eyes. 'Not his partner?' I couldn't predict which way this was going, and that, along with the flashback to last year, made the muscles at the base of my neck tighten.

'Yeah, that's right. I felt an unusual connection to this patient. I really felt his distress, you know what I mean?'

I nodded.

'But it also struck home because I was already in my thirties.' Her shoulders rose and fell. 'I suppose I was thinking that, if I started a relationship at my age, and it got serious, having kids would be a natural progression. That's how things go, isn't it?'

I didn't answer the question. Maybe she was introducing the idea of having children because it was a source of conflict in her relationship. It could have been a flashpoint. I watched her carefully for any signs she was recalling something distressing. 'Did Daniel say he wanted children?'

She hugged her knee in tighter. 'Not right at the start. After we got serious, he told me he'd previously been in a long-term relationship with a woman who'd wanted kids.'

'But he didn't?'

'Not with her, apparently.'

There was a slightly gloating undertone in her voice that sounded callous. I looked at her, careful to keep my face neutral, wondering whether her true colours were seeping through. Perhaps she wasn't quite as gentle a soul as I'd thought. 'But he did with you?'

She let her knee drop. 'We talked about it, but I was scared. After growing up in a family like mine, I wanted everything to be perfect before bringing a child into the world.'

'You didn't feel like your relationship was perfect?' I felt myself leaning forward and corrected my posture. I shouldn't look too keen.

'I already knew what divorce felt like from a child's perspective, and the man I was treating, the pain he was in – it was raw emotional agony. I was frightened of feeling anything close to that. He was in such a state I didn't know what he might do.'

She'd brought it back to the man she was treating, so, reluctantly, I followed her lead. 'You thought he might harm himself?'

'Yes, that crossed my mind, but he talked more about what he could do to get his son back. He wasn't being rational. I was worried he would go to any lengths to see the boy.'

She didn't take her eyes from my face. A bead of sweat trickled down my spine. 'When did you treat this man?' I asked. I knitted my fingers together in my lap and felt my heart pummel my ribcage as I waited for her reply.

Her lids lowered a fraction. 'Why?'

I was taken aback by the question. Then I realised mine was the unusual one. What difference did it make when she had treated the man who would go to any lengths to spend time with his child? How did that move her therapy forward?

'You're right. It doesn't make any difference.' In my peripheral vision, I was aware of Melanie leaning over her pad, making notes. 'What I meant was, did the man resolve his issues?'

'You mean did he get visitation rights?'

That wasn't what I meant at all, I realised. However hard I tried to keep my brain from going in that direction, I knew what I meant: did you treat Jimmy Bray at the same time I was working with his wife? Do you know what lengths he went to and my part in what happened? Are you toying with me and, if so, why? 'Yes. Did he?'

'I don't know. He stopped coming to his sessions and didn't reply to calls or emails, so I guess I'll never know. I do know that seeing how distraught he was made me even more nervous about throwing myself into a relationship, even with Daniel. Daniel told me he was a safe bet. He'd made all his mistakes in his previous relationship and promised he'd learned from them.' She paused. 'But trust takes a long time to build, doesn't it?'

I steepled my fingers in front of my face, trying to mask the fact that I was gulping in a deep breath. Of course she hadn't treated Jimmy Bray. I was being paranoid. But there was something else needling me. The way Laura looked at me when she spoke, it was intense. I took another lungful of air. 'I understand,' I said. 'Was there anything in particular that made you put your trust in Daniel?'

'He devised a whole scavenger hunt just for me,' she said. 'That's the day that changed everything.'

Chapter Fourteen

The Past

On the day of the scavenger hunt, the first clue came by text: Meet Cute. It was easy to decipher. I stood in front of the hotel entrance where we first met and looked around for the next clue. I asked if anything had been left for me at reception, flushing when the snooty receptionist asked if I was a guest and I had to say no. I sensed her eyes still on me as I scoured the steps and the planted borders in front of the brickwork, muttering to myself that this scavenger hunt was a stupid idea. The wind sent cold needles through my thin jacket and I wished I'd put something warmer on. The sky had turned darker in the time I'd been hovering outside and it was probably going to rain. Perhaps it was time to give up.

The thought of his lips turning down at the corners when I told him his efforts had come to nothing made me give it one last try. I replayed the evening we met in my head and retraced my steps to the side of the building where the silver cigarette bin stood.

The first time we went out, I'd asked him what he was doing lurking in the shadows that evening.

'*Surveillance on one of the business owners at the event,*' he said. '*They have links with an organised crime network funding a terrorist cell.*'

The hairs on my arms stood up. 'Wow. Who?'

He wrapped a curl of my hair slowly around his finger. The gesture felt both too intimate for a first date and oddly erotic as he stroked the strand with his thumb. 'If I told you, I'd have to kill you.' He tugged the hair, pulling me towards him, the shock of pain at my scalp superseded by the softness of his lips on mine.

Light-headed from the kiss, I eventually drew away and unwound my hair from his finger. 'You are king of the cliché, aren't you?'

'Prince Charming, king of clichés, at your service,' he said, bowing low. Then he leaned forward and kissed me again and I was lost in a cloud of euphoria.

The memory added to a glorious spike of dopamine which almost lifted me off my feet when I saw the torn side of a cigarette packet taped to the bin. I unpicked the tape and turned it over, recognising his handwriting on the reverse. 'The First Royal Banquet'.

I shook my head, but I couldn't help smiling. I could imagine him grinning when he thought about us staggering to the kebab shop at the end of our second date, both dizzy from lager and laughter. He'd joked about how he knew how to treat a girl, and I'd told him, in no uncertain terms, that I wasn't a girl, I was a grown woman, and I didn't need to be treated.

His hand snaked under my hair and held my skull, then

pulled me towards him. After he kissed me, he said, 'It's not patriarchal to want to make you feel special. You make me feel more alive than I ever have. I want to thank you for that. And what better way than a doner kebab?'

The first drops of rain tapped on my jacket when I arrived at Uskudar Kebab House, but now I'd experienced the thrill of the chase, I wasn't going to let that put me off. I wondered if this was how he felt when he was working on an investigation. A buzz ran through me when I caught sight of an envelope with my name on it hanging from the letterbox, flapping in the wind. I checked around me before snatching it, scared someone would think I was stealing post.

The envelope was damp and came open easily. Inside was the next clue, royalty-based again. Clearly he liked it when I jokingly referred to him as a prince. It occurred to me that this might be a sign of narcissism, but I took my psychologist hat off and decided that it was simply an indication that he liked being seen as a gentleman. And he liked us. If I was completely honest with myself, I liked us too. We fitted. We had chemistry, and he made me feel good about myself. In my limited experience, it was rare for a man to treat a woman with so much respect it leaned towards reverence. Why the hell was I fighting against the best thing that had happened to me in years?

The final stop on the hunt was the pub where he'd told me he loved me. When I drew close, I made a conscious decision to stop resisting my feelings. This gorgeous man had done an entire scavenger hunt just for me. He told me he loved me and demonstrated it every time we met. He was *even attentive and thoughtful when we weren't together, texting several times a day and sending thoughtful gifts.*

When I pushed open the pub door, he was standing at the bar with his back to me. I didn't know if it was the sight of his broad shoulders, or the fact that I was out of the biting wind at last, but my entire body flooded with heat. As if sensing I'd arrived, he turned towards me, and his beautiful smile, the delight on his face at just the sight of me, confirmed what I already knew. My barriers were down.

'You found me, then?' he said, striding over and lifting me off my feet, swirling me in a slow circle.

'I love you,' I whispered into his ear. He stopped, arms tight around my middle. He held me above the ground, his head nestled in my neck. I could feel his ribs rise and fall as he breathed.

'I want to remember this moment for the rest of my life,' he said. He lifted his head, then lowered me gently to my feet, before kissing me so tenderly it made me swoon. I wasn't the swooning-maiden type, my brain reminded me. But I dismissed the thought and concentrated on his soft lips on mine.

'Get a room,' a gruff voice shouted from across the bar. We pulled apart, grinning sheepishly at each other. 'Speaking of rooms,' he said, leading me to a table where his parka was draped over the back of a chair, 'I've got your prize for successfully completing the scavenger hunt.'

He dipped his hand into his coat pocket and pulled out a red keyring with a shiny door key dangling on the end.

'What's that?'

'A key.'

'I know that, but . . .' I stopped as realisation began to dawn. 'It's not for—'

'My flat, yeah.' He lifted my hand and dropped the key in my palm, then closed my fingers over the cold metal. I stared at the red rectangle hanging from my fist, lost for words. The base of my neck grew moist under my hair. 'Since my flatmate leaves his skanky pants on the bathroom floor and never rinses the toothpaste out of the sink, I'll understand if you don't want to use it that often, but I wanted to make the gesture, you know?' He shrugged and looked up at me through those dark eyelashes.

I still hadn't formulated a response, but he didn't seem to notice. 'I think this moment deserves a glass of something sparkling, don't you?' he said, standing and grabbing his wallet from the inside pocket of his coat. His police ID card dropped on to the dirty wooden floor with a slap. He stooped to pick it up. 'After that we can pop to the locksmith's and get a copy of your door key.'

My breath halted and he must've seen something in my expression because he paused. 'That's all right, isn't it?' he said. 'It's what you want, I mean?'

There was such hope in his eyes. Saying no would have felt like kicking a kitten. 'Of course,' I said, digging my keyring out of my bag and making a show of prising open the metal circles, slotting his key on with my own. The sharp end slid under my thumbnail, slicing into the skin. I ignored the sting and jangled the keys together, grinning up at him.

The broken skin under my nail still smarted an hour later when we held hands, watching the locksmith's machine scream and spark, shaping the key that would give this man access to my home.

Chapter Fifteen

I listened to Laura with a growing sense of unease. Part of her story sounded eerily familiar. While huge romantic gestures probably weren't uncommon, surely preparing a scavenger hunt for someone must be unusual? It was what Connor had done for me for our first wedding anniversary. Coming so soon after the discussion about the man who sounded eerily like Jimmy Bray, this new coincidence left me feeling off kilter.

There was a burning sensation on my skin when Laura finished her story. Why had we been allocated this insufferably warm room? She was twirling the strand of hair around her finger again. 'Who said romance is dead, eh?'

While writing in my notes, buying time until I worked out how to reply, I sifted through my friends and ex-colleagues in my head, trying to remember if anyone else's partner had also created a scavenger hunt for them. I came up blank. I'd seen one in a film, but that had had a grisly ending so wasn't likely to have inspired two separate men to create something so similarly romantic.

'Could I get a glass of water?' I said, turning my head to Melanie, who was scribbling on a pad at the desk. I needed longer to process. I turned back to Laura. 'Would you like a drink? It's warm in here, isn't it?' She was looking at me quizzically. 'I'm warm,' I said. 'Aren't you?' I was flustered and annoyed at myself for not hiding it well. I swallowed hard, resolving to manage myself better. I'd broken the flow of the session twice now, and that wasn't acceptable practice. I'd been brought in as a professional to help Laura, and that's what I needed to focus on, not joining unconnected dots my overactive imagination presented to me.

'I'll get one of the orderlies to get some.' Melanie closed her pad and walked to the door, tapping lightly on the glass to get Aidan's attention. He opened the door and she said something in a low voice to him. He disappeared from view, while Melanie leaned on the doorframe and waited. Cooler air seeped into the room at last.

If I wasn't determined to behave more calmly, I'd have been tempted to join Melanie by the door to breathe in the fresher air. I was finding it hard to shift the image of Connor's triumphant face when I eventually reached the end of the hunt he'd devised for me. That evening, we'd huddled together in the furthest corner of the pub next to an open fire, smug about having reached our first milestone.

'Here's to many more, Mrs Best, wife of mine,' Connor had said, clinking the top of his champagne flute against mine.

'Cheers to our paper anniversary.' I kissed him, then rested my head on his shoulder. I could smell that peaty fire now and feel the champagne bubbles on my tongue. I desperately wished I could talk to Connor about all the strange things going on in my head.

I needed to take control of my thoughts. That Daniel had also created a scavenger hunt was a coincidence, that's all. I reminded myself this wasn't about me and Connor. It was about Laura and Daniel. I pretended to scratch an itch and wiped sweat from my forehead.

'Does he still make romantic gestures like that?' I asked Laura. She'd already hinted that their relationship wasn't perfect, so now my aim was to find out about the current state of play, hoping that was more likely to unlock her memories. Now I'd got the ridiculous idea in my head that Laura might know more about my life than just my career, I was keen to get this case resolved as quickly as possible for both our sakes.

'Yeah, sometimes.' There was less conviction in her voice, and I sensed a drop in her energy.

'Could you give me examples?'

She released the strand of hair and put her hands behind her head, parting the ponytail and tugging. 'He organised a surprise weekend away a few months ago.'

'That sounds nice.'

'It was.' She moved her hands over her jeans, from upper thigh to knees, then back again.

I paused; the movement and her lowered eyes suggested it wasn't the perfect weekend. 'I could be wrong, but I sense a little hesitation. Was there something—' I stopped at the sound of voices in the corridor and turned to see Aidan carrying a tray with a jug of water and glasses. He put the tray on the desk. We both watched him pour water into three glasses, lift two and bring them over.

'Here you go,' he said, placing them on the table. I caught his eye and immediately looked away. I couldn't help feeling there was something predatory about that man, although I had no evidence to back up the feeling. Picking up the water, once again I was surprised to find the warmth of plastic instead of cold glass in my hand, reminding me we were in a high-security unit, housing people who could not be trusted with sharp objects. After what happened in the corridor, was it any surprise I was on high alert, looking for danger where there was none?

I smiled at Aidan, determined to put a spike in my irrational emotional response to the perfectly pleasant orderly. 'Thank you.' I took a sip then placed it on the table next to the tissues. I waited for him to exit. I wished I could ask him to leave the door open, but I'd learned enough now to know that would be downright foolhardy in a facility like this. Melanie sat back behind the desk, and I continued: 'How was that weekend away?'

Laura cupped her glass and stared into the water. 'It was lovely. Really nice.'

I stayed quiet.

'When we got there.'

'Was there a problem beforehand?' She drank, her wet swallow the only sound in the room. I let the silence grow.

'Not a problem, exactly. It's just that ... well, it was my

friend's hen do that weekend, so the timing wasn't ideal.
Daniel and I had an argument about that.'

'About which element?'

'I was sure I'd told him about the hen weekend. I was
certain I had, but he was adamant I hadn't.'

'That must've been frustrating.'

'Yeah.' Her mouth twitched to the side as if she was
annoyed.

I left it a moment before asking, 'I get the feeling that
argument wasn't fully resolved. I sense you think he did it
deliberately?'

'What?' Her nose wrinkled. 'No.'

'It was an honest mistake?'

She took another drink. 'Yeah. We argued because I asked
him to cancel it, but he'd spent so much money and couldn't
cancel without losing it all. He'd used Booking.com, that
website, you know? You can get things cheaper if you go for
the no-cancellation option. I said he should have checked
the date with me first.'

'And how did he respond to that?'

Her chin puckered. 'He knew he'd been an idiot. He kept
saying he was sorry, how he was trying to do something
nice for me and it had backfired. He said something about
how he understood why I'd want to spend the time with
friends instead of him because he always got it wrong. He
was quite upset, actually.'

'Upset?'

'He cried.' She rolled her lips over her teeth. 'It's horrible seeing a big man like that cry. Knowing it was my fault made me feel even worse.'

I kept my voice quiet. 'Your fault how?'

When she shifted position, drops of water splashed from the glass on to her jeans. She ran her palm over the wet patch as she spoke. 'I should have made sure he put the hen weekend in the calendar on his phone. I know how busy he is. Even if I had told him' – she glanced up briefly – 'and I think I did, I should have made sure he made a note of it. I can't expect him to remember everything I'm doing as well as all his stuff. That's unreasonable, isn't it?'

She looked up again, and I felt like the question was for me. The problem was, I didn't think it was unreasonable of her to ask him to remember a date she'd told him about. Even if it was, not checking with her before booking something non-refundable for the two of them was presumptuous.

'You missed the hen weekend because he was upset?'

'Well, not just because of that. We talked about it. Obviously, he said he was happy for me to go. He didn't want me to miss out.'

The way her gaze searched my face suggested she was watching for my reaction. I kept my expression neutral, trying not to show that I thought this was typical manipulation, that in my opinion, a red flag was flying high over this situation. I may be predisposed to think that way, but I was sure my judgement was evidence-based this time.

She carried on, 'But I didn't owe the hen, the bride-to-be, anything, you know what I mean?'

I nodded, wondering what she thought she owed Daniel.

'I mean, we were best friends at school, but it wasn't like I saw her all that often any more.' She swirled the water in the glass, the liquid rising higher towards the rim with every circle. 'So, I weighed up what he meant to me and what she meant to me, and it was a no-brainer, really. I chose him.'

She stopped swirling the glass and the water slopped up the sides then stilled. 'Because he was the love of my life,' she said, looking me directly in the eye.

Was the love of her life. *Was.*

Chapter Sixteen

The Past

I arrived at my front door, cursing myself for leaving the hall light on when I went to work that morning. I could have sworn I turned it off. The stained glass at the top glowed red and yellow and, despite my irritation at myself, I had to admit it was a beautiful sight to be greeted with. I was glad to be home. The NHS job I'd recently taken was proving exhausting.

I was glad that mental health issues were slowly being destigmatised and more people were seeking help, but keenly wished the funding for our department had increased in line with demand. We were sorely understaffed, and I'd seen patients back to back from the minute I'd walked in that morning. It was inevitable that listening to other peoples' suffering, without a break to process how I felt, was going to take its toll. If it wasn't for the fact I'd rearranged seeing Gaby twice already, I would have happily stayed in and had an early night.

When I turned the key in the lock and pushed the door, I stopped, surprised by the sound of loud music coming from the back of the house. Standing in the hallway, hand on the still-open door in case I needed to bolt from an intruder, I recognised the Florence and the Machine track 'Dog Days are Over' and let my hand drop. Not a burglar, then. I pushed the door closed with my bottom and walked slowly towards the kitchen.

I'd given him a key, so I couldn't really be angry with him for using it. But he'd always checked with me before coming over. He was spending more and more time here, and I was secretly toying with the idea of asking him to move in. There was something incredibly comforting about knowing there was someone to come home to, especially when that person was a gorgeous man who regularly restocked the fridge and always hung wet towels back on the radiator. He'd done far more than that, if I was honest. On top of being easy to share a space with, he was considerate and gentle, and always put me first. Since we'd been together, I felt like my trust in men was slowly being rebuilt, one kindness at a time.

I reached the doorway to the kitchen and my heart melted at the sight of him tapping his feet as he sang along, while chopping spring onions on the worktop next to the sink.

'Hello,' I said.

He turned, putting the hand holding the knife across his chest. 'Christ, you nearly gave me a heart attack. What are you, some kind of ninja?'

I laughed. 'I didn't know you were coming over tonight, I've—'

'I'm making Thai green curry. Thought you'd benefit

from a nutritional meal cooked by somebody else since you're working so hard,' he shouted. 'Just a minute.' He lifted his phone from the table and pressed the side button. The volume of the music lowered and it occurred to me he must've connected his phone to my Alexa. I didn't remember giving him the password, but I must have.

'That's so lovely,' I said. 'But I'm having dinner with Gaby tonight. I did tell you.' I remembered texting him after Gaby and I made the new plan. I'd cancelled last time because he'd bought us last-minute theatre tickets that were non-refundable.

His mouth fell open. 'God, right, sorry.' He turned to the chopping board and pulled an apologetic face. 'I must've forgotten. You definitely told me?'

'I definitely told you.' I walked over to join him and saw piles of trimmed green beans. The smell of fresh lemongrass made me stop. 'God, you're doing it all from scratch?'

He pecked me on the lips then lifted the lid of the food recycling bin. 'No biggie.' He picked up the chopping board and moved it towards the bin.

'Don't throw it away,' I said, horrified at the waste.

He held the board in the air, frowning as though confused. 'But you're going out?'

'Yeah, but you can't throw all that food out . . . We could have it tomorrow, or something.'

He put the board back down and let out a resigned sigh. 'Nah, it's never the same the next day. Don't worry. It's probably for the best. I'd be poor company anyway. I'm not in a great mood.'

He hadn't looked like someone in a bad mood when I arrived. 'What's up?'

'Oh. Nothing. Don't worry. Don't you need to get ready? Do you want a lift, or are you driving?' *His voice was flat, all the bounce from when I'd come into the kitchen gone.*

I looked at my watch. I could spare ten minutes. 'Come on.' *I turned to see a bottle of wine already open on the table, two glasses beside it. He really had gone to a lot of effort. I poured us both a small glass and he took his with a ghost of a smile.* 'What's up?'

'It's nothing really,' *he said, sitting down.* 'I don't want to burden you. I don't want you to think I'm only with you because you're a brilliant psychologist.'

'Ha, thanks, but I think that might be a slight exaggeration.' *Despite my protestation, I glowed at the praise.* 'What's up, mister?'

He wiped his hands on his jeans then shrugged. 'It's just ... sometimes the past just catches you up, doesn't it?' *He glanced quickly up at me, then down at his hands.* 'Look, it's fine. You've got enough emotional baggage to process after seeing patients all day. You don't want to come home to more of the same.'

He went to stand, but I stopped him. 'Please,' *I said.* 'Tell me.'

He glanced over at the vegetables. 'Okay. It's just ... well, when I was chopping that lot, I had a kind of flashback to when I was younger. Mum seemed to be in the kitchen all the time. I tried to imagine my dad ever cooking for her, and ...' *He ran his hand over his face.* 'It would never have *happened. Never in a million years. Even when she was ill, she was still treated like she was his servant.'*

'I hear you,' I said, taking his hand and squeezing it. Over the last months, we'd disclosed snippets of our pasts to each other; our upbringings were one of the things that had connected us. In truth, he was the first person I'd ever disclosed my secrets to, and the fact that he had a difficult family background made me feel a synergy I had never experienced with anyone before.

He looked at me with his trademark intensity. 'I want to be different,' he said. 'I don't want to be anything like him.'

'I know.' I moved closer, taking him in my arms. His back shuddered under my hand, and I held him tightly, breathing in the smell of his skin mingled with lemongrass and garlic.

'That's why doing this kind of thing for you is so important to me,' he said into my neck. 'I'm desperate to prove to myself that I'm worthy of you.'

'Of course you're worthy,' I said. 'More than worthy.' It was a strange word to choose. The thought he held me in such high esteem made me feel a little taller.

He raised his head and looked at me through glassy eyes. 'I'm sorry. You're out fixing heads all day, then you come home to this mess. You could really do without this.'

'Not at all. It's not as if you've got an easy job, is it? You're saving the world from baddies.' That raised a smile. I handed him his glass. 'Have some medicine.'

'On prescription?' He lifted the glass, then stopped. 'Actually, I shouldn't if I'm going to drive home. Won't be saving the world from the bad guys if I lose my job for drink driving.' A tear dropped from the corner of his eye and ran down the side of his nose. He wiped it away with the back of his hand and shook his head. He closed his eyes, as if trying to manage his emotions. 'I'm sorry,' he said. 'I have to keep it together all day at work. Whatever they say in the papers, the Met is still a hotbed of machismo. No signs of weakness allowed.' He sniffed and looked up at me. 'I hope you don't see this as weakness. I feel like I can be entirely truthful with you, be vulnerable, you know?'

'I know. Of course I want you to be completely open with me, about everything.' I was flattered that he could show me the most tender side of himself. And I couldn't ask him to leave when he was feeling like this. It would be heartless, especially since he'd planned such a special evening just to prove he wasn't like his dad. 'Stay,' I said. 'I'll rearrange seeing Gaby. It's fine.'

'You really don't have to.'

A catch in his voice made me even more certain I was doing the right thing. 'It's fine.'

When he kissed me, I tasted the tannin of the wine on his lips. He mouthed a silent thank you and went back to slicing spring onions.

I climbed the stairs to my bedroom to message Gaby. I should have called, but the embarrassment of cancelling for the third time and at such short notice made me cowardly.

Again????!!! came the immediate response. The grey dots

danced on the screen. When did you last see any of your friends? xx

That was a strange question. I pondered it as 'Kiss with a Fist' pounded through the floorboards from the kitchen.

Chapter Seventeen

In the canteen after the therapy session with Laura, I went over in my mind what I'd say to Harvey if I was in a supervision session with him. I could see my responses in today's session had sometimes been emotional rather than clinical. When Laura talked about the man who wasn't allowed to see his child I'd seriously questioned whether she was toying with me. I could see that wasn't entirely rational. One thing a psychologist had to be was rational.

And the coincidence of the scavenger hunts had completely thrown me off balance. It was perfectly natural that any similarity between my and Laura's experiences would cause an empathetic reaction in me, but until now, I thought I'd successfully acknowledged the feelings and either dismissed them or used them to help me understand Laura better. Now I analysed my responses, I could see they were extreme. I had never needed an hour with my supervisor more.

Julie put a tray of food on the table before me with a warm smile. 'There you go, love.'

I looked up at her, a little confused by the familiarity.

She scratched the back of her head, the stubble there rasping under her nails. 'Sorry, I mean Emma. I call everybody "love". Terrible habit. Unprofessional. Sorry.'

'It's fine,' I said. There was a softness in her eyes, something motherly, like she understood I was conflicted and wished the best for me. She wasn't that much older than me, but there was something maternal about her, like she was used to looking after people. I assessed she was about forty-five, though I suspected she was trying to mask her age with bleached blonde hair tied up over an undercut. This interaction was the most human I'd had in days and it made tears prick behind my eyes. God, I was tired. I wanted to see Connor. I needed a hug. 'This looks great, thanks.'

It didn't. The jacket potato was overflowing with the vegetable chilli I'd asked for, but now it was in front of me, the kidney beans looked like red-grey bullets and the sauce was pooling on the plate, orange fat separating from sludgy brown gravy. I speared a piece of red pepper and forced myself to chew.

Across from me, Melanie was shovelling her food in. I envied her, imagining what it would be like to be a person whose anxieties didn't always affect their ability to eat. I contemplated why I was still so anxious in the staff canteen; it was probably the safest place in the whole institution. But one look around the featureless side room, and into the main canteen, where people with blue lanyards ate in stony-faced silence, and it made sense. Heaton Place was bleak. From the basic accommodation and the stark treatment rooms to this soulless eatery, even if there were no patients ready to drag my key fob from my neck nearby, it still felt like somewhere people were held, not healed.

It occurred to me then that since I'd arrived, I'd felt like I was on one of those weird reality-TV shows. *The Truman Show*, but aimed at people who got off on misery porn. The thought made me smile internally. It was like I'd been plucked out of my life and dropped in this bizarre set, given a top-secret mission which I had to complete in double-quick time to win the prize. Any amusement dissipated when I remembered the prize wasn't mine to win. It was Laura who would win or lose. If I didn't complete the mission, her life as she knew it would end. Yep, I thought, there were plenty of reasons why an anxious stomach might shut up shop.

'The scavenger-hunt story was interesting,' I said to Melanie. 'It reminded me of . . .' I paused. Her plastic fork had stopped halfway to her mouth and she was looking at me so attentively it was unnerving.

'Go on,' she said, putting the fork down on her plate.

'Well, it reminded me, as if we need reminding in our job, that relationships are complex beasts. That sounds like a very lovely thing to do, but I get the feeling there's something else at play.' Something told me not to share that Connor had done the same thing for me. It was the narrowing of her eyes, the creases at the corners fanning out towards her hairline. She looked infinitesimally too interested in what I was about to say. I didn't want to be analysed by her. If I was going to seek therapy, it would be with Harvey. 'What do you think was going on between Patient X and Daniel?' I felt silly saying 'Patient X'. Nobody was close enough to hear.

She dug back into her potato, twisting it to release the white flesh, then scooping up sauce and raising it to her mouth. She squinted as she chewed, clearly giving my question a lot of thought. 'Not sure. What about you?' Or perhaps not.

'The crying and blaming himself after the mistake sounded like manipulation rather than contrition to me,' I said.

'Interesting.' She took another mouthful. 'So, you think, what? He was abusive?'

Abusive. The word held such weight. Did I suspect Laura's partner was habitually cruel? 'Possibly,' I said. I pushed another forkful of food into my mouth and chewed. The pulp of a kidney bean powdered on my tongue. It was an effort to swallow. 'Could you arrange for me to speak to whoever is in charge of her detention?' I said.

Melanie stilled. 'Of course. Can I ask why?'

She looked nervous. I put my hand out to reassure her. 'I don't want to complain about anything. It's nothing like that. It's just that I'd really, really like to speak to my supervisor, Harvey.'

'I'll try again,' Melanie said.

'You've already asked? I thought—'

'Yes, I mentioned it yesterday. I agree with you, I think it would be a good idea, I mean, it's standard practice, isn't it?'

I could have kissed her. I was so relieved to have her support. 'What did they say?'

Her lips tightened and she wrinkled her nose. 'They basically said I should be supervising you better myself.'

'Oh.' My heart dropped. 'I didn't mean to make things difficult for you. Sorry. I hadn't considered that's what they might think.' I remembered what she'd said about applying for another job and hoped this wouldn't affect her reference.

She gave a half-shrug but didn't meet my gaze. 'It's fine, honestly. Like I said, I think you should be allowed to talk to someone you trust.'

'It's not that I don't trust you,' I said, quickly, appalled that this generous woman might be doubting herself because of me. 'It's just . . .' Just what? I trust Harvey more? Of course I did, but the real problem was that I wanted someone outside this extraordinary situation to tell me whether I was just being paranoid about the things Laura had said that kept replaying in my mind. 'It's just that I'm used to working with Harvey.'

'I get it.' She set down the knife and fork and spread her fingers on the table. 'And I wish the management did. They gave me this spiel about how they'd thought I was ready for this challenge but maybe they'd been mistaken, yadayada.' She wobbled her head to lighten the revelation, but I knew then I'd put her in a very difficult situation.

'Do you want me to speak to them?' I said. 'Let them know I'm more than happy to be working with you?'

'No,' she said. 'Really, it's fine.'

I remembered what she'd said about wanting to prove herself and feared I'd overstepped again. I should try to be more like this self-reliant young woman. I was beginning to

121

see why her career was advancing so well; she didn't look to other people to push her forward; she took control for herself. At that moment, I decided to pull my big-girl pants on and rely on myself for a change. It occurred to me that I had been leaning on other people for too long; Harvey professionally and Connor at home. It was time for me to step up and make my own decisions. 'It's absolutely fine. I'll wait until I get home to talk to Harvey.'

'You sure?'

'Absolutely.'

I still wasn't used to having people fetch and carry for me, so when Julie picked up my tray when Melanie and I rose to leave, I put my hand out to stop her. 'You really don't have to.'

'It's no bother,' she said. She eyed the food I'd left. 'I wish you'd eat a bit more.' There was that softness on her face again.

'Maybe later.'

'I'll bring you an extra pud up if you're eating dinner in your room.' She winked and went with Aidan to scrape off the food and stack the trays, before they followed Melanie and me up the steps towards the glass walkway. I would definitely eat dinner in my room if it meant one less traverse through the hideous tunnel.

'Can you do something for me?' I said to Melanie, ignoring the perspiration starting to trickle down my back the further up we climbed.

'What's that?'

'I wanted to do some research into memory and trauma,

to make sure that I'm using the right approach. We don't have much time and I want to check if there are any new techniques I could use.'

'Good idea, although I've been impressed with your work with the patient so far.'

While the compliment was welcome, it didn't shift the feeling that there was always a chance I might make a mistake. I'd done it before, and I was more tired now than I had been when I'd fallen asleep before sending in the paperwork about Shannon Bray and her son needing to be moved to a shelter immediately. 'Thanks,' I said. 'But no research is wasted, is it? Might be useful for the book I'm planning to write, if nothing else. Ordinarily, I'd be able to use the texts I've got at home and Doctor Google.'

'Good old Doctor Google.' She smiled.

'Do you have any resources here, or could I do some research on the internet on one of the computers?'

'Great idea,' she said. 'I'll ask Sonia in the office when it would be convenient.' She glanced behind and lowered her voice. 'She's a bloody tyrant, that one. Runs the office like a military regime.'

Unlike Gail on reception, I thought bitterly, who can't tell one bloody phone from another. We'd arrived at the entrance to the walkway. I squinted against the light blazing through the glass. Melanie stepped on to the frosted floor as though it was just another carpet tile. I forced myself to do the same.

Blood boomed in my ears as I put one foot in front of the other. I was congratulating myself on having reached halfway without hyperventilating when a crashing sound pierced my eardrums. Unbalanced by the shock, I lurched to the side, reaching out my hand to stop myself from falling while, in my head, glass shattered all around me and I was sure I was a split second away from plummeting through the air to my death.

My palm met a surface so cold it burned. Another crash sounded. I reeled. Then hands were on me, solid arms wrapped around my waist. A deep voice said, 'It's okay. It's all right.'

I straightened, my breath coming in sharp bursts. I twisted to see Aidan, his face silhouetted by the glaring light of the sky behind him, his wolf-like eyes bright. I could smell stale cigarette smoke on his breath. His grip was tight, too low on my waist. I pulled back. He lifted his arms, holding his palms up as though I'd made a silent accusation. The skull tattoo with the key for teeth looked like something from a horror film. He saw me looking and dropped his arms. 'It was the wrecking ball. That's all.' He turned and pointed across the courtyard to where an orb dangled on a thick chain from the spindly arm of a crane.

'You okay?' Melanie's eyes scrutinised my face.

'The noise,' I said. 'Gave me a fright.' I ran a shaky hand through my hair, trying to regain some composure. 'I'm fine. Just a bit jumpy. I get like this when I'm tired.'

She kept her eyes on me for a beat, then turned away, stepping closer to the glass. 'They've started to demolish it, then.'

I followed her gaze and saw that the left-hand side of the

barracks opposite was missing a chunk out of the top, as though a giant creature had come along and taken a bite from the stone. The image swam in and out of focus. My stomach pitched. 'Can we . . .' I started to move towards the far end of the tunnel, desperate to be back on more solid ground.

'You really okay?' asked Melanie when I let out a long breath on reaching the other side.

'Yeah, like I said, I'm just tired.' I was desperate to be in my room, alone. I might not be able to speak to Harvey, but at least I could call Connor. I yearned to hear his voice, for him to tell me he missed me and couldn't wait until I was home.

I'd rarely been so relieved to hear a click as the lock released and my bedroom door opened. I said my goodbyes and closed it behind me, immediately crossing the room and picking up the phone from my desk.

I expected to see a reply to my text to Connor, but there was nothing showing on the small screen. I pressed the key to the messages inbox. Nothing. Indignation fought with the tears pushing behind my eyes. I couldn't believe he hadn't texted back. I momentarily considered putting the phone down in protest. I could get back to the chapter I'd started reading on mastering structure in non-fiction and see how he liked it when I went dark. But the feeling passed quickly. I didn't want to think about the book I was planning to write. I wanted to hear my husband's voice.

I dialled his number. The ringtone sounded. I shifted position, then moved again, unable to settle when I imagined

Connor choosing not to pick up the phone because he was still upset with me. He wouldn't do that. Our arguments were never left unresolved. We weren't that kind of couple. With a spike of adrenaline, I understood that if I was dismissing the idea he wouldn't choose not to pick up the phone, that left me with the uneasy sense that he couldn't answer for some reason. I ended the call and redialled. The phone rang, and rang and rang.

Chapter Eighteen

Wednesday

I was drying myself after a shower when a knock rattled on the door. Pulling the towel around me, I left the bathroom, goosebumps rising on my arms when I reached the bedroom. I hated the fact this part of Heaton Place still had the original old radiators. Not only were they inefficient, they clanked and groaned day and night, regularly waking me from my already fitful sleep. The ones in the modern building were too hot, but at least they were quiet.

I opened the door a couple of inches and looked through the gap. Melanie was standing in the corridor in a black suit and white shirt with tiny black dots.

I started. 'God, am I late? I thought today's session was after lunch.' I shivered as water from my wet hair dribbled over my shoulders and down my back like icy fingers. I couldn't conduct therapy with wet hair.

'It is,' said Melanie, holding her palm out and smiling. 'Don't panic.'

'Phew.' I tried to laugh it off, but my adrenaline had spiked, weakening my knees. I hated being late and dreaded anyone thinking of me as unreliable. I was too amenable, I knew that, but try as I might, I hadn't been able to eradicate the people-pleasing element of my personality. I presumed that's what came from growing up in a domestic war zone. 'You had me worried there for a sec.'

She held out a tote bag printed with the unit's emblem. 'Present for you.'

Uncomfortably aware of my nakedness, I pressed the towel to my chest, reached out with my other hand and took the bag from her. 'What's this?'

'Scary Sonia in the office said she could only accommodate you at eight this morning, and I knew how tired you were, so I didn't want to make you get up and ready so early, so I did some research for you.'

Once again, I swelled with gratitude for this wonderful woman. Pulling my elbows in to pin the towel in place, I opened the bag and peered in at the printed A4 pages. 'Thank you. That's so kind.' I didn't mention that I'd been awake for three hours already by eight. I'd been trying and failing to focus on a chapter in my book on creative non-fiction, but none of it was going in. I must've reread the same page a dozen times. Despite me calling every hour, Connor still hadn't got back to me and I couldn't make my mind stick on anything else. Maybe reading up on how to move forward with this case would distract me from checking the phone.

'No problem,' she said. 'Happy reading. I'll swing by and collect you a bit before two. Julie will drop off some lunch at twelvish.'

'Great, see you then. Thanks again. You're a complete star.'

I threw the bag on the bed, glanced at the phone again, then went into the bathroom to finish drying off, wishing I'd had the sense to close the door to keep the steam and heat in the poky room.

An hour later, I'd read most of what Melanie had printed off. I was reassured that what I already knew about the neuroscience of PTSD was correct, that during trauma the amygdala undermines the hippocampus's ability to lay down memories. It can lose connection, so whatever conscious memory is created is often highly fragmented. Laura might never be able to provide a coherent narrative about what had happened that day.

I read on, any hope that there was anything I could do to help Laura diminishing. If the memories weren't there, no amount of therapy could help retrieve them. I was about to admit defeat when the final article made me sit up on the bed and harness what little concentration I had. The piece explained how victims of trauma could have implicit memory of the emotions they experienced and those memories could potentially be triggered by something that emotionally put the sufferer back in that trauma-inducing situation.

That made complete sense. That's the direction I had started to go in when I was asking her about Daniel. I was surer than ever that their relationship was not the idyll she'd initially tried to portray. She'd almost said as much before going off on a tangent. I wondered now whether her talking about her patient was a deliberate ploy, not to let me know she was aware of my mistake, but to move away from her uncomfortable feelings about Daniel. I paused, reminding myself he may have absolutely nothing to do with her situation. I was in danger of leading her if I didn't keep that in mind. I concluded it was now my job to get her to access her memories of other times she'd felt in danger, but without being too overt.

I opened my notebook and started to scribble down questions. I would go back to her childhood again. Surely the atmosphere she talked about would elicit some of the same feelings, if I was right about her relationship. As I wrote, I warmed to this line of questioning, not least because the less we talked about Daniel, the less chance there was of me finding a parallel with my life with Connor.

Last night's broken sleep had been peppered with disturbing dreams involving both of us. It was probably all to do with not being able to get hold of him, but if I could avoid Laura tapping into my subconscious more than I tapped into hers, I would consider that a good afternoon's work.

At the beginning of that afternoon's session, Laura strode into the room, her gait nothing like her nervous shuffle on Monday. 'Hello, Laura. How are you today?' I said. Her eyes were bright. She was clearly better rested than yesterday. I was glad one of us was.

'Okay, thanks.' She sat in her usual seat and crossed her legs. 'How are you?'

She emphasised the 'you' and, for a second, it felt like she was already trying to lead the session. Momentarily, I wished our positions were reversed, in the therapy sense, at least. Despite my usual reticence, I had an almost over-whelming urge to tell her about how tired I was, how I hadn't been able to eat a full meal since I'd arrived, how my dreams were plagued with dreadful scenes of conflict. I wanted to let out the fact that I still couldn't get hold of my husband and was growing increasingly worried about his radio silence; and the reason behind it. 'Fine, thank you.' I closed my pad and crossed my legs, mirroring her. 'I'd like to start today's session with a game of best and worst.'

'Best and worst?' She raised an eyebrow.

'Yes.' I wasn't surprised she hadn't heard of this strategy, since I'd made it up that morning. I really only wanted her to access her worst memories in the hope they might trigger something from the night she was found. It was already halfway through our available time and I needed to get results, not least because I wanted to get home to my husband. But that strategy could cause overwhelm, setting us back, so I was aiming for an element of balance. 'Could you tell me your best childhood memory?'

'Ah, right.' Her gaze trailed up to the window above me. 'Hmm, that's a hard one.'

'Hard?'

'Yeah. It's interesting.' I could see by the narrowing of her eyes that she was analysing herself as she spoke. 'Because every good memory has . . . what you might call an attach-ment.'

'An attachment?'

'My best memories are of snuggling up with my sister.' She smiled and squeezed her arms into her sides. 'You know, when you're both in a single bed and there's not enough room so you kind of squiggle up, making bottoms and hips fit together, faces slot into necks, that kind of thing?'

I nodded. It felt like she was one step ahead, already conflating the good with the bad. I knew exactly what she meant. I could smell Sarah's hair as Laura spoke and feel the smooth skin above her collar bone next to my cheek. I swallowed hard and concentrated on the movement of Laura's lips as she continued.

'And we'd be all cuddled up, laughing, me pulling my arm out from under her because it had gone dead, her telling me off for getting my hair in her mouth, and then . . .' She rubbed her hand across her chin. 'Then we'd hear it.'

'Hear what?' The room was too hot again. I glanced up at the wire grille across the window, wishing there was some way of prising it open.

'The silence.' Her voice was low. The smile was gone, replaced by a deep crease between her eyebrows. Her eyes were dull and I knew she was back there, in that single bed with her sister. I knew because that's where I was too, with mine. 'It sounds strange to describe silence as a noise, doesn't it?'

It didn't sound strange to me. I remembered silences so loud that only the ringing in my ears would drown them out.

'Then there would be a rumble of voices, like thunder

at the start of a storm,' she continued. 'Nicole and I would stop messing about. I hated it when she grew still. I would try to tickle her, or blow a raspberry on her cheek or something, but she would push me away and lift her head off the pillow to listen.' She closed her eyes. 'It sounds ridiculous, but I used to wish there would be shouting, or screaming, but there was only ever this weird quiet, like the ominous calm before a thunderclap.'

'It didn't feel calm?'

'It felt like the threat of a storm, you know what I mean? That heaviness in the air, the crackling electricity.'

Metaphors were common in therapy. It was one way of putting a little emotional distance between the traumatic experience and the self. If a patient used one, I always tried to follow their lead. 'You wanted to protect Nicole from the threat of the storm?'

'Yes. But I couldn't.'

I felt Sarah's arms around me. When the storms raged in our house they were thunderous, lightning cracks of slaps and backs slammed against walls. Sarah would cradle my head against her chest, covering my ears. She would rock me and make shushing noises. I could feel the seam of her nightdress where it would press into my wet cheeks. 'I'm sorry your best memories are so tied up with your worst. That must be hard.'

'Oh, they're not the worst,' Laura said. She sat back, then looked away. 'It got far worse than that.'

Chapter Nineteen

I was aware of the buzz of the strip light overhead as I braced myself for whatever revelation Laura was about to make. I was ready for a dark secret from her childhood. The way she'd approached it made me think she was about to disclose sexual abuse. I'd heard it more times than I cared to remember from women who suffered at the hands of their partners. In some cases, their early lives had been blighted by an abusive male family member, and the experiences they shared with me still existed inside me, like layers of tar in the lungs of smokers. Their suffering had built up in me over the years, clogging my airways until, sometimes, I found it hard to breathe.

Laura leaned forward. 'I need to tell you something else,' she said in a low voice. 'Something strange is happening. You're making me see things differently and it's making me question everything.'

I'd anticipated many things, but I hadn't expected her to turn things back to me. I recalibrated my thoughts, noted the word 'making' and wondered if she was resentful of me in some way. It wasn't unusual for a patient to become angry with their therapist for encouraging them to bring forward and sit with painful feelings. I never enjoyed it when that happened. I acknowledged the need within myself to be liked, especially by the woman in front of me now. In any other situation we would be peers, colleagues, perhaps friends. I reminded myself that her liking me shouldn't feature on my list of priorities right now. 'What are you seeing differently?'

'Well, my childhood, for example, and the passive aggression, particularly the way my dad behaved. I've done the work, hours of analysis, what effect that's had on my life. But now, talking to you, things are getting blurred.'

'Blurred?'

'Yeah. For example, I've started to remember times when Dad came home from work in a bad mood and everything we did was wrong. He made us feel like he'd be fine if it wasn't for the fact we were untidy, or noisy, or' – she raised her hands and let them slap back on her legs – 'or anything he could pin on us. It was so manipulative. We'd end up apologising for things we hadn't done, but really, he was the problem, not us.'

'Okay. How does that blur things?'

'Yesterday, when you asked whether Daniel had purposefully booked a weekend away because I was supposed to go on that hen do, it got me thinking . . . about manipulation.'

She'd brought things back to Daniel. There must be a reason for that. I had to work to keep my voice level. 'What in particular were you thinking about?'

'Well, it wasn't the only time.' She tugged her ponytail tighter. 'It happened on a few occasions.'

'He forgot you had plans ... or?' This was it; she was about to disclose something vital. I could feel it on my tingling skin.

'That's the thing. I always gave him the benefit of the doubt. I mean, I've been out with enough men to know they don't all book theatre trips, cook dinners, arrange romantic meals out, so the fact that sometimes the things he arranged clashed with plans I'd made seemed like a small price to pay for all the good stuff. I chose to think it was nothing more than coincidental, just honest mistakes.'

'And now you think differently?'

'Coincidence can be seen in terms of a statistical equation, can't it?'

I wanted her to be specific. This sounded like a diversion. 'Go on.'

'There's that birthday paradox thing, where it's been proved that if there are twenty-three people in a room there's about a fifty per cent chance that two of those people will have been born on the same day.'

I blinked. Was she trying to say that she did or didn't believe him? 'Okay.'

'So that shows coincidences are more likely than you'd think. I mean, there're three hundred and sixty-five days in a year, right? So how can it be fifty–fifty with only twenty-three people in a room?'

I'd found the maths part of my psychology degree the most difficult and, on top of the brain fog of exhaustion, I was struggling to keep up. 'So, you're saying that, despite it seeming like a huge coincidence, it isn't?'

'That's what I started to think, but then I did the maths in my head last night.'

More maths. Great. A yawn crept up on me. The effort of keeping it contained made my eyes water.

'You see, by the time we'd become a proper couple, my social circle was already pretty small, so the likelihood of me arranging something and him arranging something on the exact same day was tiny. It could happen once, maybe even twice, but he was so difficult about me seeing other people that I only made plans about once a month.'

'You say he was difficult about you seeing other people. Difficult how?' The questions in my pad remained unasked, but I was compelled to keep going on the path she was leading me down, certain it would be fruitful if she would just be specific.

She lifted her hands to the side as though there were a multitude of examples she could pick. 'Sulking if I went out without him. Moaning about friends taking up too much of my time. Complaining that I'd rather spend time with other people than with him. Getting upset if I looked at my phone when a message came in.' She blew out her lips. 'He always couched it in pretty language, spinning it so I couldn't come back at him without appearing dismissive or cruel.'

This was it, the truth about their relationship. At last, we were getting somewhere. 'How did he do that?'

'He'd say it was because he loved me so much he couldn't bear to share me. He worried about me. Couldn't stand to think of anything bad happening to me. Those are nice things to hear, really, aren't they? Until they're the things stopping you from seeing your friends, or even your own mother.'

I'd listened to stories of these tactics being used on so many women before, it made me want to sob. I wished I could tell Laura that what she was describing was a recognised pattern of control and coercion, but I wanted it to come from her. 'And you realised this last night?'

Laura scrunched her mouth to the side. After a moment she said, 'The thoughts solidified last night. It became tangible, rather than just a feeling, but, if I'm honest, I've known deep down that something wasn't right for a long time.'

Blood pulsed in my ears. This was a huge step forward; the lifting-off point for discovering what had led to her being found covered in blood that night. I was sure of it. I stilled to try to get a sense of what she was feeling. Her hands rested on her lap and she sat, face serious, her chest rising and falling steadily. I waited for the air to thicken with emotion, but the space between us didn't throb as I expected. Light shone through the window, illuminating the tissues on the table, but Laura didn't reach forward to take one to dry her tears. There were no tears. I could sense no change in her at all.

Women I worked with usually broke down when they came to a new understanding of their situation. Talking about it was like cracking open their hearts and bleeding while reliving the worst times of their lives. It was usual for them to cry, explode with rage, self-flagellate for allowing themselves and often their children to suffer at the hands of a controlling man. I always found it deeply upsetting to hear.

But Laura was calm. Watchful.

The only person who seemed to be struggling to contain their roiling emotions, I realised, was me.

A long moment passed. 'I'm sorry you felt isolated and manipulated,' I said. I was risking kickback by blatantly stating what she was describing, but time was running out and I needed to harness this forward motion. 'Would you say that kind of behaviour escalated?'

She shrugged, the movement seeming incongruous. 'Depends what you mean.'

I remained quiet. She dropped her head to the side and looked towards the window, the reflection of the grille making a crisscross pattern on the surface of her eye. 'After a while, he started to go out without telling me where, or when he'd be back. Then he wouldn't return my calls, didn't answer texts, things like that. He'd finally come back and say how much he missed me, how he couldn't bear to be without me. When I told him how upsetting I found it when I couldn't contact him, the apologies turned to accusations. He'd say I was possessive and demanding, that I was trying to control him. He went on and on until I could see his point. I was nagging, and that's not an attractive trait, is it?'

The sound of the tinny ringtone I'd heard so often over the last three days replayed in my head. Despite my situation being completely different, I could well imagine how hard that must have been for her.

'Were you nagging, or were you asking to be treated with due respect, do you think?'

'I must've been nagging, because, one time I had a go at him, and he disappeared. Puff' – she opened her hands in front of her face – 'he was gone.'

'Daniel disappeared?' My scalp tightened. If that was true, then maybe I'd been heading in the wrong direction all along. It was already Wednesday afternoon, so half my allocated time was already gone. 'Altogether?'

'For five days,' she said, seemingly oblivious to the loud breath I released. 'But for all that time I had no idea where he was. I didn't know if he was alive or dead. It was agony. I should probably have been stronger, insisted he treated me with more consideration, but, in the end, when it happened more regularly, I kind of got used to the fact he would go off grid.'

'That sounds like a difficult way to live,' I said. Not being able to contact Connor for three days was consuming my thoughts.

'Yeah' – she gave a bitter laugh – 'you probably think I'm an idiot for staying.'

'I would never think you were an idiot.' I felt I needed to make sure she knew that. If she was the victim of an abusive man, he was the one at fault, not her. For the abuse, at least. I'd have to reserve judgement on whatever I discovered happened as a result.

'I'm not so sure, to be honest.' She slid her fingers together, eyes on her slowly circling thumbs. 'I suspected he was cheating on me,' she said. 'I began to think he was with another woman when he wasn't with me. Why else would he not answer his phone when he was away? You're married, right?'

She nodded at the platinum band on my left hand. I resisted the urge to twist it, feel its solidity. 'I am, yes.'

'If you couldn't get hold of your husband for days on end, you'd suspect he was either up to something he didn't want you to know about or that something bad had happened to him, wouldn't you?'

She looked directly at me, eyebrows raised. Once again, I had the uneasy feeling she was choosing her words for impact. My gut told me she knew I couldn't get hold of Connor. More than that, the static shocks under my skin told me that she knew why. I took a breath. That thought process wasn't rational. I had to keep my mind from connecting dots that didn't exist or I would never be able to do my job. And my job was to help Laura. 'This isn't about me,' I said, as calmly as I could. 'I'm here to help you retrieve the lost memories.'

'I want that to happen as much as you do,' she said. Her laser-like gaze told me that was true.

Back in my room after the session, I paced the floor with the phone pinned to my ear, the incessant ringtone almost drowned out by the echo of Laura repeating, 'You'd suspect something bad had happened to him, wouldn't you?' Despite my best efforts to manage my thoughts, the volume of her voice in my head grew every time I pressed redial.

Chapter Twenty

Thursday

A crunching sound roused me, then an unbearable pressure bore down on my back teeth. The grinding sent needles of pain through my jaw. My molars shattered. I froze in horror at my teeth disintegrating, turning first to bony spikes, then to powder in my mouth.

A bang made me open my eyes, the terror of the dream still visceral. The crunching sound came again. I ran my tongue over my teeth, my heart racing. They were all there, solid and hard in my dry mouth. The relief was short-lived when I assessed the rest of my body and discovered I was just as bone-tired as yesterday. More so, even. I closed my eyes again, tears of exhaustion leaking from the corners on to my cheeks. Breathing slowly, I got my bearings and groaned. I was at Heaton Place, in this uncomfortable bed, in this miserable room, for the fourth bloody day.

I forced my weary body to climb out of bed, shivering as the chill of the room reached my skin, and took the couple of steps to the window to see what was making the noise. The wiry carpet tiles itched the soles of my bare feet.

I wondered how many other staff had woken up in this pitiful room before me and questioned their life choices like I was questioning mine right then. Light spilled in under the navy roller blind, illuminating the painted stone of the wall. Cracks showed in the paintwork. I put my nail into one and flaked a piece off, revealing more dirty white paint underneath.

The blind's cord was pinned into the wall with what looked like huge staples. The cord juddered in my hand and made a clicking sound as it lifted to let in the silver light of a rainy day. There was another bang, then a sequence of thuds. My room was in the corner of the courtyard and I could only see the high wall to the right and one side of the barracks opposite, which was still intact, as far as I could make out.

I angled myself to the corner of the window, my breath fogging the glass. Raindrops blurred the stone building and the gravel below. There was the low growl of an engine. I stood back and looked for a way to open the window to get a better view. It was an old sash window which had been double-glazed with one large sheet of thick glass. There was usually a sliding mechanism with this kind of secondary glazing, but I couldn't find a way of shifting the layer of glass aside to get to the sash. The metal lock and the grubby ropes to lift the bottom half of the old window taunted me through the transparent barrier.

'Typical of this place,' I seethed. 'Everything useful is behind a layer of something else and impossible to unlock.' I half laughed at the metaphor. That was psychotherapy in one grim nutshell. I considered making a note of the observation for my book, but even the thought of picking up a pen and engaging my brain long enough to record the point made my jaw tighten with a yawn. I'd spent hours trying to absorb the information in the book on the bedside unit and still didn't know where to start. If I couldn't effectively read a book, what hope did I have of writing one? In that moment, I didn't want to be a psychologist, never mind write about it. I wished I worked on the tills at Tesco instead.

A clanking sound inside the room made me jump. It was just the old radiator next to the desk coughing into life. I walked over and put my hand on the painted metal. It was tepid at best, certainly not hot enough to make any material difference to the chilly temperature of the room.

I fell back on the bed and pulled the duvet over me, searching for the place on the mattress I'd left minutes before, hoping to find a warm spot. I grabbed the phone from the bedside cabinet, willing there to be a message from Connor. I was sure the weird dreams I'd been having were because I was increasingly concerned about him not replying to me. But there was no message. No missed calls. Nothing. Laura's words from yesterday came back to me, and I allowed the thought that had been worrying away at me to break the surface, like a nail scratching an itch until it pierced the skin: Connor might not be intentionally ignoring my calls and texts. Something might have happened to stop him from replying. Jimmy Bray's snarling face appeared behind my eyes. I pushed it away. I was being ridiculous.

He was safely behind bars, and if he did want revenge on me, he wouldn't have waited until now, and he wouldn't target Connor, surely?

The thought that Laura might know Jimmy Bray resurfaced. And what she'd said about Daniel being with another woman ... was she suggesting Connor was cheating on me? My breath hitched at the images my brain immediately presented of Connor naked, his hands sliding over another woman's body.

I shook my head. The pressure to unlock Laura's memories was getting to me, that was all. Time was running out and what happened in the next three days would alter the course of a woman's life. I couldn't misstep, which meant I had to get my head straight. My thoughts were just that – thoughts. None of what my brain offered was real. What was real was that I had made significant progress with Laura, and I needed to hold on to that.

Wrestling to rescue what was left of my rational brain, I worked out the days in my head. Connor had gone to Copenhagen the day I came to Heaton Place, so he was due back today. I now regretted that we'd decided to get rid of the landline.

'We've both got mobiles,' Connor had said. 'It's a waste of money.'

It had seemed like a logical move, but he wasn't answering his bloody mobile, and if we still had a home phone I'd at least be able to leave a message telling him where I was and insisting he got in touch. The need to speak to him pulsed in me, primal, like thirst.

I hadn't slept well in days and I was running out of time to discover what had happened the day Laura was found covered in blood. I was certain that the only thing that could make me feel calmer was speaking to Connor. If I could just get through to him, I would know he was safe, and he would know exactly what to say to put my mind at ease. He was an expert at showing me when I was being irrational and he'd talk me down, make the peculiar coincidences I was picking up on make sense. I tried his number again, curled into the fetal position and waited. Tears of frustration and despair ran down my cheeks, seeping on to the handset and into my hair as the ringtone droned on.

Chapter Twenty-One

Melanie knocked for me ten minutes before the session was due to begin. I dropped the phone in the tote bag. To hell with professionalism. I wanted it to hand. I hoped she wouldn't notice that my eyes were swollen from crying.

'You okay?' she said.

Hoping a psychologist wouldn't read the room was clearly futile. 'Fine. You?'

She nodded, looking unconvinced. I wished I'd packed my make-up bag when I came here. I couldn't disguise my emotions, but I could at least try to physically mask them. I usually wore at least foundation, mascara and a neutral-coloured lipstick for work, but I hadn't packed any in my rush to leave. Melanie only wore a hint of grey eyeshadow and pale pink lipstick, and neither Julie nor Laura wore make-up that I'd noticed.

'Ready?'

'As I'll ever be.'

'Grab your lanyard, then we'll get off.'

'Oh, right, yes.' I put my hand to my chest where the

identity card usually sat and looked behind me into the room. I didn't remember seeing it that morning. 'Give me a second.' I went over to the cabinet next to the bed. There was nothing but my book and a plastic cup with a dribble of water at the bottom. I bent to look under the bed. Nothing there. I glanced behind me at the desk, but already knew it wouldn't be there because I was certain I could remember putting it by the bed. 'It's not here,' I said, rubbing at the still-sore skin on my neck where the ribbon had been yanked.

'What do you mean?' Melanie's voice was understandably troubled.

I lifted the edge of the thin duvet and folded it back. 'I can't find my lanyard. It's not where I left it.' I swooped the duvet all the way off but found nothing but the creased white sheet underneath.

'Is it in the bathroom?' said Melanie, from the doorway.

'I don't think so,' I said, concern rising. 'I'll check.' I let the tote drop on to the floor, and went through to the small en suite, making my eyes focus on the surface above the sink, on the toilet cistern. I even dragged back the flimsy curtain and looked inside the tiny shower cubicle.

'It's not here,' I said, panic narrowing my throat. 'It can't have just disappeared.'

Melanie's mouth was a serious line. 'Could you have dropped it on the way back from yesterday's session?'

I put my hand to my chest again, imagining what I could possibly have done with it. 'I don't think so.' I tried to visualise taking it off and putting it beside the bed. I was sure I had. I went to the cabinet and tried to push it aside to look behind it, but it was attached to the floor by metal brackets screwed through the carpet tiles. 'I'm sure I put it here.'

'This is a secure mental health unit,' said Melanie. 'That lanyard is a weapon in the wrong hands.'

Did she think I didn't know that, after what happened in the corridor? I dropped to my knees and searched the carpet again. 'I'm sorry, but I'm sure I remember taking it off last night and putting it by the bed.'

'It definitely isn't there?'

I stood, defeated. 'Sorry, no.'

'Okay,' she said, in a voice that told me it was anything but okay. 'I'll have to delay the session and go and tell Management.'

'I'll come with you,' I said. It was the right thing to do. I'd lost it. I should make my own apologies.

'No,' she said. 'Until that key fob is deactivated, everyone needs to stay in their rooms.'

A chill ran through me. Banging and wailing often disturbed me when I was lying in bed at night. The thought that someone unstable, potentially criminally unstable, might have picked up a key fob I'd been careless enough to lose was terrifying. I looked around the small room, the thought of being locked in tightening my chest. I'd rather go with Melanie to make my apologies in person than stay here on my own. 'I'm so sorry,' I said again.

Melanie nodded. 'I'll be back as soon as I can.' She closed the door and the lock clicked into place.

I sat on the bed, hands clamped between my knees, trying to recall when I'd last had the lanyard. Then I remembered: it was just before I tried calling Connor again last night. An image of dragging my hair out from under the thick ribbon and placing it next to the plastic cup on the bedside unit appeared clearly in my mind. I stood and ran to the door, grabbing the handle, hoping to catch Melanie before she reached the end of the corridor. I tugged the handle down and pulled but the door didn't budge.

My mouth went dry. The cold handle shifted up and down, but the door didn't move. I didn't know what scared me more, the fact that someone had been in my room and taken the lanyard while I was sleeping, or that I was now locked in the room with no means of escape.

Chapter Twenty-Two

A screaming sound rang out. My heart leapt in my chest. I tried the door again, but it was still locked. The alarm was coming from the corridor, but the speaker must have been close to my room because the high-pitched wailing pierced my eardrums. I covered my ears with my hands, my cold palms pressed tight against the side of my head.

This was because of the lost lanyard, I was sure. But it wasn't lost. It had been stolen, and now the whole facility was on lockdown and there was no way for me to tell Melanie what had really happened. I went to the window, but I couldn't see anything through the rain spatters except the wall and the side of the barracks opposite. I looked up at the bank of swollen clouds, but my eyes kept being drawn back to the door. I couldn't get out, but could someone else get in? Someone with my stolen key fob?

My gaze fell on the desk chair. Should I wedge it against the handle like I did when I was in hotel rooms on my own? From a young age, Mum drummed into me that a woman on her own in a hotel is automatically at risk. Because of her anxiety, I'd always been hyperaware that all the staff would be aware when a woman is staying on her own. Other guests could be watching to see which women ask for a table for one when they eat, what floor they press in the lift, which room they let themselves into. I was always agonisingly aware of anyone who passed me in a hotel corridor, feeling their eyes on me when I slipped into my room. Every knock at the door had me peering nervously through the spyhole, heart pounding. It had got to the stage where I avoided staying away without my husband.

I took my hands from the side of my head, the screech of the siren making me wince. I lifted the chair and shoved it against the door so that the handle couldn't be moved down, but I didn't feel any safer. Someone had been in my room. Who?

My imagination conjured horrifying pictures of wild-eyed men watching me while I slept, then picking up the lanyard and planning what they would do the next time they let themselves into my room at night. Perhaps someone had been in when I was in the shower. Maybe they had crept into the bathroom and seen me while I was washing my naked body.

Suddenly, the sound stopped, leaving my ears ringing with the ghost of it. I strained to listen for sounds in the corridor, but couldn't hear anything but a tapping from the radiator and the slashing of rain against the window. Checking that the chair was firmly in place, I took the plastic cup into the bathroom and filled it from the tap, my hand shaking as I raised it to my arid mouth.

A knock at the door made my hand jolt so violently the water surged out of the cup and splashed on to the linoleum floor. 'Who is it?' I said, putting down the cup and stepping gingerly towards the door.

'Only me.' It was Melanie's voice.

I shifted the chair away. 'Come in.'

'Disaster averted,' she said. 'Phew.'

'Someone came into my room and stole the lanyard,' I said over her.

'Sorry, what?'

'I remembered taking the lanyard off and putting it next to my bed.' I pointed at the unit. 'I put it there last night. I remembered after you'd gone. Someone must've been in my room and taken it.'

Melanie shook her head. 'You can't have done,' she said. She put her hand into the inside pocket of her jacket and drew out a blue lanyard. She dangled it in front of my face. 'Because one of the orderlies found it near the therapy room and handed it in.' She swung it from side to side like a hypnotist's watch. 'Look,' she said, allowing it to still. 'It's yours. I just wish I'd checked if it had been found before I made the lockdown call. Could have saved us all from those wailing sirens.'

I took it from her, holding the laminated rectangle in my trembling palm. There was my name, and that awful, haunted photograph of my face. 'This was taken from my room,' I said. 'Sometime between last night and this morning.'

'Emma, an orderly found it and handed it in. That's all. Nothing more sinister than that.'

'Which orderly?'

Melanie's nose wrinkled. 'I didn't ask. What difference does it make?'

I needed her to take me seriously. 'I am absolutely certain I took this off and put it by the side of my bed last night.'

'I'm not trying to be difficult, but that's not what you said earlier,' said Melanie. 'You were rushing around the room trying to remember when you'd last seen it.'

'Yes, but then I remembered.' Did I, though? I thought I did, but it was possible I was remembering another time I'd taken it off. Memories were slippery things. I knew that better than most people. Each time a memory is made it is re-formed, possibly changed a little. Could I say for certain that the lanyard was by my bed last night? Would I swear to it under oath? And I was so, so tired. My thoughts were becoming disordered, not that I was about to admit that to Melanie.

'I know it's not ideal, getting the entire place locked down,' said Melanie, holding the door open, 'but it was only for a few minutes, and I'll be the one taking the blame, since it was my team, not you.'

Heat rushed to my cheeks. 'God, I'm so sorry. I hope it won't affect your reference.' I couldn't believe I'd put her in that position.

'I'm sure one black mark won't kill me,' she said. 'Keep hold of it in future, though.'

I nodded, running my finger over the smooth laminated card, still unsure of how I could possibly have lost it without physically lifting it off myself. Why would I have done that? It didn't make sense.

'Why don't we get along to the session and say no more about it?' said Melanie. 'I'm painfully aware that we don't have much time left. The detective in charge of the case rang for an update this morning. I probably shouldn't say this, but I feel like the police and the press are circling like vultures, just out of sight, waiting for a feeding frenzy.'

The image played like a movie in my head. I saw Laura pinned out in a star shape, her stomach sliced open, guts spilling on to the scorched earth beside her. I heard the flap of enormous wings and a shriek as a vulture's sharp beak plucked out an intestine and dragged it skywards, as more birds descended, until a multitude of black wings blocked out the light.

I shook my head to dislodge the image and slipped the lanyard over my head, lifting my hair over the ribbon. 'That's a lot of pressure. Do you want me to speak to them?' I said. I didn't know what I could add, but thought I should show willing, since I was the one who'd been brought in to handle the treatment. It didn't seem fair that Melanie was the one fending off the questions.

'Ah, thanks, but I told them we'd had a breakthrough yesterday. Laura admitting Daniel was coercive and manipulative felt like a turning point to me.'

'I agree,' I said. 'Three days left to find out what happened that night. Not long, is it?'

Melanie pulled in air through almost-closed lips and nodded. 'Let's hope it's long enough.'

I picked up the tote and followed her into the corridor, where Julie and Aidan were waiting. They stood further apart than usual and I sensed an atmosphere between them, but after the last half an hour, I couldn't expend energy worrying about those two.

As we approached the glass walkway, I became more aware of the sound of our feet on the carpet. Julie and Aidan's feet matched the pounding rhythm in my head, which grew louder as the light from the tunnel loomed at the end of the corridor.

The urge to yawn tugged at the base of my throat. I opened my mouth to pull in more oxygen, but the satisfied throat tightening that signified the lung-full end of a yawn didn't come. I tried again. I couldn't find enough air.

My head swam. I stepped on to the frosted base of the tunnel. How could it still be so painfully bright when the whole glass shell was wet with rain? Droplets moved, not only downwards but across, like filmy insects crawling along the exterior, trying to find their way in. I attempted to fill my lungs again, gulping in air, but I still couldn't drag it far enough into my diaphragm.

I searched my brain for a strategy to calm me. *Find something external to focus on, something static*: I heard Harvey's voice in my head. I turned to look across the court-yard to the barracks. But nothing was still. The building blurred and shifted with the water. I tried to see past the rivulets, to focus on the solid stone, the building that had been a safe haven for soldiers, that had stood for decades, centuries even, but it was distorted, alive and moving.

I forced myself to walk on, pushing away the thoughts of the chasm of air beneath my feet. One step. Another step. My vision pulsed, blurring my focus. I looked again, trying to adjust my eyesight, and saw the barracks wasn't just distorted by the rain on the glass – half of it was missing. The right-hand side of the building stood proud and sturdy, but all that remained of the left was a jagged scar of protruding stones and mangled metal rods.

The clocktower rose over the rubble, like a head balanced on a body severed in half, its face still showing the same time, as if too stunned to move.

Chapter Twenty-Three

My relief when Melanie put her fob to the therapy-room door was palpable. I held it together until she, Aidan and Julie left to collect Laura, then, following the satisfying click of the door lock, I collapsed into the chair and laid my head on the desk. For once, I welcomed the heat radiating from behind me. My fingers were white with cold and the chill burrowed through to my centre. I was utterly drained of energy. I'd hoped crossing the walkway would get easier each time, but instead of desensitising me, my anxiety was spiking so high it was becoming unmanageable.

I'd diagnosed myself with anxiety not long after Sarah took her own life. It was no surprise that my coping mechanisms were overloaded after my sister, the one person who had loved and protected me my whole life, jumped from a bridge on to a busy motorway. When she'd brought the man who went on to become her abuser home for the first time, Mum and I had been surprised that her new boyfriend was more than a decade older than her.

'You didn't tell me he was an old man,' I said, after he left.

'He's not old, he's thirty.' She laughed and poked me in the chest. 'You only think he's old because you're immature. And, anyway, he's charming and funny and he loves me.'

Despite how besotted she was, it had come as a shock when she decided not to go to university after her exams then moved in with him a couple of months later. A few months after that, she stopped coming home, then stopped answering her phone when we called.

It was her boyfriend who reported her missing when she didn't come home one evening. He gave the appearance of being the distraught, loving partner, desperately worried about her. We were all taken in by him, until the police arrived at our door to tell us how she died. Then there was a post-mortem, and the catalogue of old injuries was discovered by the pathologist: previously broken ribs, cigarette burns on the inside of her thighs.

I did some research on her boyfriend then, and soon discovered details of previous accusations against him. Without Sarah to attest, the police told us there was nothing anyone could do. When the injustice began to overwhelm me, I decided not to focus on him for a second longer. Instead, I made it my mission to do what I could to help women in abusive relationships. If I'd known what Sarah was going through, I might have been able to help her. Since it was too late for her, I made a silent promise to her that I would do what I could for others.

I started at home. That wasn't easy. Dad never forgave me for standing up to him. He blamed me for Mum leaving him too, saying I turned her against him with my radical feminist ideas. I tried hard not to care about the cruel accusations he levelled at me. I told him once that, if he hadn't made us think controlling behaviour was normal, then Sarah wouldn't have accepted it in her own relationship. I could still see the look of disgust on his face before he turned and walked away. The feelings when he died were complicated. How could I possibly be so bereft when I knew what he was, what he'd done to Mum – to all of us? Even though they were divorced by then, Mum still arranged his funeral. She said she understood why I wouldn't go.

Following the inquest into Sarah's death, my fear of heights got so bad it affected my everyday life. I imagined peril everywhere. The visual imagery of everything that could go wrong was like a constant motion picture in my head. Reluctantly, I eventually admitted it to Harvey, and we did a lot of work on my generalised anxiety. I'd thought I was doing well at controlling that, but Harvey helped me see that my brain had tried to contain any mental distress by focusing on one specific area, and that area was heights.

Of course, he was right. I'd seen clients who were absolutely fine unless they were faced with a pigeon, or buttons. I understood them completely because I was generally symptom free unless I had to face heights. It was no surprise, really, since every night I saw Sarah leap to her death in my dreams.

The cognitive behavioural therapy Harvey and I did alleviated the anxiety so significantly that I'd classed it as a fear rather than a phobia until what happened to Kai Bray. But recently the anxiety was spreading again, infecting my thoughts, my sleep, my body, my ability to function. And the visual images were spiralling out of control, even when I was awake.

With my cheek against the hard surface of the desk, it occurred to me that I was in no fit state to be in charge of Laura's case. Perhaps I should tell Melanie I was struggling. But then I'd be the psychologist whose mental health stopped her from working. How would that impact my private practice? What would happen to my career? And what would happen to Laura? I knew there was a chance she'd hurt someone, maybe fatally, and I was running out of time to uncover exactly who that was. That was the reason I had been brought here, but I also had a strong suspicion she might be the victim of an abusive man. I owed it to Sarah to see this through. I'd made a promise and I would not break it. I sat upright. This would be over in two days. Next week I could arrange to see Harvey, maybe get some medication to take the edge off the anxiety. Connor and I could take a holiday. I just needed to take it moment by moment until this job was done.

I only had a few minutes to compose myself. I did some breathing exercises and a posture release stretch in an attempt to soothe the tension nagging at the base of my neck and across my shoulders. Before stowing my tote bag under the desk, I checked the phone one more time. The screen was blank. 'Where are you, Connor?' I said to the phone through gritted teeth, before slipping it back in the bag.

I sat myself in the usual spot on the sofa facing the desk,

putting my pad and pen on the seat beside me and counted my breaths in and out until I heard the tread of feet in the corridor. The top of Melanie's head appeared through the glass pane as she leaned down to unlock the door. Laura entered, looking fresh and rested. Her cheeks glowed pink, as though she'd recently come in from the cold.

'Hello,' I said, making sure my voice was strong. 'How are you today?' I smiled. 'You look well.'

Laura glanced at Melanie, but Melanie had her back to her, making her way to the desk. Laura turned to me. 'Thank you.' She ran her hand through her glossy ponytail. 'It would be easy to give up making an effort in here, but you have to do what you can to cheer yourself up in a place like this, don't you?'

'Cheer yourself up' struck me as an odd phrase. I was tempted to ask if she remembered why she was being detained. If I was being held in this unit because I'd been found covered in someone else's blood, and I couldn't pinpoint how or why, I imagined it would take more than a clear complexion and shiny hair to lift my spirits.

I checked myself. That was not an empathetic response. Unconditional positive regard was the least any patient should expect from me. She took a seat then leaned forward, her hands knitted together in front of her. 'I've been thinking about yesterday's session,' she said.

My pulse quickened. This is what I needed, more detail on the escalating abuse. Those recollections could trigger memories of what happened that night and my work here would be done. 'Go on.'

'I feel like I was unfair about Daniel, that I gave you the wrong impression about him.'

No. She could not backtrack now. I clenched my fists in my lap. 'Unfair how?'

Her fingers opened and closed, as if warming up for a fight. 'I feel like I made him out to be some kind of monster . . . and he's not.' She paused. 'I mean, he's not perfect, but nobody is, are they?'

'No, nobody's perfect.'

'And we have a good time when we're together, especially when it's just the two of us, which it is most of the time. And he's kind, when I'm not feeling—'

An ear-splitting crash from outside made me turn my head towards the window. Behind the wire grille the glass was splattered with rain. I kept my eyes on it for a beat, trying to calm my buzzing nerves. I turned back to Laura, noting she looked perfectly relaxed. 'Demolition isn't exactly the ideal background noise to therapy, is it?'

'I prefer something more ambient,' she said, smiling.

'You were about to tell me about times when Daniel is kind.'

'Yes, for example, when he took me to Berlin two months ago.'

Heat rushed up my neck. 'Sorry, you went to Berlin two months ago?'

'Yes, the first week of February. Daniel had to go for work, so I took a few days off to go with him.'

Two months ago. Eight weeks. Precisely when my husband was working in the German capital.

'I've always wanted to visit Berlin. Did you get to see much of the city?' I sensed Melanie look up. She was probably wondering why I was asking about tourist destinations instead of delving into Laura's subconscious. I didn't care.

'Yes, when he wasn't working, we did one of those walking tours. It was fascinating. We went to the Brandenburg Gate, the Reichstag, the Memorial to the murdered Jews. God, that was harrowing. The East Side Gallery was brilliant, but we did that on the following day because it's a bit further out.'

Dread tightened its grip on me with every sight she listed. 'Where did you stay?'

She looked up to the left, pursing her lips, then said, 'It was a hotel called the Catalonia Berlin Mitte. It was on the East side, not far from Alexanderplatz. It's a really cool hotel, all exposed brickwork and aluminium tables. It had amazing graffiti on the walls upstairs.'

Every muscle in my body tightened. It could be a coincidence that Connor had also stayed at the Catalonia Berlin two months ago, but it didn't feel like one. First Laura talked about a man who sounded a lot like Jimmy Bray, then the scavenger hunt, Daniel disappearing and not answering calls, and now she was talking about the exact same itinerary my husband had followed while staying in the same hotel. It felt targeted, like a carefully planned drip-feed of disclosures to make me aware that she knew everything about my life . . . and Connor's. Why? Stomach acid rose up my throat, catching at the back of my mouth and making me cough. I stood, afraid I'd start retching. 'Sorry,' I said.

'I need the bathroom. Sorry.' I didn't care if it was unprofessional to interrupt the session this time. I needed to get out of that room.

'Emma.' Melanie sprang up from behind the desk. 'Are you okay?'

I tried to swallow down the bitter liquid and coughed again. 'I'm fine.' I walked towards the door, pulling on my lanyard ready to press the fob against the lock. 'Sorry,' I muttered. 'Just give me a minute.' I tugged the door, but it was still locked. I pushed the fob against the pad again, sweat itching my scalp.

'Let me,' said Melanie. I stepped back so she could try her fob. The door instantly clicked open. Aidan and Julie were staring between me and Melanie. 'Could you escort Emma to the ladies, please, Julie?'

'Course.' Julie's face was screwed up in concern. 'Come on, love.'

She took my elbow and led me along the corridor in the direction of the toilets. My vision blurred, swirling colours seeming to reach for me from the walls. I was relieved when Julie held open the door and I could rush inside, past a bank of sinks and into a cubicle. I lowered the toilet lid and sat down, pulling my hair away from my shoulders, glad to feel cooler air on my neck.

Julie's Crocs squeaked on the linoleum inside the room. I wished she'd stayed out in the corridor. I wanted to hold my head in my hands and moan. I wanted to rock backwards and forward and sob, and most of all I wanted to scream *What the hell is going on?* at the top of my lungs.

Because something was going on. It wasn't just my anxiety leading me to see connections where there weren't any. I wasn't fortune-telling or catastrophising. Surely even a rational mind, free of the pressures I was under, would conclude this was all far beyond any conceivable coincidence. There was no statistical probability that could place the woman in that therapy room in the same city as Connor at exactly the same time, in the same hotel, doing precisely the same sightseeing in the same sequence he'd described to me when he got home. Even if there was, something below the surface, deep down in my subconscious, was telling me something was wrong with the situation I had willingly walked into at Heaton Place.

Why, of all the psychologists in the country, many of whom would jump at the chance to treat this case, did she insist on seeing me? Who the hell was Laura Winters, I asked myself, as fear crawled over my skin, and what kind of twisted game was she playing with me?

Chapter Twenty-Four

'Are you all right, Emma?' Julie's voice echoed in the bath-room.

I let my hair fall back over my shoulders and grabbed some toilet roll, wiping away the sweat that had collected along my hairline. 'Yeah, I'm fine,' I said. 'Won't be a sec.' I stood, lifting the lid of the toilet and throwing the tissue inside, then flushing. I took a breath and unlocked the door.

When I stepped out of the cubicle Julie was leaning against a sink, her hands on her broad hips. 'You sure you're all right?'

'I'm fine. Don't worry.' I went to the furthest sink near the window and ran the cold water. I squeezed synthetic-lemon-scented soap on to my hands and washed them, shifting my body away from Julie in the hope she wouldn't see me hold the inside of my wrists under the icy water. The freezing sting on my skin was something tangible I could focus on. I needed it to bring me out of my head, away from the turmoil of my thoughts and firmly into this room.

Turning off the tap, I glanced around to find Julie holding out sheets of blue paper. I smiled at her and took them, forcing myself to be aware of the rough texture on my palms. The dusty, chemical smell of paper hand towels immediately took me back to primary school. A vision of being in the school toilets with a group of my friends appeared to me. We must've been around eight or nine and had recently learned about ouija boards and all things supernatural from someone's older sibling.

One rainy lunchtime, on a day very much like today, we got one of the girls to lie flat on the floor by the coat pegs and tried to lift her off the ground using only one finger each. And it worked. Using just one finger each, six pre-pubescent girls raised another to around ten centimetres off the floor. The memory comforted me, somehow, as if it was reminding me that strange things happen all the time; we just tune them out or make them fit logic so we feel safe in our self-structures.

'When you were younger, did you ever play that game where a few of you try to lift someone using one finger?'

Julie's mouth opened in a surprised smile. 'You know what, I did.' Her eyes brightened. 'I'd completely forgotten about it, though. I bet every little girl tries that at one time or another.' She laughed. 'It's weird. In my head, it worked. But it can't have done, can it? I mean, it's not possible, is it?'

I shrugged. 'I remember it working too.'

'I'm going to ask my Marnie when I next speak to her, see if she did it when she was at school.'

'Is that your daughter?' I remembered Aidan mentioning

a Marnie before and wondered about the connection. It would feel like prying to ask. I looked around the bathroom, at the lino floor with scraps of blue hand towel under the sinks and grubby edges where the flooring met the white-painted skirting board. I took in the window with the same impenetrable secondary glazing as in my room, and the bank of sinks, the one I'd just used with a droplet of water hovering at the end of the chrome tap, and found I could breathe more easily. My chest was less tight. The prickling in my brain lessened.

'Erm, yes.' Julie looked down at her blue Crocs. I could see her greying white socks through the holes. I sensed Julie felt she'd overstepped some kind of professional mark, mentioning her family, so I didn't push her.

I kept concentrating on the tiny details of the room to stay grounded. The memory of school felt like a gift my brain offered at exactly the right moment, reminding me that not everything can be explained. In terms of science, I also knew that our conscious mind is such a tiny part of what makes up the whole. The pseudoscience suggestion that we only use ten per cent of our brain was a myth, but I believed research that said that, of the hundred billion neurons we have, ninety-five per cent were firing unconsciously. My visions and conscious thoughts, the ones that were raging out of control, were only the tip of an enormous iceberg, and I knew that trying to direct them was like trying to direct a kayak on a stormy ocean.

Drying the last of the water from my hands, I told myself that my conscious, rational brain had lost control. I was finding connections and reading into things that weren't necessarily there. But, try as I might, I couldn't get past the litany of coincidences. And if my subconscious was trying to tell me something, maybe I should listen.

'Feeling better?' Julie said, brightly. I imagined her with Marnie. I bet she was a lovely mum, firm but fair. I pictured a younger version of Julie, fair-haired, stocky and always ready with a cuddle and a smile.

An urge to hug Julie took me by surprise. 'Much better, thank you ... but I'm still a bit queasy. I think I might need to postpone the rest of the session.'

Julie's mouth twitched. 'I don't know if ... I'm not sure that ...'

I was as aware of the limited time we had left as the rest of the team, but I was also aware of what it took to be a good psychologist and, right now, my head was not in the right space for the work and there was only one solution I could think of to remedy that. 'Don't worry, I'll go back to the therapy room and explain to Laura. It's important she knows I'm not feeling well, that I wouldn't just abandon her.' Stopping a session or even postponing one could cause problems in therapy. If a patient already had abandonment issues, and the therapist appeared to leave without clear and valid reasons, and sometimes even if they did give good reasons, it could damage the therapist–patient alliance. Not that Laura seemed to have issues in that area.

I still had no real idea what to think about Laura. After

the revelations that morning, I wanted time to gather my thoughts and manage my spiralling anxiety, and in order to do that, I needed to go home and see my husband in the flesh.

Chapter Twenty-Five

Despite the time constraint, now I'd made the decision to go home and see Connor before continuing the work with Laura, I surged with a new sense of purpose. I followed Julie along the corridor back to the therapy room, this time noticing the bright pictures pinned to the walls.

'Art therapy?' I said, eyeing one rather disturbing painting with bold swirls of reds and blacks.

'Yes,' said Julie, striding ahead, her shoulders tensely curled. I waited for her to say more, but she remained silent, picking up pace so I had to take long steps to keep up.

I leapt at a shattering sound to my left, then fell against the wall. Something that felt like hot snow peppered my cheek. I turned to see a chair leg wedged in what remained of the glass panel in a therapy-room door. Beyond the scarred wood of the chair leg, two orderlies were restraining a young woman who didn't look much older than a schoolgirl. The action seemed to happen in slow motion as one man took her arms and raised them above her head and the other grabbed her ankles. They manoeuvred her to the floor while she tried to kick out. The orderlies turned away as she spat frothy white globules at their faces.

Julie took my arm. 'Come on.' She led me a few doors along before stopping and assessing me. She reached out and lifted something from my hair near my ear. 'You'll need to make sure you get all that glass out of your hair.'

I raised my hand to my cheek gingerly, sure I'd find sharp slivers of glass sticking out. 'Can you see any in my face?'

She moved closer, scrutinising my skin. Her warm breath smelled of coffee. 'I think you're okay,' she said. The proximity felt too intimate, and I exhaled a lungful of air when she took a step back. 'All fun and games here, isn't it?'

I glanced back when I heard the bottom of a door scraping glass along the floor. The young woman emerged, looking even more diminutive now she was flanked by the orderlies. I would never have guessed she'd have the strength to smash a chair through a window. Looks could be deceiving.

My heart rate was still galloping by the time we approached the therapy room. Aidan stood with one shoulder leaning against the wall, his back to us. The bass of his voice reverberated in the corridor, but I couldn't decipher what he was saying. Julie coughed. He turned at the sound, flattening against the wall, his eyes trailing the length of my body in that unnerving way of his. Melanie stood at the other side of the door, the pinched look on her face turning to a smile when she addressed me. 'You okay?'

'Not really,' I said. 'Did you see what happened down there?'

Melanie nodded. 'We heard it. You weren't caught up in it, were you?'

'Other than needing to brush glass out of my hair, you mean?' I gestured for her to come closer. She did, a concerned expression on her face. 'I need to curtail today's session,' I said. The urge to tell her what was disturbing me was almost overwhelming, but I had nothing but my suspicions to report. I had a strong sense that I would be the one who looked like she was suffering a mental health crisis if I explained what was happening in my head.

'Are you unwell? Is there anything I can get you?'

I shook my head. 'Just exhausted and a bit shaken.' I realised the event in the corridor just now could play into my hands. 'I know it's far from ideal to cancel a session, especially since we don't have much time left, but being sprayed with glass has left me a bit wobbly and I need a clear head to be able to tune into what Laura's going through. I'm sorry, I know it's not ... but I don't feel like I'm in a position to do that this morning. Maybe we can make the time up tomorrow. Do two sessions? I'll let her know. It's not fair to keep her waiting in there. She must be wondering what's going on.'

'It's Thursday,' Melanie said through tight lips. 'We only have until Saturday.'

'I am aware of that but, as I said, we can make the time up tomorrow. Could you please look into when the room is available?' I walked past her, ignoring the strained look on her face, and into the room. Laura was sitting where I'd left her. She looked up, her eyes wide, with an expression that struck me as feigned innocence. The uneasiness in my gut returned at the sight of her. 'I'm very sorry, Laura, but I'm going to have to cut our session short this morning.'

Laura glanced at where Melanie stood in the doorway, then back to me. 'Oh, okay. Are you—'

'I'm not feeling too great. Nothing to worry about – I'm sure I'll be back on form tomorrow.' I kept my tone clipped and professional so as not to invite further questions. 'You'll be escorted back to your room now and we'll reconvene as soon as the room's free in the morning.' I wondered then if Laura had been told that she only had two days left to use our therapy to remember what happened in her kitchen that night; if she knew that the birds were already circling, preparing to descend. I hardened my heart, deciding that wasn't my problem. My mental health had to be my first priority, and the only way I was going to protect that was by speaking to Connor face to face. When I told him all the things Laura had said that made me uneasy, he would have an explanation. It's what he did – put things right; showed me where I was going wrong.

Laura stood, shoving her hands into the front pockets of her jeans. 'I hope you feel better soon.' She smiled weakly and walked to the door, turning when she got there. 'I hope it wasn't anything I said.' Before I could reply she turned left out of the room, followed by Melanie, and I heard the lock slide into place.

What the hell did she mean by that? I threw myself on to the chair behind the desk. To my annoyance, the desk was bare. I wanted to see Melanie's notes, see what she was making of what Laura said. The certainty she was toying with me was back with force. I stood and walked to the sofa, picking up my pad from where I'd left it on the cushion. I was sure I'd left the pen on top, but it wasn't there. I kneeled on the floor, the thick fibres of the carpet tiles scratchy under my palms as I dipped my head to look underneath the sofa. The pen lay next to the wooden leg.

As I retrieved it, a sickening thought occurred to me. Melanie and Aidan had been standing outside in the corridor when Julie and I came back from the bathroom. Laura had been in the room on her own. With a new prickling inside my skull, I opened the pad I'd been using since I started to treat Laura. The first page was filled with my handwriting, neatly spaced, all perfectly coherent sentences. I turned to what I'd written today. Stomach acid burned up my throat when I saw the scrawled letters in untidy capitals, 'BERLIN????' Underneath, in barely legible script, I'd written, 'SHE'S MESSING WITH MY HEAD!!!!!'

It would be clear to anyone reading these pages that whoever had written them was not in a good place mentally. And Laura wasn't just anyone; she was a trained psychologist. She was the one who had brought me to this place, away from my home and my husband; the husband I now couldn't get hold of. The room suddenly felt like the core of an inferno. Thank God I'd made the decision to go home. I couldn't escape Heaton Place quickly enough.

Chapter Twenty-Six

I was still staring at the scrawl on my pad when the sound of the therapy-room door unlocking made me look up. The metal click of the internal bolt passing through the door to the frame used to make me nervous. Now I found it comforting. How quickly I'd become institutionalised. That was another good reason for escaping Heaton Place. I looked up to see Julie standing in the doorway. 'You all right, love? You look pale.'

She'd clearly got over her concern about being over-familiar and the kindness in her voice made my knees weaken. 'I'm really not feeling great,' I said. I picked up the pad and pen and went over to the desk to collect the tote bag. 'I could do with a night in my own bed, to be honest.'

'I hear you,' she said. 'I do a week on, a week off here, and it always takes me a couple of nights to get used to that thin mattress. I bought a topper for mine. Helps a bit. Do you want me to see if I can get you one?'

She lifted her eyebrows, then turned at what sounded like a deliberate cough from outside the door. It must be

Aidan, quietly hovering around, as always. Julie turned, and when she looked back her face was flushed. 'Although, you won't be here long enough to need one, will you?' she said.

'True.' I picked the tote up from beneath the desk. The off-white cotton sagged. I lifted it, confused by the lightness. I took it between my hands and patted the limp fabric. Fear made my vision stutter, like a film caught in a projector. It was empty. The phone was gone. I opened the top and shoved my hand inside. I felt nothing but rough cotton. I dropped to my knees, searching the floor under the desk.

'What's wrong?' said Julie, coming into the room and leaning over to see what I was doing.

'My phone . . . the phone Melanie gave to me. It's not in my bag.' Moisture filmed my skin. Why was this bloody building so relentlessly hot?

Aidan appeared in the doorway. 'What's going on?'

'She's lost her phone,' said Julie.

'No, I haven't,' I said. 'I brought it down with me in this bag. I remember checking it before Laura came in.' I turned the bag inside out. 'But it's gone.'

'Is it in your pocket?' asked Julie.

I stood and patted down my jeans, knowing there was no way I would have forgotten moving the phone out of the bag. 'No. I know it was in that bag.'

Aidan went to the sofa where I'd been sitting and lifted the cushions one by one, then dropped into a plank. The key-teeth of the skull on his forearm stretched into a mocking smile. He sprang back up. 'It's not down here.'

'It was in this bag,' I repeated.

'Are you sure?' Julie's voice was soft.

'Fucking certain.' Julie started, but I wasn't in the mood to apologise. 'Somebody's taken it.' I didn't mean *someone*, I meant Laura. When everyone was out of the room, Laura had stolen my phone. My brain presented an image of her pressing the keys, grinning as she read my increasingly desperate texts to Connor.

'You can't let a phone out of your sight in here,' said Aidan. 'It's one of the basic rules.' The sneer in his voice made me wonder if he spoke to all senior staff like that. I added it to the list of things to mention when I escaped from Heaton Place for good.

With sickening clarity, I was suddenly absolutely certain that Laura had stolen my phone so she could call Connor. I pictured her lifting the handset to her ear in my mind's eye, then smiling at the sound of his voice. Why would my imagination allow him to answer her, but not me?

'Have you got a car here?' I said to Julie.

'A car? Why?' Her top lip lifted, showing pink-grey gums.

'I'd like a lift to the nearest station. I need to get back to London.'

Aidan joined us at the desk, crossing his arms over his wide chest. 'We don't have cars. Not here.' The stench of his stale tobacco breath crossed over the desk.

'Can you call me a taxi, then?' The two of them looked utterly perplexed. 'Please?'

'We can't look up numbers for taxis,' said Aidan, his cold eyes shifting from me to Julie and back. 'It's the rules, innit? We'll get you back to your room, then ask Melanie to come and see you. We're not . . . it's above our pay grade.'

I stopped myself from rolling my eyes. Since when had calling a taxi been above someone's professional remit? A look at Julie's worried face made me regret being harsh. These two were orderlies. Their pay wouldn't be much over minimum wage and their shift patterns sounded brutal. How did someone maintain a personal life when they worked a week on, a week off? How did they maintain relationships beyond these walls? I found it hard enough when Connor worked away for a few days at a time.

At the thought of Connor, my stomach shrivelled to a tight fist. I shoved the pad and pen into the bag and made for the door. 'Okay. Please tell Melanie I need to get a train back to London. It's urgent, tell her. I need to go now.'

Chapter Twenty-Seven

So many questions paraded around my head as I marched up the stairs to my room. I inhaled as deeply as my lungs would allow, before stepping into the glass walkway, accepting the dizziness and the nausea, clamping my teeth together and telling myself it was temporary, it would pass. Through the dirty glass I noticed the crane had moved to the other side of the barracks across the courtyard, ugly gouged-out track marks showing its trajectory across the gravel. The wrecking ball swung ominously, the contents of my stomach swilling from side to side along with it.

Patchy scrubland spread out past the rubble on the missing left-hand side of the building, revealing a single-track road which snaked off into the distance, eventually joining a wider road with traffic speeding along. The desire to be in one of those cars racing away from this stultifying place with its locked windows and hideous walkways made me light-headed. I'd been trapped here for an interminable time. That's how it felt, like I was somehow stuck here, caught in a toxic cycle of attempting to help Laura while she tried to thwart me. The promise I'd made after Sarah's death came back to me. But what if Laura wasn't the victim of abuse? What if she was a murderer trying to cover up her crime? So much of what she said left me with more questions than answers. And some of those questions needed to be put to Connor. That thought fuelled my determination to get back to London that afternoon.

Once in my room, I splashed cold water on to my face. I raised my head and saw a ghost of a woman in the mirror. Semicircular dips, purple as bruises, sat under my eyes and pallid skin clung to my protruding cheekbones. An image of Sarah, lying in the coffin in the funeral home, appeared behind my eyes. The make-up artists had done their best to make her look presentable, but there was a visible dent in her forehead and her skin was waxy, her cheeks rouged in a pink she'd never choose herself, and all I could see was the deadness of her. The lack of life.

Saliva flooded my mouth. I leaned over the sink, thinking I might vomit at the memory of how very gone she was. In that room with floral wallpaper and gentle classical music playing through a speaker in the ceiling, I'd had a disgusting urge to lift her eyelid, to see if I could find a single spark of the girl who'd held me to her when storms raged in our house.

A knock at the door made me jump. I rubbed my face quickly with the towel. Melanie's head was poking around my bedroom door when I left the bathroom.

'You all right? Your face is red,' she said.

I lifted the towel, which was still in my hand. 'Just washed my face.' I didn't want to waste any time on small talk. 'I need to get back to London. Today,' I added, in case she didn't understand the urgency.

'Has something happened?'

The list of strange coincidences rattled through my head. Should I tell her? No. I would see Connor, he'd clear it all up and Melanie wouldn't need to know about any of it until I had firm explanations. I couldn't wait to stop thinking I was going mad and get on with my job. Or perhaps not. Maybe I should just walk away from this case. I tried to remember if I'd signed a contract before agreeing to take it on. 'No, nothing specific. But I need to see my husband as soon as I can.'

She pushed the door and came further in. 'It's only two more days, Emma. Are you sure this can't wait until—'

Another two days might seem short to her, but my pitching thoughts were making seconds feel like hours. 'No.' I hung the towel over the back of the chair. 'I need a lift to the station now, please. Do you have a car here? If you could give me a lift, I'd be very grateful. If not, could you please call me a cab?'

Melanie hesitated then said, 'Laura's treatment is important. She needs consistency.'

'I understand that, and I will come straight back after I've seen my husband.' Something told me I should reassure her of this, whether I meant it or not. 'I just need to speak to him first.'

Her face relaxed with the news I wasn't bailing on her. 'Okay. I'm free now, since our session was cut short, so I can give you a lift.'

'Great. Thanks. Do you know how regularly the trains run?'

'I mean I'll take you to London.'

I stopped and looked at her. 'You don't have to take me all the way.'

'It's no bother,' she said, smiling. 'If it helps to get the treatment back on course, then I consider it part of my job. I've got some errands to run, so I can get on with those while you talk to your husband. Best get on our way soon though, if we want to miss the traffic.'

I weighed up my options: get a lift to the station, then take the train and then the tube or a bus to Bow, or sit in a nice warm car all the way there. If I took the train at least I'd have time on my own to think. But I was so tired. I glanced through the window. The dark clouds promised more rain. Springtime in England, doing what it does best: misery. 'If you're sure, thank you.'

'I just need to finish a couple of jobs here, but that shouldn't take more than fifteen minutes. Then I'll be ready to go, okay?'

I wanted to leave that second, but nodded. The door closed and I sat on the bed and waited.

The fresh wind on my face was welcome as we walked to the staff car park behind the facility. Melanie stopped by an oldish Audi A1 and clicked her key fob. The lights flashed and there was a clunk as it unlocked. She opened the passenger side and leaned in to grab handfuls of wrappers and empty paper coffee cups. She brushed crumbs off the seat with her spare hand. 'Sorry it's such a mess,' she said, walking to the back of the car and opening the boot. I listened to her throw the detritus inside and slam it shut, then she climbed into the car beside me and turned the key in the ignition.

She pressed a button on the dash and a console appeared on top. 'What's your postcode?' she said. I told her and watched her twist a dial and press numbers and letters into the satnav. As her finger moved, I thought about the car; it didn't fit with the image of Melanie I'd created in my head. I'd got used to thinking of her as in charge, but she was young to be a supervising psychologist; I remembered thinking that when I first met her. Despite her age, I'd always found her to be professional and focused, so I'd expected her to be the kind of woman who kept every area of her life ordered. If I was honest, I expected her to have a newer, cleaner car. A more prestigious one. Clearly her priorities lay elsewhere. Her career, maybe.

The pressure on my chest lifted a notch when we drew out of the car park, allowing me to take a full breath for the first time in days. Melanie drove slowly along the uneven track at the back of Heaton Place. I looked up at the old stone barracks where my room was, then at the glass walkway leading to the square, modern treatment centre next door. As we passed, I was sure I saw movement on the walkway. Twisting in my seat, I looked back to see two figures in blue scrubs. The body shapes made me certain it was Julie and Aidan. A third figure appeared behind them. My heartbeat intensified when the figure stilled and stared down at the car.

It was Laura, I was sure of it. But why would she be on the walkway behind the orderlies who were meant to watch her? I strained my eyes to see more clearly, but with every turn of the car's tyres, the figure staring down at me got smaller until all I could see was a dark streak against the brooding sky.

Chapter Twenty-Eight

The air conditioner blew out warm, comforting air and Melanie hummed along to a melodic tune I recognised. 'Is this Beth Orton?' I said.

'Yeah, I love this album. My mum used to play it when we drove down to Cornwall in the summer holidays.' Melanie smiled at the memories playing in her head. A recollection of my family driving to St Just one summer crawled out from under a rock in my brain. I saw Sarah and me clinging to each other in the back of Dad's Ford Focus, begging him to turn around and pick Mum up. He'd forced her out of the car by the side of a country road for spilling a drop of coffee on his trousers when she handed him the cup from the top of the flask. My childhood despair and desperation were still so accessible, raw like an unhealed wound. I remembered the plasticky new-car smell and the flood of relief when his huge hands shifted on the steering wheel to turn the car around. Then I saw my mother, shivering in her thin summer dress on the grass verge, quietly crying. When she got in the car, Dad pretended it was all a prank and told Mum she should have known that and to stop being a killjoy. I remembered his grin as he looked back at Sarah and me, making us laugh along and join in the charade of Mum not being able to take a joke.

By the time we reached the A20, the warm car and thrumming engine tempted me to sleep, but the anticipation of seeing Connor and getting to the bottom of what was going on made it hard for me to keep still. When I tensed at the sight of red taillights ahead and pressed my foot on an imaginary brake pedal for about the fortieth time, Melanie said, 'You're very jumpy. Are you sure you're all right?'

'Yeah, sorry.' I pulled my leg back.

Predictably, there was a queue of cars when we eventually approached the Blackwall Tunnel. We crept forward minutely, every paltry rotation of the tyres adding to my desire to be home.

'You seem agitated.' Melanie looked across at me when the traffic was at a standstill again. 'You can tell me if something's wrong, you know.'

'Thank you, I know,' I said. I could see the old tunnel entrance ahead, its yellow-and-red brickwork half obscured by ugly grey gantries with illuminated speed restrictions telling us to go at twenty miles an hour. Chance would be a fine thing. A car on my left indicated to join our lane, nudging its bonnet towards the front of Melanie's car. Melanie sighed and stepped on the brakes, allowing the car to pull in ahead of us. Even in my perturbed state, I found it interesting that she allowed the same thing to happen twice more before we were even a car-length ahead.

I'd passed through the Blackwall Tunnel hundreds of times, and I always found people's responses to this stretch of road said a lot about their personalities. I was the kind of driver who hung back and offered the space to people who indicated but didn't try to push their way in. If I felt bullied, if someone did what the person by the side of us now was doing, edging their enormous 4×4 dangerously close to our near-side panel, I would stubbornly creep forward, close to the bumper of the vehicle in front, so there was no chance of them getting ahead.

Connor never let anyone in. He seemed to think it was an affront to his manhood if someone tried to get ahead of him. The 4×4 took its place in front, then flashed its emergency lights as a thank you to Melanie. It occurred to me that, at this rate, we wouldn't reach the mouth of the tunnel until midnight. I clamped my lips shut so I didn't ask her to stop being a sap and get a bloody move on. I wondered about her suitability as a supervisor. If she was this easily intimidated and bullied, I couldn't imagine how she'd got a leadership role.

Eventually we were spewed out at the other side of the tunnel and the traffic moved more steadily until we turned left on to Bow Road, past the Blind Beggar and up to the lights after Mile End tube station. My stomach churned quicker when we turned right, past the pizza and kebab places where Connor and I would call on our way home from a night out. We drove under the bridge then, to my relief, at last Melanie was indicating into Copperfield Road.

When our modern townhouse, tacked on to the end

of a row of Victorian terraces, came into view, my pulse thundered. I was almost scared to get out when Melanie pulled up outside. It was only days since I'd been here, but it seemed considerably longer.

'Want me to come in with you?' asked Melanie, turning off the engine.

'No, thanks.' I looked at the black railings with their regal gold tops and my front door beyond, then opened the car and stepped out. I stopped, realising I'd left without my keys. What an idiot. No phone, no keys. I was losing my grip on adulting altogether. I pressed my finger on the doorbell, ready, oh, so ready for Connor to open the door. I could almost feel his arms around me, smell his skin as I pushed my head into his neck. Tears gathered in my eyes in anticipation of knowing he was safely back from his trip, that I was safe with him.

I waited. Connor didn't come. I pressed the bell again, then knocked, hoping Melanie couldn't see my tears when I looked around and gave her a tight smile. Still the door didn't open. I rapped my knuckles against the wood once more, then gave up and opened the cover of the lockbox we'd installed for the fortnightly cleaners, half hidden behind the bay tree to the side of the door. My fingers were shaking when I punched in the code and I had to press reset and try again. I sensed Melanie's eyes on my back as I eventually unhooked the keys from the box and fumbled the one for the front door into the lock.

The door swung open. In the hallway the scent of the jasmine diffuser I kept on the radiator cover was too strong.

That was the wrong smell. I should be smelling coffee, or burnt toast. I should smell shampoo and soap. I should be breathing in a scent that told me Connor was home and waiting for me.

'Connor,' I said, taking a step into the hall. I was met with silence. Envelopes skidded across the wooden floor as I stumbled inside. 'Connor,' I shouted, poking my head around the sitting-room door. It was exactly as I had left it. The book I'd been reading the week before was open, balanced face down on the arm of the chair. 'Connor,' I shouted again, panic flowing up my throat, strangling my voice. 'Where are you?' I rushed through to the kitchen at the back of the house, desperate to find him silhouetted against the window, dropping slices of bread on a plate for a sandwich, but knowing, in my frothing guts, he would not be there. He wasn't. The kitchen was cold and empty and smelled of bleach and cleaning fluid, not cooking.

I sensed someone behind me and turned to see Melanie standing in the kitchen doorway, brow furrowed, mouth a downturned arc. 'Emma,' she said, 'are you—'

'He's not here,' I said, letting tears fall freely. 'His flight should have landed hours ago, but he's not here.'

'You don't know where Connor is?' Melanie said gently. 'That's what's upsetting you?'

'He wasn't answering his phone,' I said, 'but I thought he must've lost it or something.' I looked around the room. It looked so clean, so empty. 'And I was sure he would be here.'

Melanie's gaze moved across the kitchen. 'You thought he'd be here, if you came back?'

I let out a sob, realising that I only half thought he might be. I'd hoped, more than thought. 'I'm worried . . .' I said, gripping on to the worktop, 'that something's happened to Connor. Something really, really terrible.'

Chapter Twenty-Nine

'Emma, breathe.' Melanie put her hand on my back as I bent over, gripping my knees, trying to get air into my lungs. She took her hand away, and I missed the warmth of it. I stayed down, watching my tears drop on to the floor tiles.

'Can you tell me why you're so upset? What's going on?' she said, after a minute. 'You seemed to think your husband would be here. Is that right?'

I nodded.

'Any idea where else he could be?'

I stood, feeling a sudden headrush. 'I don't know.' I gazed around the room, still hoping to see some evidence that Connor had been home. I went over to the bin in the corner. It was one that opened automatically when it sensed movement, and the lid creaked up when I hovered my hand over it. The black bag inside appeared to be empty. I dug my hand in, hoping to find a discarded boarding pass or anything that told me he'd got off that flight and had been home. The bag rustled as I searched to the bottom. There wasn't a single thing inside.

'What are you doing?'

'I don't know,' I said, 'I need to see if ... I don't know where Connor is.' My home didn't feel right; this was my kitchen, but it was wrong, somehow. Like a jigsaw cut with a faulty tool, nothing fitted.

'Shall I make us a cup of tea?'

I almost laughed at the absurdity of the question. That was how foreigners thought British people acted in a crisis: sit down with a nice cup of tea and everything will sort itself out. 'I don't want tea. I want to know where my husband is.'

As though she hadn't heard me, Melanie started to fill the kettle. The running water matched the static fizzing in my brain. 'What did he say when you spoke to him?' said Melanie, clicking the switch on the kettle.

'When?'

'At Heaton Place. That's why you wanted the phone. You were going to ring him, weren't you?'

That felt like a lifetime ago. I thought back to sitting on the thin mattress dialling Connor's number over and over again. 'I didn't get through.'

'Did you text him?'

I wanted to scream, *Of course I bloody texted.* 'Yes,' I said. 'He never replied. It's not like him at all. He's the kind of man who stays in touch. He likes to know where I am, what time I'm coming home, that kind of thing. He wouldn't go off grid. He just wouldn't.'

'Did you leave a voicemail?' Melanie opened and closed cupboards until she found our jar of teabags. The ingrained sense I should help her almost made me stand. This was my kitchen after all, but I didn't want a cup of sodding tea, and anyway, my limbs were lead weights.

'He's never had voicemail. Doesn't like the fact they can be hacked. Always says people will ring back if it's important.' Tears bubbled under my words. 'But I did keep ringing back, and he never answered.'

Melanie glanced over at me, then took two mugs from the cupboard above the kettle and dropped a teabag in each. The roar of the kettle boiling filled the room, then dropped to a burble. 'I can see this is very upsetting for you,' Melanie said, pouring steaming water into the cups.

Her voice was measured and calm and I wanted to tell her not to try her psychologist shit on me. I didn't need her to tell me how I was feeling. I had the words for what was going on inside me: I was confused, frustrated, scared. The suction sound of the fridge opening distracted me from my tortured thoughts, and I watched as Melanie unscrewed the cap of the milk and sniffed the top. It must have been all right because she poured a little into each mug.

The milk hadn't soured. That's how little time had passed since Connor and I were here, in this kitchen together. Acknowledging that sent hot needles through my brain. Try as I might, I couldn't get a handle on what was actually happening, but one thing I did know was that it all began the minute I was called to Heaton Place to treat Laura Winters. The thought swelled so big it burst out of me. 'I think it's something to do with Laura.'

Melanie turned. A teaspoon she was using to stir the

tea stilled in her fingers, pale brown liquid dripping from it. 'What?'

'She can't have said all those things by accident. There are too many, I don't know ... hints.'

Melanie frowned, then went back to stirring. 'What do you mean, hints? Hints at what?'

I sat at the small table where Connor and I ate our meals. I looked at the chair he usually sat in and my heart keened for him. 'I made a mistake on a case last year,' I said. 'And I think Laura knows about it.'

'We all make mistakes,' said Melanie. 'We're only human.'

'No. This was a big mistake. It ended up with a man kidnapping his son and threatening the police with a machete. You must've seen it in the news. Jimmy Bray.'

Melanie laid the spoon beside the mugs on the work surface. It would leave a stain. Connor hated mess. 'Ah, right. I know the one you mean. You were the psychologist who didn't file the papers in time?'

'Yes.' The shame hit me again. That poor boy, seeing his father wielding a huge knife at the police, then being dragged away. 'And I think Laura knew and was using it to ...' To what? Destabilise me? Make me feel unsafe?

'It was on the national news, Emma. Lots of people would be aware of the case, and even if Laura knew it was you, how would she benefit from that information?'

I didn't know. That was the problem. 'That's not the only thing,' I said, wiping my hand over my face. 'I think she knows Connor.' I had come to the disturbing conclusion that she knew him very well indeed.

'Your husband, Connor?' Disbelief showed in Melanie's voice.

'At the first session, when Laura described Daniel, she could have been describing Connor.'

'Tall, dark and handsome?' Melanie placed a mug in front of me and sat down in Connor's chair, wrapping her hands around her tea. 'That's not a huge coincidence, is it?'

I wanted to yell at her to get up. Who did she think she was, coming into my house, searching through my cupboards and sitting in my husband's chair? 'Connor was working in Berlin at the same time Laura was there.'

Melanie narrowed her eyes. 'I understand how that seems like a coincidence, but I once bumped into my history teacher on a beach in Marbella, so ... you know ... and Berlin's a big city, I'm sure a lot—'

'At the same hotel.'

'Oh.' She sipped her tea.

I leaned forward, looking her directly in the eye. 'I think Laura has an agenda. Do you know why she refused to see anyone except me?'

She shook her head, then looked down at her mug, blowing on the steaming tea. A patch of pale brown bubbles juddered across the top to the edge. 'Only that she thought you'd be able to help her.'

I dug my nails into my palms. I needed answers, not vague platitudes. 'But why me specifically? If whoever this Daniel is *is* abusive, there are far more eminent psychologists working in the field than me.'

'Don't underestimate your reputation.'

I looked away, annoyed by her response. I knew my reputation didn't merit being the only person who could treat dissociative amnesia. If that's even what Laura had. I was beginning to wonder. 'Connor went to exactly the same sights in Berlin, in the same order as Laura described.'

'So did hundreds of other people, probably. It's a tourist hotspot.'

I wanted to add the part about Daniel not wanting children with his last partner, but that wasn't specific enough to make sense to Melanie. Now I remembered it, it pierced me again. I was sure she was telling me that his last partner was me. 'No. She targeted me and sent messages to me throughout our sessions, letting me know she . . .' I stopped. I sounded like those conspiracy theorists who call into radio shows trying to make people see how they were being gaslit by the establishment. But I believed there was a conspiracy, of one at least.

'What exactly are you saying, Emma?'

'She knew I wouldn't be able to get hold of Connor on the phone. I don't know how, but she knew and she taunted me with it. Then she said that Daniel was cheating, but I think she was really telling me . . .' I exhaled a shuddering breath. Whether I sounded insane or not, I truly believed what I was about to say: 'I suspect Laura is having an affair with my husband.'

The incredulity on Melanie's face made me falter for a moment. 'What?' She laughed nervously. 'Oh, come on, Emma. Seriously? You have to see that's absurd.'

'It's not, though, is it? I don't think it can all be explained by chance. I'm serious, Melanie. I think Laura is having an affair with Connor and that she's playing with me.'

'Why? Why on earth would she do that?' Melanie sat back in Connor's chair, her arms flung wide. 'Surely you can't possibly believe she was really seeing your husband?' she said. 'And why would she toy with you? It doesn't make any sense.'

'I don't know,' I said, more certain than ever that, however improbable it sounded, Laura knew exactly what she was doing.

'What motive could she possibly have?'

A feeling of dread crept through my body. Laura had been found covered in someone else's blood. I couldn't get hold of Connor. There were too many things tying the two of them together. Alarm careered through my veins as I understood for the first time what was really frightening me: I was afraid that the blood found on Laura was my husband's.

Chapter Thirty

Melanie was staring across my kitchen table at me as though she thought I was mad. There was no way I was about to disclose any more of my thoughts, especially not the one currently making excruciating fireworks go off in my brain.

'That's a bit far-fetched . . .' She paused and started again, 'Don't jump to conclusions. It's been a tough few days. You're tired. You're not thinking clearly.'

I knew I was thinking more clearly than I had since my first day at Heaton Place. 'Okay. How do you explain Connor going missing?'

Her shoulders lifted, the lining of her suit making a rustling sound. 'Is he actually missing, though?'

'He would never worry me like this,' I said. I didn't say that he'd find it hard to insist I was always where I said I was if he pulled this kind of stunt. He liked to keep the upper hand. Not that I ever quizzed him. I was now thinking that perhaps I should have.

Melanie brought her phone out of the inside pocket of her jacket. 'Why don't you try ringing him again?'

I cursed myself again for leaving my phone on reception when I arrived at Heaton Place. Melanie unlocked hers and passed it to me. I tapped out Connor's number and pressed the call icon. I held the phone to my ear and listened to it ring. Melanie bit her thumbnail, a hopeful look on her face. The phone continued to ring. My insides hollowing out, I switched it to speakerphone and laid it on the table between us. The tinny sound filled the kitchen. I crossed my arms over my chest, still willing Connor's voice to interrupt the monotonous tone, but knowing, in my bones, that it wouldn't.

'You said he was flying back today.' Melanie tapped the screen to end the call. The echo of the sound still rang in my ears. 'Maybe his flight was delayed. It could just be that he's still in the air. His phone may be on airplane mode.'

I straightened. That could be it. 'I don't know the flight number, but it was from Copenhagen to Stansted and it was due in first thing this morning.'

Melanie took up the phone and started to tap on the screen. 'There was only one flight from Copenhagen to Stansted this morning.' I watched her bitten fingernail stab at the device. Her face dropped. 'It landed on time, apparently.'

'Then where is he?' I looked around my empty kitchen, despair filling the hole at my centre. 'He should have been home hours ago.'

'Maybe he missed the flight,' Melanie said.

'Can you check?'

She looked back to the screen. 'There's a number I can ring.'

I nodded. I would have offered to call myself, but I couldn't guarantee I would be able to make myself understood through the tears which, to my embarrassment, had started again. She pressed the screen, held the phone to her ear, and after a moment she said, 'Hello, yes, I wonder if you can help me. I'm looking for a passenger who should have arrived this morning.' She gave the flight number and waited, looking across at me, then down at the table. A muffled voice was barely audible at the other end of the line.

'No, I understand,' she said. 'But could you at least tell me if any passengers were missing from that flight?' She wrinkled her nose. 'Okay, yes, but ... okay, so could you tell me if the flight was full? Did everybody who booked a seat board the plane?'

Time shifted and warped, taking my balance with it. I stumbled to the box of tissues on the windowsill, pulling one out, then starting as a spider fell from the tissue on to the side of the box. It lay on its back, spindly legs in the air, like a dog playing dead. I turned when Melanie spoke again.

'Okay,' she said. 'I understand.' She nodded as though the person she was talking to could see her. 'Yes, thank you. Thanks then, bye.' She clicked off the call and turned her head to me. 'She wouldn't give me any details, but she did say there was nothing unexpected about the flight from Copenhagen to Stansted. I don't know if that means everyone who was supposed to get on did, but that doesn't tell us if anyone cancelled, or ... ' She trailed off.

I pulled another tissue from the box, not caring if a nest of spiders had set up home in there, and wiped my face. 'Try his number again,' I said. 'Please.' Melanie tapped the screen and let the phone ring. I leaned my back against the sink, aware of my heart pumping hot blood around my body, feeling it course through me, right to the tips of my fingers.

After a long minute, she stopped the call. 'Have a drink,' she said.

Nothing could compel me to sit in a chair and drink tea when I didn't have the first clue where Connor was. 'What if he didn't go on the trip? Like you said, he might have cancelled his ticket.' The thought was a beam of light. I ran from the room, into the hall and up the stairs. I marched past the little home office on the landing, past the spare bedroom and into our bedroom. My feet halted in the doorway. The cream duvet cover with black geometric print was smooth and flat on the bed. Connor always left his side of the bed open, climbing out and starting his day without a thought for how the place looked or, more to the point, who would make things neat and tidy as he preferred. I was the one who always folded it back in place.

When did he last sleep in our bed?

We'd had two cupboards designed and built to look like beach huts, each side of the chest of drawers. I went to his and wrenched open the door. I dragged hangers along the rail, checking to see if his favourite clothes were there. The feel of one of his cotton shirts in my fingers, combined with the thick geranium and leather scent of his aftershave made me want to climb inside and wrap myself up in his clothes.

'Any clues?'

I flinched at the sound of Melanie's voice. I didn't want

her in my bedroom. It felt intrusive. I dropped the sleeve and continued to hunt through the wardrobe. The clothes were all there, as far as I could tell. Both pairs of his Diesel jeans were stacked on top of the others on the shelf as normal. Everything was normal. Except it wasn't.

'No.' I walked past Melanie into the spare room and dipped down to look under the bed. My airways seemed to close when I saw the small black case he took on work trips on the carpet next to the two larger cases we took on holiday. I blinked and looked again. It was still there.

If Connor hadn't even got on the plane in the first place, where the hell was he now?

Chapter Thirty-One

When I stood up, my vision swam. I sat on the spare-room bed, one hand on the iron frame. I tried to channel Harvey's voice, telling me to focus on something solid. I closed my eyes and concentrated on the twisted orb on the end of the frame, the smooth, cold surface of the painted metal. But my brain kept screaming at me, *Connor didn't go to Copenhagen. Why did he lie to me? Where is he now?*

'Emma.' I opened my eyes to see Melanie standing in front of me, a confused look on her face.

'His case is under the bed,' I said. 'He didn't go to Copenhagen.'

She worried at her thumbnail with her front teeth. 'Maybe we should just go back to the—'

'We need to ring the hospitals.' I stood, a new urgency driving me. The only rational explanation was that Connor had had an accident. I was ashamed of myself. I'd been so busy treating Laura that I'd completely neglected to care for my own husband. He could be lying in a coma right now, or sitting in a hospital bed feeling abandoned and alone.

A memory of Mum in a hospital gown, her usually tidy hair in knotted rat's tails hanging beside her gaunt face, appeared in my mind. Dad had had her sectioned after Sarah's death, mistaking cataclysmic grief for insanity. Perhaps they were the same. She left him when she was released from hospital. He put that down to madness too, blaming me for putting ideas in her head, although it was probably the most sane thing she'd ever done. I missed my mum. Whatever Connor said about her, she was still my mother. 'Where's your phone?'

'In the kitchen, but don't you think—'

I didn't wait for her to finish. I ran down the stairs, aware of her light footsteps following mine. I picked the handset up from the kitchen table. It was locked. I thrust it at her. 'Can you look up the numbers for' – I closed my eyes and tried to think of the names of all the local hospitals 'the Royal London Hospital, the Queen Elizabeth ... Try Whipps Cross and Guy's as well.'

She took the phone and nodded, but I could see she was reluctant. I wanted to snatch it back and do it myself, but when I'd given it to her, my hand had been trembling and I knew I wouldn't be able to control my voice when I spoke. 'His full name is Connor Joseph Best and his birth date is the third of January 1988.'

She tapped at the screen and I watched, hope fading as she made call after call. Nowhere had admitted a Connor Best.

'Look,' she said, after tapping off the final call. 'I honestly think we'd be better off going back to Heaton Place.'

'I can't,' I said. 'I can't go back until I know where my husband is. I won't,' I added, watching her mouth close, swallowing down whatever she was about to say.

She looked around the room as though searching for inspiration. 'What about his friends, or colleagues? Maybe they'd know something.'

I tried to think of Connor's friends. He'd always kept his social life separate from our home life, saying he liked to keep me to himself, that our time together was precious, not to be squandered on nights out with people he didn't care about in the same way.

'If you don't know their numbers, we could try looking them up on social media,' Melanie said.

'All right, yes. There's Billy and Josh. He sees them regularly, and there's George from work.'

'Okay, let's start with Billy.' Melanie tapped on the Facebook icon on her screen. 'Do you think he'll be listed as Billy or William? What's his last name?'

I couldn't come up with a single surname. I'd never met any of these men. 'I don't know.' My cheeks burned with the humiliation of not being able to tell her my husband's closest friends' names.

She spoke quickly, as if sensing my mortification, 'Maybe you could call your friends, see if they've heard anything?'

My friends. I went through my internal contact list, trying to remember when I'd last been in touch with any of my friends. Too long. I didn't know a single number off by heart, and there was no point contacting them on social media to ask about Connor. He'd never been keen on the people I introduced him to. They wouldn't have a clue where he was. They might have forgotten either of us existed.

My mind spun back to sitting in the therapy room with Laura. She was talking about the way Daniel had made it difficult for her to stay in touch with her friends, how he accused them of not liking him, saying they were trying to put a wedge between the two of them. It had become easier to just cancel plans to keep him happy. Now, I had to admit to myself I saw the same behaviour in Connor.

Had I spent years helping other people recognise signs of abuse in their relationships while, all the time, ignoring the signs in my own?

Chapter Thirty-Two

I forced all the new, disturbing thoughts about the true state of my marriage from the front of my brain. I had to find out where Connor was, and everything else would have to wait. I was now viewing my home more like a crime scene, somewhere I had to forensically search for evidence. Walking along my hallway and into the sitting room, I scanned for clues that might help me work out where Connor could possibly be. I glanced into my therapy room, but I knew he wouldn't have ventured in there. The room was pretty much defunct now anyway. When Connor moved in, he'd become increasingly uncomfortable with me seeing patients at home. Now I mainly worked with women at support centres, or at an office off the Bethnal Green Road on a time-share basis.

For reasons I couldn't quantify, I didn't want Melanie in there either. When all this was cleared up and Heaton Place was a distant memory, I wanted that room to be my sanctuary again, unsullied by this grim episode. Maybe I'd reintroduce the idea of seeing patients at home again when

I saw Connor. *If I saw Connor*, my mind offered, shifting the dread up a notch.

I took my book from where I'd left it splayed over the chair arm, closed it and slapped it down on the coffee table. Losing my page was the very least of my problems. Melanie walked to the table and peered at it. 'Is that an old arcade game?' she said.

'Yeah.' I glanced down at the dark glass centre with buttons and joysticks on two sides, feeling the same antipathy I had when Connor spent a fortune on it without consulting me. My mind placed another pin in the map of our relationship. I'd have to examine it later.

'Very cool.'

I wasn't in the mood to discuss home decor. 'I need to speak to someone at his office,' I said. The realisation I didn't have a single friend I could call on was still stinging. 'They'll know if he's been in.'

Melanie sat in the armchair and opened her phone again. 'Do you have a direct number?'

'No,' I said. I held my hand out for her phone. 'I can find it, though.' We both looked at my shaking fingers.

'You're upset. Let me,' she said. Grateful, I told her what to look up and she searched for a minute, then tapped in a number. She moved the phone to her ear, but I held out my hand again. 'Can I?'

She looked reluctant but handed it over. I sat on the leather sofa, lifted the handset and willed the ringtone to end. Eventually, a woman's voice said, 'Hello.'

'Hi,' I said. I closed my eyes and tried to keep my voice

211

steady. 'Could you please put me through to Connor Best?' It was all I could do not to cross my fingers.

'I'm sorry, Connor isn't in the office right now. Can I take a message?'

I let out a shuddering breath. 'It's his wife, Emma. Could you tell me when you're expecting him back in? I need to speak to him urgently and his mobile isn't connecting.' I didn't want to admit he wasn't picking up.

'Oh, hi Emma.' Her nasal voice sounded familiar. I supposed I must've spoken to her a number of times over the years. That reassuring thought brought tears to my eyes. 'I don't think he has any meetings scheduled. I don't remember seeing him in the office, now you come to mention it.'

'Would you do me a favour? Could you ask around and see if anyone else has seen him and call me back?'

'No problem,' said the kindly voice. 'Give me ten minutes. Shall I call back on this number?'

'Yes, please,' I said. 'Thank you.'

Melanie looked at me expectantly. 'Anything to report?'

'She's going to ask around and get back to me.' I put the phone on top of the stupid table, the clack of the cover against the glass the only sound in the room.

Minutes stretched. I stared across at the yellow-brick house opposite. I'd made friends with Bukola and Nigel when they lived there. I'd invited them over for drinks once and, when they left, Connor complained about how much they drank and how dull their conversation was, which surprised me. I thought we'd had fun. I didn't invite them

212

again. They moved soon after and the new people hadn't been in long. I didn't know any of the neighbours, really. I supposed that's how it was in London. That's how it was living with Connor in London, my mind suggested.

I glanced down at the phone. Only two minutes had gone by. How? It seemed like at least an hour. A teenage boy cycled past the window. He was probably on his way to meet friends in the park at the end of the road, I mused, or on the lookout for a woman walking alone along the canal towpath at the far end of the park. One or the other. When had my thoughts got so dark? I knew when. It was after Mum had identified Sarah's body and we knew that the world could be as bad as any nightmare. Connor said that my worldview was skewed because of the way Sarah died; the reason I believed she took her own life. He told me I was negative and suspicious of anyone with a penis. He argued that I was always looking for the worst in people and expected men to prove themselves before I trusted them. Maybe he was right. Or maybe I was.

I could hear the wet tug of Melanie biting her nails. In my peripheral vision I saw her lower her thumb and run a finger over the nail. She mustn't have been satisfied because she returned it to her mouth and the nibbling sound started again. I wondered what kept her gnawing away. I recognised it as self-soothing behaviour. If she was neurodivergent, it would be called stimming, but I rarely met anyone, neurotypicals included, who didn't have some quirk of repeated behaviour. We all have anxieties we need soothing, after all; the things that make us pick our skin, or tap our pockets to make sure we haven't lost our phone. It's just that, for most of us, those worries are a waste of mental energy. They come to nothing. But when Sarah died, my worst fear had come true. And now I was terrified something equally horrifying had happened to Connor.

We both jolted at the sound of the phone ringing and vibrating against the glass. I snatched it up and accepted the call. 'Hello.'

'Hi, is that Emma?'

'Yes.' I held my breath.

'I've asked around, but nobody's seen Connor, I'm afraid.'

I bit my lip to stop the tears. 'Okay, did he tell anyone where he was going?'

'Sorry, not that they said. I think everyone presumed he was on holiday.'

'Right. Okay. Thanks for getting back to me.' I clicked off the call, not wanting the receptionist to hear the sobs I could no longer keep in. 'Nobody knows where he is,' I spluttered. 'It doesn't make sense.'

Melanie continued to bite her nail. Eventually she said, 'Maybe we should get back to Heaton Place.'

The suggestion seemed absurd. I couldn't just accept my husband had completely disappeared and go back to that God-forsaken facility as if nothing was happening. 'I need to go down to his office,' I said. That was the only sensible thing to do. The woman on the phone obviously hadn't spoken to the right people. I needed to find George. He'd know where he was. I could kick myself for not asking the woman to speak to Connor's friend, George. 'It's about half an hour in the car.'

I looked at Melanie, expecting to see her getting ready to leave with me, but she was sitting very still. 'I don't think that's a good idea,' she said quietly.

'What?' Of course it was a good idea. It was the only idea I had.

'Think about it. Connor isn't taking your calls. He didn't tell you where he was going.'

'That's exactly my point. He would never—'

'Do you want everyone at his workplace to see you like this? Is that what he'd want?'

She dropped her head to the side and I saw myself through her eyes. I put my fingertips to my wet cheeks. I hadn't slept properly in days, had red, puffy eyes and couldn't keep my emotions from exploding out of me. Connor would be mortified if this version of me turned up, exposing our personal business to anyone who'd listen. He prized his professional reputation and was always keen to manage how things *looked*.

'But I don't know where he is.' My voice came out weak and faltering. 'I think I should call the police,' I said. 'Do you think I should call the police?' I didn't trust myself to make the right decisions any more.

'And say what?'

I threw my hands up. 'That he's missing.'

'He's a grown man,' she said. She wrinkled her nose. 'Forgive me for this, but is it possible that his intention was to go AWOL?'

'What?'

'I'm sorry, Emma, but it must have occurred to you that he's made a conscious decision to disappear?'

'No, I don't think that. I don't believe for one second he would put me through any of this.'

'Deep down, is that really true?' She shuffled forward in her seat and looked at me intently. 'You obviously think he's capable of having an affair – you even mentioned you thought he might be seeing Laura.'

There was an incredulous tone to her voice that made me want to scream. 'That was in response to what Laura said, not because I'm paranoid about my husband.'

'Think about it with your psychologist hat on,' she said, her intentionally soothing voice making me clamp my teeth together so I didn't wail. 'Could it be possible that your subconscious knew he was having an affair with someone? Maybe that fear, along with not being able to contact him, made you conflate your troubled relationship with Connor with your professional relationship with Laura.'

'No,' I said. 'That's not what's happening here. You can't explain this away as counter-transference. And anyway, even if Connor was having an affair, he would never be barbaric enough to just disappear. He wouldn't just leave me desperately wondering where he was.' I wiped my cheeks dry with my sleeve. 'He's not a cruel man.'

'Isn't he?' said Melanie, sitting back and letting the question hang in the air.

Chapter Thirty-Three

After an exhausting discussion, I reluctantly let Melanie persuade me to get back in the car. Going back to Heaton Place was against every instinct I had, but I didn't know what else to do. My phone would arrive back there with Gail tomorrow, and finding a message from Connor on it was the only hope I had left. We agreed that if there was no sign of him and I still couldn't get hold of him, then I should file a missing person report. Having a plan made me marginally calmer.

Melanie called Heaton Place to say we were on our way back, then got in beside me and started the engine. We drove in silence, the reverse journey seeming even more interminable than the one earlier in the day. With my head resting against the window, I watched the afternoon light fade and soon the trees lining the road were just shadows, their spindly branches like witchy fingers reaching for the car.

Eventually we turned on to the track leading to the facility. I sat up at the sight of blue lights flashing in the courtyard near reception. I sensed Melanie tense beside me. 'What's going on, do you think?'

'I don't know,' she said. 'Could be a new patient being admitted, or there might have been an incident.'

I strained my eyes to see, but the blue lights dipped in and out, giving me only glimpses of police cars and a larger van. 'Looks like there might be an ambulance.'

'A lot of our patients are brought in by ambulance, with police escorts.'

'Is that how Laura arrived?' I asked, imagining how terrifying it must be to be in the midst of a psychotic break and have all those strangers, disorienting lights and noise.

'Yes, that's how our patient was brought in, poor woman.' She looked across at me, her face illuminated in eerie blue light, then plunged back into darkness. 'It must be a frightening experience.'

Gravel crunched under the tyres as we neared the building. A huge shadow loomed to my left, as though rising out of the ground and soaring over the car. 'What's that?'

Melanie dipped her head to see through the passenger side window. 'The clocktower, I think. The rest must have been demolished.'

I looked up at the dark remnant of the old barracks, feeling a peculiar sympathy for what remained of it, then back at Heaton Place. There were dim lights at some of the windows. The only section fully lit was reception, and that light was lost as we drove behind the building to the staff car park. When we left the car, Melanie walked towards the entrance to the staff quarters, finding her key fob at the end of her lanyard.

'Melanie,' I said, stopping and putting my hands on my hips, surprised to find the bones now protruded, since I hadn't been able to eat properly for days. 'I need to talk to Laura.'

She turned to me. 'Not now. There's too much going on. We'll have to wait until the morning.'

'No,' I said. 'Right now. I don't care what's going on, I need some answers.'

'I'm as keen as you are to resolve this, believe me. We've got forty-eight hours left to work with Laura. Forty-eight hours!' Her shadowy figure threw its arms wide. 'I don't know how this ends and I'm finding it all incredibly stressful, but now's not the time. It's late and there's clearly some kind of incident. Just leave it until the morning.'

I balled my fists and dug the knuckles into my thighs. 'I'm going to see Laura,' I said, striding in front of her. 'I have too many questions in my head. I'm too tired to spend another night trying to work it all out.' In truth, I was finding it hard to put one foot in front of the other. I hadn't been able to eat a full meal in days, and I was so exhausted. There was a constant ringing in my ears and my head throbbed. I reached the door to the staff quarters first and held my fob against the metal panel. I pushed the door, but it was still locked. I tried again, then dropped the fob against my chest. 'Why doesn't this fucking thing ever work?' I slammed my fist against the doorframe.

Melanie sighed and pressed her fob against the panel. The lock clicked open. She pushed on the wood, but stood, barring my way. The light in the stairwell came on, making her a silhouette. 'You can't see Laura tonight. Not in this state.'

'Please get out of my way,' I said, ready to barge her if I had to. I'd had enough of being blocked at every turn.

'No.' She crossed her arms and stood with her legs wide. 'I can't allow you to see my patient until you're in a calmer state.'

'I thought she was my patient,' I said. I didn't want a confrontation with Melanie. I liked and respected her, but I was at the end of my tolerance.

'She's both of our patient, but I'm the permanent member of staff and the supervising psychologist.'

'Please move,' I said. 'Enough is enough. I'm going to see Laura right now, whether I have your permission or not.' Melanie dropped her head, then shifted to the side, allowing me to pass. I started up the first flight of steps. My purpose faltered when I realised I didn't actually know where Laura's room was. 'I'd appreciate it if you could take me to her room, now.'

I turned at the sound of crying. Melanie stood at the foot of the steps, a hand covering her face. 'What's the matter?' I'd never seen much emotion from Melanie. She'd always been measured and pragmatic.

'If I take you to see a patient now, at night, when you're in this kind of mood, I'll lose my job.'

'I'll take full responsibility for my actions,' I said, needles of guilt adding to my headache. 'I'll say I gave you no choice.' I was giving her no choice. It wouldn't be a lie.

She shook her head. 'That won't matter. They'll sack both of us for going against protocol.'

'Surely visiting a patient isn't that far out of our remit?' The rules in this place were exasperating.

She rubbed her forehead. 'It's not just that.' She leaned her back against the wall. The motion-sensor light clicked off, leaving us in darkness. 'I didn't tell anyone we were leaving Heaton Place today.'

That didn't make sense. 'But you called in to tell them we were on our way back.'

'I rang Julie.'

'Julie?' I didn't get it. 'Why is that a problem?'

She sniffed. The sound of her teeth tugging against a nail made me cringe. 'There's a process. There's always a process here, and it's usually a long one. Since you wanted to go quickly, I didn't bother getting the authorisation for two members of staff to be off site, I just went to ask Julie if her and Aidan would keep an eye out and fudge it if anyone asked where we were. There's always got to be a ratio of staff to patients here. It's safety protocol, but you really wanted to get back to London, so I didn't ask for official permission, or wait for them to bring in cover. I didn't sign us out, which is a sackable offence in itself. I just asked Aidan and Julie to cover for us.'

I heard more sniffing. The tiredness was making my head

too heavy for my body. I was annoyed at the protocols, but even I had to admit that not getting authorisation when there had to be a ratio in a place like this was a pretty stupid thing to do. But she'd done it for me. 'Does anyone else know we've been off site?'

The light came back on as she shook her head. 'No. Just Aidan and Julie.'

'They won't tell anyone, will they? We're back now, so does it matter if I see Laura?'

'This place is full of cameras. If we contravene another rule and we get caught and they look into things, it won't take them long to discover we've been missing most of the day.'

I glanced up to see a black orb above the doorway. If anyone was watching now, they'd be able to see exactly when we came in and out. Melanie followed my gaze then covered her face with her hand again. 'I can't believe I've been so irresponsible. I worked so hard to get this position. This could end my career.'

'Hey,' I said, over the sound of her crying. 'It's okay.' I let out a resigned sigh. 'I'll wait until tomorrow to see Laura. You're right: I'm too tired and overwrought now anyway.'

She dropped her hand. 'Thank you.' She stepped towards me. 'And you won't say anything if anyone asks if we've been off site?' She walked quickly ahead of me. 'When there's been an incident, they sometimes do door-to-door checks.'

'Even in the staff accommodation?' I was struggling to keep up.

'Yes, everywhere.'

'Okay,' I said, feeling like the lies were stacking up too quickly for me to give them as much thought as I probably should.

Chapter Thirty-Four

When we got to the next set of stairs, Melanie opened the door with her fob and marched up. She walked with purpose, apparently fully recovered from her earlier bout of emotion.

I was out of breath when we reached my corridor. Aidan was leaning against the wall outside his room, staring at a phone screen. He slipped it into his pocket when he saw us. 'Animal Crossing,' he said, looking sheepish. 'I'm addicted.'

'I thought there was no internet inside here,' I said, still feeling petulant about not having my own phone.

'That's not an online game, is it?' Melanie said.

'Nah,' said Aidan, looking down at his blindingly white trainers. 'Just, you know, an app.'

Melanie took her phone from inside her jacket. 'And I have to keep mine on airplane mode, which reminds me.' She made a show of going into settings and switching it to airplane mode.

'But if there's an internet block, why do you have to disable the Wi-Fi?'

'Protocol,' said Melanie. 'Just to make certain. So many bloody rules in this place.' She shook her head as though it was all ridiculous.

Aidan moved to Julie's door and knocked. She came out and joined him, looking from him to Melanie and then me. 'Glad you're back,' she said, crossing her arms. 'You all right?' I wasn't sure if she was talking to me or Melanie; her eyes flitted between us both.

'All good,' said Melanie. 'Thanks for covering for us. Sorry to put you in that position. We won't do it again, will we?'

She looked at me and I felt like I had to say, 'No, sorry about that. Thanks.' Even though I didn't knowingly break the rules or ask anyone to cover for me.

'DCI Okoro is on the prowl,' Aidan said in a low voice. My ears pricked up. If a DCI was involved, it was likely to be a murder investigation. What was going on four flights down? Maybe it was for the best that Melanie had steered us directly up here.

'Shit,' said Melanie. 'Has he been to this floor yet?'

'No, he's working his way up, though, so it's good you got back when you did.'

'What does that mean?' I said, not liking their anxious tone.

'Not sure, but I'd rather not muddy the waters by being caught breaking the rules. If we want to make it look like we've been here all day, we'd better get to wherever we'd usually be at this time,' said Melanie. 'I'll leave you here and get down to the canteen. That's where I'd be expected to be. If you want to—'

'I'm fine in my room,' I said. I wasn't usually anywhere because I didn't belong in bloody Heaton Place. The headache was a painful drumbeat now and I just wanted to lie down in the dark.

Julie put her fob against the pad next to my door. 'There you go, love. I'll bring you up something to eat a bit later.'

Melanie hesitated. 'Sorry for all the lies,' she said. Something in her expression told me she really meant it.

'No worries,' I said, glad to slip into my room and close the door behind me. I lay on the bed, unable to release the tension in my back and shoulders even when I tried my breathing exercises. I was hyperaware of the sounds of the facility. Doors opening and closing crashed inside my throbbing head. A woman was crying, and it sounded so close by it could have been coming from inside my room.

I listened for footsteps and, when they came, fifteen minutes later, followed by a sharp knock at my door, I was ready. I set my face to what I hoped was a relaxed expression and opened the door to a tall man with a black goatee beard. He introduced himself as Detective Chief Inspector Sam Okoro. I thought of Melanie's earnest face and bitten nails and knew I would do what I could to keep her out of trouble.

'Emma Best?' he said.

'Yes.'

'Sorry to disturb you. We were called to an incident earlier today and I'm just checking everything is . . . as it should be.'

'Yes.' I smiled. 'Everything's fine, thank you.'

'Nothing out of the ordinary today?' he said, fingering the lanyard hanging around his neck. It had the Heaton Place logo with the word 'Guest' printed on the ID card. 'You've been here all day, have you?'

'All day,' I said. 'Nothing unusual to report.'

He nodded slowly. 'Thank you, Emma.' He did a half-turn as if to leave, and I started to close the door, but his head turned back in my direction. 'You're quite sure?'

'I think I'd remember,' I said, with forced cheerfulness. But when we had both wished each other a goodnight, after I pushed my door closed I lay on my bed with a new edginess.

The reflection of blue lights flashed on to the painted stone under my closed blind. I watched the lights flicker, my thoughts careering around my head so quickly I couldn't catch hold of one. Soon car doors slammed and the lights slowly faded away. The room was pitch black, and I was so very tired, but I couldn't close my eyes. Something told me I shouldn't. I still had no idea where Connor was, and I had the feeling that, in lying to the police, I had just made everything a hundred times worse.

Chapter Thirty-Five

Friday

The next morning, when a feeble light crept under the blinds, I stared at the chipped white paintwork convinced I'd hardly closed my eyes. Sleep now seemed like something other people did. People who hadn't made life-altering mistakes that could be used against them, who knew where their loved ones were, who didn't feel like the inmate of a secure unit was toying with them. The pressure to get the truth from Laura before it was too late pressed down on my chest. The police and lawyers wanted answers, but I felt like I wanted them more.

I blinked, dry lids scratching across my eyeballs, trying to dispel the images that had come to me in bursts of vivid, horrifying dreams. But I couldn't shift the scene my brain had created of Laura as a snake winding herself around first Connor, then me. I turned on my back, watching the light spread across the roughly plastered ceiling, formulating a plan to get to the bottom of what was really going on. Today, Laura wouldn't be directing the session; I would.

At 8.30 a.m., I followed Melanie to the glass walkway

in what, in one of my patients, I might diagnose as a fugue state. Sweat sheened my skin as soon as my foot touched the frosted-glass floor. The clouds were lower today, threatening to engulf the building, the dark ones hanging ominously overhead, sending out the lighter, misty ones to do their dirty work. I tried to focus on the barracks opposite, but there was nothing left but the clocktower. It was shrouded in a grey haze, the sides ragged where the rest of the building had been torn away.

I made one foot follow the other, listening to the soles of Aidan's trainers and Julie's Crocs squeaking behind. My brain threw me a picture of the glass cracking and all of us falling through the air. I saw Aidan's arms flailing and heard Julie's desperate screams as she called out for her daughter.

Melanie turned to me. 'All right?'

'Fine.' Another three steps and we were back on the carpet. I could breathe again. I presumed today's session had been scheduled so early because we had to make up the time from yesterday, but it was deeply inconvenient. I was exhausted and I needed to be working at full capacity in order to face Laura.

'I'm going to pick up my phone straight after this session,' I said.

'Are you sure Gail's back today?'

I stopped. 'You're the one who said she'd be back on Friday.' I flung my arms out. 'It's Friday.'

Melanie carried on walking ahead. 'Oh, did I? Hopefully she is, then. Remember it's not a nine-to-five job, though, so she might not be in yet if she's on lates.'

229

I growled inwardly and set off to follow her, reminding myself I only had one more day of this place, then I could re-enter the real world, where, with any luck, I could take actions that weren't thwarted at every bloody turn.

Approaching the therapy room, I thought about how the balance of power was skewed in this therapeutic arrangement. I planned to even it out. Inside, I sat on the sofa facing the desk, and scanned the room I had come to see as a kind of prison. A man's face appeared in the glass in the doorway. His jaw was slack, mouth drooping open over a bloated expanse of skin making his chin and neck one pale mass. He looked into the room, but his eyes had the lifeless quality of the heavily sedated. He jolted forward, then out of view, his face replaced by the fleeting heads of orderlies. I felt an ache of sympathy for the man; the prisoner. Glancing up at the wire grille over the window, I realised I felt as trapped as him, as much a prisoner as Laura was. I mused that should make me more empathetic to what she was experiencing. It didn't.

The strip light on the ceiling flickered. It made a buzzing sound, then went out, leaving the room in the eerie pearl light from the window. It buzzed again and came back on, illuminating all the dead flies in its casing. I looked away from the mess of insect remains and opened my notebook, preparing for battle.

Quiet voices drifted in from the corridor. I kept my head down, trying to focus on my notes. The words distorted and shifted on the page. God, I was tired. I kept my eyes on the dancing letters as the lock clicked and I sensed people in the room. I wasn't prepared to start the session with a welcoming smile. I was all out of welcomes.

A sniffling sound surprised me. I looked up to see Laura standing in front of the closed door, holding a tissue to her nose. 'Laura, hi.'

She didn't speak, just moved towards her usual seat. When she sat, she closed her eyes and took a long breath. 'I've remembered something.'

Thank God. Tears of my own pricked behind my eyes. If Laura had remembered what happened, then this could all start to make sense.

'Not about that night, but before.'

I stiffened, feeling like someone had offered me the key to my cell door, then snatched it away again. 'Go on.'

'It's about Daniel. About his abuse.'

Chapter Thirty-Six

The Past

The hall light was on when I got home, shining through the stained glass. My shoulders tensed. I rolled them before putting my key in the lock and prepared my smile. I should be grateful. It would be a lonely old life if I didn't have him, I reminded myself. I'd allowed my introvert side to get the better of me recently, and it wasn't as if I saw anyone else much these days.

'Honey, I'm home,' I sing-songed into the hallway. I breathed in through my nose, trying to detect if he'd started to cook. He used to make dinner when he was in earlier than me, but these days he was always busy working on his phone, leaving me to prepare food for both of us. It was hard to argue that I would like to share the housework out more evenly when he said he was working on matters of international security. I'd once asked how Candy Crush counted as a terrorism threat, but apologised for my inappropriate gag after he threw me a withering look.

'Hey, you.' He came through the kitchen doorway carrying a rectangular box. He kissed the top of my head.

'Where do you keep your screwdrivers?'

'Eh?' I shook off my coat and hung it on the banister. 'What do you need a screwdriver for?'

He held the box aloft. 'Camera doorbell.'

I frowned. I hadn't asked him to get a camera doorbell.

'This isn't the safest neighbourhood, is it? Someone at work was talking about a spike in break-ins around here. I spoke to a bloke in the Flying Squad and he said these things really put people off; not the professional gangs, but the ones who are just chancing their arm.'

'The Flying Squad is a real thing? I thought it was made up, for TV or something.'

He shook his head. 'Oh, to be as innocent as you. The Flying Squad investigates robberies. I'm trying to make sure you're safe when I'm not here to keep an eye on you.'

'Right ...' The phrase 'keep an eye on you' made me want to laugh. I didn't need to be kept an eye on. I wasn't a small child, or a pet. He was smiling expectantly, as if waiting for me to rub his tummy and tell him what a good boy he was.

'So ...' he said.

'What?'

'Where do you keep your screwdrivers? I've charged it, so I just need to screw in the fixing.'

I shook my head. 'That's kind of you, but I think I'd feel more nervous if my phone was lighting up with alerts every time the postman came. I reckon it would make me more twitchy, not less.'

'I thought about that,' he said, pulling his phone from

his back pocket. 'And that's why I've put the app on my phone, then you won't be bothered by it, but I can be sure you're safe.'

'I'm not one of your OCGs. I don't need to be spied on.' It came out before I could stop it. His expression darkened and I wished I could rewind the words, like when I pressed the thirty-second back button when I missed a bit of a podcast. 'I mean, that's kind and everything, but I don't want you to be bothered either.'

He tucked a strand of hair behind my ear. A tug at the root stung. The unease I'd been feeling recently, a sense that I should keep the peace, rose to the surface of my skin, lifting the tiny hairs.

'I want to make sure you're safe.'

'I'm fine,' I said, ducking past him and walking away towards the kitchen. I took a glass from the cupboard and ran the tap, holding my finger under the stream of water until it was ice cold.

'You can't say that for sure, though, can you?' I wilted at the sound of his footsteps following me into the kitchen. 'Do you know how many weirdos might be out there watching you? You work with people with messy heads. You can't tell me none of your clients has ever thought about following you home.'

I froze, watching the water swirl around the plughole.

'You work with very troubled people,' he said. 'And I've seen too much to be naïve about what people are capable of, especially unstable ones.'

'Don't.' I filled the glass and turned off the tap. 'That's

not fair.' He used to be so flattering about my work. I missed that. I drank the cold water, concentrating on the liquid on my tongue, sliding down my throat.

'I just want to look out for you, that's all.' I sensed him move closer, and then his hands were on the top of my arms, rubbing up and down. 'It's my job. It's become part of my DNA. I need to know you're safe when I'm not with you.' His fingers circled my arms, his grip tight, trapping me. I wanted to drag my arm away. My heart thundered in my chest. But that response was silly. He was one of the good guys. He was only trying to take care of me. He didn't know his own strength. There was no menace in it.

'I love you,' he said. 'Keeping you safe is my priority.'

'Under the stairs,' I said, smiling up at him. 'The screw-drivers are in a red plastic box under the stairs.'

He released me, but as I listened to him go back to the hall and open the under-stairs cupboard, I could still feel the imprint of his fingers digging into my flesh.

The sound of his key in the door made me tense. I shifted on the sofa, berating myself for being such an idiot. The arguments we'd been having recently were normal for any couple. It was healthy to have conflict ... as long as res-olution followed. The trouble was, the resolution always seemed to be me apologising to him.

'How was your day?' he asked, walking into the front room, kneading his temples with the heels of his hands.

'Fine, thanks. Yours?'

'Grim,' he said. 'Interrogating some arsehole who thinks

he's cleverer than you and not being allowed to smash his face into the desk is a challenge I could do without, day in, day out.' His tone was dark. I could easily imagine his fingers twitching under the interrogation desk, him desperate to slam them into the face across from him. Too easily.

'Sounds tough.' I smiled sympathetically then looked back at the screen of my phone.

'You been up to anything interesting?' he said.

I didn't look up. I didn't like lying to his face, but last time I met up with Gaby he made such a fuss, insisting she was trying to turn me against him, that it was just easier to stay quiet. 'Nah. Just loafed around here.'

It was the stillness that made me raise my head. He was standing above me, and when I looked into his face, I saw utter contempt. I swallowed. 'You going to get a conviction?' I said.

'Probably.' His voice was brittle. 'Liars generally get caught in the end.' His threatening tone sent a chill over my skin. I waited. Eventually, he sighed and shook his head wearily. 'Why, oh why, do you, of all people, feel the need to lie to me?'

A sour taste filled my mouth. 'I didn't.' I knew it was pointless to carry on pretending, but a part of me was furious that he was challenging me. I was an adult. I could come and go from my own home as I pleased.

He took his phone from his pocket and clicked a square fingernail against the screen. 'Really?' He turned it towards me and a black-and-white video of me walking up the steps and unlocking the door played out. 'Eight minutes past four.'

I stood, fury igniting inside me. 'What the hell do you expect? I'm just trying to keep the peace. You don't like my friends, you don't even like me talking to my own mother, so it's easier to keep it quiet.'

'You're being ridiculous,' he said. 'And you know why I've got an issue with Gaby.'

'She's my best friend.'

He laughed, 'And you call yourself a psychologist! Jesus, how do you hold down that job? That woman is toxic, and you haven't got a clue.'

'She's not—'

He flung his arms out to the side. 'She's been trying to split us up since the day we met. She's a bitter, jealous bitch who can't bear to see you happy.'

'That's not true.' It wasn't true, was it? Admittedly, she wasn't the biggest fan of our relationship and she was pretty negative about the stuff I'd had qualms about myself. That's why I stopped confiding in her. I just wished I hadn't told him what she'd said in the early days, then he might not have turned so completely against her.

'So, it was Gaby you met up with this afternoon?' He spoke slowly and deliberately, not taking his eyes from mine.

I was tired. I just wanted to curl up with a book then go to bed. All this drama was too much. I was on high alert all the time and it was so bloody draining. 'Yes. I met Gaby for a coffee. I'm sorry, I should have told you.' I hoped admitting it and apologising would put an end to it.

'Gaby?' he said again.

I squinted up into his face, confused by the question in his voice. 'Yes.'

'You sure?'

'What?'

'Well, you're clearly happy to lie to my face, so how do I know it was Gaby you met this afternoon, and not some other bloke?' He scowled, lifting his palms as if to emphasise the question.

I fought back my indignance. 'Of course it wasn't another bloke.'

'You say that.' He was towering over me now.

'Yes, I fucking do.'

'But I can't trust what you say, can I? You've just proved that.'

I barged past him, planning to march up to my bedroom, but he grabbed my arm and tugged me back. 'That hurts.' I panted, my breaths coming fast and short. His hand was tight around my wrist. 'Get off.' I pulled my arm, but he gripped it tighter. My skin burned under his fingers.

'Why should I believe a liar?' He spat the words at me.

'What do you think you're doing?' I looked from my wrist to his face. 'Get off.' I tried to drag my arm away. 'Get your hands off me.' He let go suddenly and I stumbled backwards, falling and hitting my head on the sofa arm, feeling my teeth bite down hard on my tongue.

I lay on my back on the floor, stunned. I ran my hand across my mouth, then looked at my blood-streaked palm.

'Oh God!' He fell to his knees beside me. 'Are you all

right? Oh my God, you're bleeding. Shit, are you okay?'
His words tumbled out as he leaned over me.

I stayed still, numbed by shock. He lifted me into his arms
and cradled me, kissing my forehead, then my wet cheeks.
When I looked up, his face was covered in my blood too.

'You know I hate it when you lie. I'm sorry. I deal with
liars all day long, and it grinds me down.' He spoke quickly.
'And, honestly, it takes me back to when Dad used to gas-
light Mum. I can't bear to think of us being like them. I
can't bear you lying to me. You won't ever do it again,
will you? I need to be able to trust you. You're the most
important thing in the world to me, you know that. This
would never have happened if you hadn't lied to me. You
won't ever do that again, will you? I need you. I love you.
I can't lose you.' He was crying, his face twisted and wet.

I shook my head. Metallic blood seeped over my swelling
tongue. I opened my mouth to speak, but stopped. What
could I say, anyway? He was right. I had lied to him. I was
the one who had caused the argument. All he'd done was
ask me an honest question.

I let myself rest back in his arms. I closed my eyes, his
sobbing confirming how sorry he was. I was to blame too,
really. And I hit my head when I fell. He didn't push me.
'I'm sorry,' I said. 'I won't lie to you again.'

His breathing slowed. 'You promise?' he whispered,
kissing me tenderly on my forehead.

'I promise.'

Chapter Thirty-Seven

'So, you're saying there was an escalation of coercion and abusive behaviour?' I said when she'd finished speaking.

With a whimpering sound, Laura nodded. She held the corner of the tissue between her fingers, pulling at the white triangle. Something made her actions feel inauthentic, but I couldn't pinpoint what. Once again, I thought of all the women I'd sat with while they bared their souls; how I felt their emotions, palpably, in the room. But I felt nothing for Laura. I tried to harness some empathy but couldn't find any.

I was angled towards her but could see Melanie in my peripheral vision. She was leaning forward, watching. 'Was he regularly violent?' I said.

Laura tugged the edge of the tissue, ripping the fibres apart. 'Not regularly,' she said. 'It was more ... he didn't like to be challenged.'

'Challenged how?'

'Like if I answered back or did something he didn't like.'

'That sounds like a difficult situation to navigate.' I kept my voice even, but I still didn't sense that she was telling me the whole truth. I needed to know what had happened that night. I decided to go in for the kill. 'Did it come to a head, Laura?'

'Kind of,' she said. 'The night I found something.'

Time stretched. I was convinced she was enjoying making me wait. When I couldn't bear it any longer, I said, 'What did you find? What happened?'

'He said he was working late.' She laid a torn piece of tissue on her thigh and ripped another piece slowly and evenly. 'He's been doing that a lot recently.'

I watched a white fragment float from her fingers to the floor, the inside of my head shouting at her to get on with it. I stayed still and listened.

'But I found a receipt.'

'A receipt?' I couldn't stop myself. 'What kind of receipt?'

'I can't believe I'd forgotten about it . . . about all of it, all the stuff that had been creeping in. The way he'd been behaving towards me.'

'What specifically?' This felt like manipulation, like she was teasing me. The clock above the door ticked the seconds away. I wanted to bellow at her that in twenty-four hours our time would run out, so she should get to the point and tell me how she came to be covered in someone else's blood.

'All kinds of things, really. In the end it got . . . more insidious.'

I wanted specifics. I wanted her to tell me what the hell was going on. 'Tell me about the receipt, Laura.'

'It was for a restaurant,' she said, her voice wavering. 'It's such a cliché, isn't it? I found a receipt for a fancy restaurant in my partner's wallet.' She looked at me directly then said, 'That's when I had proof Daniel was having an affair.'

Chapter Thirty-Eight

The Past

The second bottle of wine at the restaurant was probably excessive, especially at that price, but it's not every day you celebrate your birthday. In the cab home, life felt blurred at the edges, that thirteen-per-cent-proof kind of soft focus, and I felt lighter than I had in months. I was ridiculously proud of myself for not spoiling the evening by bringing up any of the things he said I'm always nagging about. It had been fun. Like the old days. Even when we were home and the door closed behind us, I didn't get the usual crawl of nerves.

I watched him sit on the bottom step and unlace his shoes. He looked so handsome in a suit. I hadn't mentioned the waitress eyeing him up tonight because I knew it would annoy him. But her gaze had lingered on him, making me watchful to see if he returned the interest. He hadn't. Not much, anyway. Not enough to start an argument about. Not on my birthday.

'Nightcap?' he asked, standing and stretching. His shirt untucked from his trousers, revealing a trail of dark hair

from his navel to the narrow leather belt. I hoped to feel the tingling I used to get when I anticipated sex. Nothing. That was disappointing, because he would definitely want sex tonight. His drive was higher than mine and I'd realised long ago it was easier just to comply. I didn't know where my libido had gone and I could see why it upset him, thinking I didn't find him desirable any more. He had no idea how hard I worked to show I did.

'Yes,' I said. 'Why not? What do you fancy?' I followed him through to the kitchen. He took his phone and wallet out of his pocket and put them on the table, before hanging his jacket on the back of a chair and opening the cupboard, lifting bottles of spirits and examining the labels.

His phone buzzed on the table. I glanced at the screen. Little Miss Sunshine. My stomach flipped. I reached for it, just as he turned and snatched it up.

'Who's that?' I said, trying to keep my voice neutral.

'Work,' he said, slipping the phone into his trouser pocket.

'It said "Little Miss Sunshine".' My voice slurred on the 's's.

He plucked out a bottle of Jack Daniel's and clonked it on the table. 'It's that miserable cow in Forensics.'

I swallowed, suddenly able to focus. 'You told me she was called Paula, and why would she be messaging at this time?'

'Jesus,' he said. 'Have you made a list of every woman I've ever mentioned? Isn't that a bit . . .' He made a winding motion with a finger next to his temple. 'Here we go again. You're going to spoil tonight with more of your petty jealousy.' He grabbed a glass, slammed the cupboard door and

poured himself a large measure. 'It's an ironic nickname, if you must know, a joke. Maybe that's why you don't get it. You could give bloody Paula a run for her money in the misery stakes, you know. You should enter a competition to see who would win moaner of the fucking year. My money's on you, to be fair.'

He didn't look me in the eye all the time he spoke. When he turned away I knew he was lying. His phone buzzed again.

'I'm going to the loo. Maybe you could try to be less of a suspicious nutjob when I get back.'

Who announces they're going to the toilet at home? Whatever he said, I knew he was going to check his phone. It was my birthday; tonight should be about me. I'd done my best to believe him when he said he was working late over the last few months, and I usually ignored the messages and calls that he always left the room to return. But tonight was meant to be special.

I was in my mid-thirties. I always thought I'd have a couple of kids by now, but I was still waiting for him to deem it the right time. In that moment, I knew it was never going to be the right time, and the loss gouged a hole in my middle. Looking around my spotless kitchen, the surfaces sparkling exactly how he liked them, I knew this tiled floor would never be strewn with plastic toys. He wouldn't tolerate the mess, the disruption to his life. He wouldn't allow anything to knock him off the highest rung of the ladder. I realised then, that he would clamber over anyone or anything to maintain his top-dog status. He'd climbed over me and now he had his foot on my neck as I looked up.

I glanced towards the hall, the shame of allowing him to treat me this way burning, furnace hot. His wallet sat, squat and full on the kitchen table. I listened for footsteps, then not hearing any, I lifted his wallet and opened the section where he stowed his receipts. The first was for tonight's meal. The next was for petrol. A noise made me freeze. I glanced towards the hall, but all I could hear was his voice from inside the downstairs toilet, quiet, but definitely there. He was speaking to someone on the phone. The bastard. I plucked out the next receipt. It was for the same restaurant we'd been to this evening. I searched for the date. Two days ago. When he said he'd been working on a case.

'What the hell do you think you're doing?'

His voice made my brain jump in my skull. Nerve endings tingled on every inch of my skin. I held the receipt in quivering fingers. 'What's this receipt for?'

He marched over and tore it from my hand. 'How dare you snoop in my wallet?'

'Who were you talking to?'

'I wasn't talking to anyone.'

The sneer in his voice made me question myself. 'I heard you,' I said. I had. I was sure I had.

He stood closer, dropping his voice, 'I think I need to have a word with your supervisor. You're clearly delusional. That's got to be dangerous in your profession, hasn't it? A psychologist who's completely lost her grip on reality. Fuck me, you've reached a new low.' He shoved the receipt into *the compartment then snapped the wallet shut centimetres from my face. 'I think it's time for you to apologise, you mad bitch.'*

It was those words that flipped the switch. In my head, his voice echoed Chloe's, a patient I'd seen earlier in the week. She'd presented at Accident and Emergency with lacerations on her wrists and ankles where her husband had tied her to the radiator in the kitchen, then beaten her with a wooden spoon for suggesting he got his own ketchup out of the fridge. Her teenage daughter had untied her, and Chloe had taken the bus to the hospital without even putting shoes on her feet.

In the report I read it said her husband had turned up at the hospital screaming that she was a mad bitch. According to him, she was lying. She was just a mad bitch. When I met with her, she'd spent most of the session explaining to me what she'd done wrong. 'He works hard,' she said, as I tried not to focus on the spoon-shaped welts on her cheek. 'It's not too much to expect his dinner when he gets home is it? It wouldn't have killed me to get the ketchup for him. I'm a lazy cow, that's my problem.'

But that wasn't her problem at all. Her problem was that an abusive man had got inside her head. When the police arrived, they were no help. She wouldn't press charges, so they said their hands were tied. I even saw one of them suppress laughter at the pun. So much for people like him keeping vulnerable women safe.

'Get out of this house,' I said. It came out as a whisper. 'This again?' His lip curled. 'You going to have one

of your little paddies? Throw your toys out of the pram because you've got some deluded idea in your head?' He reached for the glass, but I got to it before him. I raised it above my head and smashed it to the floor.

He leapt backwards with a yelp. 'You've lost it,' he shouted. He gave a forced laugh. 'All right, I'll pop out for half an hour while you clean this lot up.' He pointed a finger so close to my face I could smell the garlic from the prawns he'd shelled earlier. 'You'd better have your apology ready for when I get back.'

He dragged his jacket from the back of the chair and strode into the hall, then out through the door.

As the latch clicked into place, a new energy flooded through me. I wasn't delusional. He was just trying to make me feel like I was. And, to my shame, I'd fallen for it. I saw the trajectory of our relationship clearly for the very first time. He'd used a trick as old as abuse itself. First he'd captured me with intensive, performative love, then, little by little, he'd undermined me, infiltrating my thoughts until it was his voice I heard in my head, not mine.

Well, it ended now.

The words of all the women I'd seen over the years who'd suffered at the hands of abusive men crowded into my head and started to scream. All the pain, all the fear and suffering. The lies they told themselves because those men had dripped poison into their minds, replacing the women's language with their own so they blamed themselves, apologised for causing their own broken bones and split lips. Said sorry for being frigid while the bastards raped them night after night.

I burned with fiery outrage for all the times I'd been made to feel like I was stupid or a fantasist. All the times I'd lain there while he pumped away inside me, making noises like I enjoyed it, ignoring the stinging and painful slamming, willing him to come quickly so I could get some sleep.

I looked down at the shattered glass at my feet. The base was still intact, one shard spiking up. The way I felt in that moment, if he came back into this house expecting an apology, he was more likely to find that piece of glass embedded in his throat.

Chapter Thirty-Nine

'I think Daniel took another woman to Fulvia.' The strip light flickered again as Laura finished speaking. We all looked up. It buzzed then settled, shining its yellow artificial light on the three of us as I sat, rigid, incredulous. I couldn't believe what I was hearing. It was literally unbelievable. I glanced across at Melanie to see if she'd heard the same thing I had, but she was just looking from me to Laura, her expression unreadable. But then, she hadn't been at Fulvia with her husband on the night Laura was talking about. I had.

'What was the name of the restaurant again?' I said. I hadn't misheard, I just couldn't get my head around it. This was no mere coincidence. This was as targeted as a missile.

'Fulvia.' She kept her eyes on me, focused, deliberate. I was one hundred per cent certain she knew that was the restaurant Connor had taken me to on my birthday. It was the last evening out we'd had together and, somehow, the woman across from me now was fully aware of that. My guts churned. Laura knew everything about me, about

Connor, and where he was now. There was no longer any question in my mind.

'You found a receipt for two people on the tenth of March for a restaurant called Fulvia?'

She nodded, fiddling with the remnants of the tissue. Even that seemed contrived now, an artificial attempt to appear anxious. I wanted to rip it from her hand and tell her to give up the act. It was fooling no one. Although, another glance at Melanie suggested that wasn't true. Lower lip caught between her teeth, eyes bright, she looked rapt.

'It's an Italian restaurant. It's nice – expensive, though. Do you know it?' Laura said, with a calmness that made me want to grab her by the neck and squeeze.

I looked down at my notes, pretending to read, but the letters blurred. I dug my nails into my palms. I would not cry in front of this woman. This *patient*, I reminded myself. 'I do.' I reached for a tissue from the box on the table and blew my nose, rubbing at the corner of my eyes as I did. I was playing for time. I had to unravel her reasoning and get to her motives. What exactly was Laura's agenda? There was no doubt in my mind she had one.

'I can't believe he took another woman there.' She sounded close to tears again. This woman should have been an actress, not a psychologist. She'd win a bloody Oscar.

'Can you be certain it was another woman?' I said, more for myself than for her. Perhaps Daniel had been a few tables away from Connor and me, having a perfectly innocent business meeting. I knew that wasn't the case, though, because Daniel didn't exist. Daniel was Connor and she was the devil.

'It's not the kind of place you go for a business meeting, unless you want to get your colleague into bed. It's all candles and soft lighting, isn't it?'

I looked at her. She was watching me. Not looking at me, watching me. Her blue eyes were trained on my face. Sitting across from her now, I couldn't believe that just a few short days ago she had reminded me so much of Sarah. Not any more. Sarah was kind and gentle. She was guileless and trusting. I always wondered whether, if she'd been less inclined to see the best in people, she would have recognised the signs of abuse early in her relationship and might still be alive today. But I'm a psychologist, trained to read the subtext of words, decode body language, sense the emotions of other people, and I had been sucked in by this scheming monster, so what hope was there for a trusting teenager? Skilled and devious people will make you see what they want you to see.

This woman was the opposite of Sarah. She was swollen with guile, pulsating with it. It was bursting from her, erupting from every orifice. I was certain now that every last thing she said was minutely engineered to have maximum impact on me. What I couldn't fathom was why? Whatever her motives, I had to admit her trick was working. I couldn't help but visualise Connor's face when he sat across the table from me at Fulvia, his cheekbones highlighted in the candle-light. I could smell the chicken cacciatore he'd ordered on the evening of my birthday, taste the tang of the Chianti we'd shared.

My instinct told me to stop the session there and then,

to turn to Melanie and explain every last one of the out-rageous things that made me absolutely certain that Laura was playing some kind of twisted game with me. There was no longer any question in my mind that she had asked for me to treat her, had me brought to this God-forsaken place, for some nefarious reason, and my gut told me it was inextricably linked to Connor's disappearance. Because he had disappeared, and that realisation made every cell in my body scream in pain.

Laura sat back in what I translated as a challenging pose. *Look how relaxed I am*, her body language said, smugly, while her potential motivations spun through my mind. Was she involved with some kind of criminal gang who were holding Connor hostage? Was Jimmy Bray behind it? Maybe this was some kind of payback for what he thought I was plotting to do for his wife and child. A partner for a partner. In my mind's eye, I saw Laura seducing Connor, pretending to start a relationship, then luring him into a trap set by Jimmy Bray from behind bars. But what would Laura get out of that arrangement? And why would she be caught covered in Connor's blood? I looked over at the locked door. Surely no amount of money was worth faking a psychotic break and being detained in a place like this?

Eyes back on my pad, I dismissed the idea. It was ridic-ulous. Things like that only happened in films. The only plausible explanation was that Laura was having a pas-sionate affair with Connor, that she'd hurt him somehow and then had me brought to Heaton Place as some kind of sick revenge for the way he had treated her. The thought that it was more than likely Connor would treat another woman badly hit me in the solar plexus. That's another thing Laura's stories had brought home to me; her experiences with whoever this Daniel was were chillingly similar to mine with Connor. In the last few days I'd come to understand something I'd known deep down but had been avoiding facing for years; Connor was not a good husband. He was not even a good man.

As Laura rested her head on the back of the sofa, I felt her gaze still on me, and I was sure she knew exactly who Connor really was. What he was. Perhaps she blamed me, or resented me for not standing up to him and allowing him to think he had the right to treat women as his personal playthings. Maybe that's what all this was about: revenge. In that moment, that was the only thing that made sense.

But I had no proof she'd ever met my husband. What I needed was evidence. Without it, all I had to offer was a set of bizarre coincidences and a feeling in the marrow of my bones. I knew, and I suspected Laura knew, that if I began to accuse a patient of mind games, I'd be the one under scrutiny. It would be my career in jeopardy. Maybe that's what she wanted, I thought, as I watched her tear the last of the tissue to shreds. Perhaps she wanted to destroy my practice. Maybe that was part of the plan. But how would that benefit her?

I needed to be smarter than her. I couldn't tell Melanie any more of my suspicions, or anyone else, until I had concrete evidence that Laura was intentionally messing with my head. I was sure it was her that had taken my lanyard from my bedroom to make me feel like I couldn't trust myself. I didn't know how she had managed to take my ID and key fob, but I did know my phone had gone missing when she was the only person in the room.

That's where I would start. That would be the evidence I needed to prove what I had begun to believe to my core, that Laura had hurt Connor and now she was trying to destroy me.

Chapter Forty

I asked Julie to stay behind while Melanie and Aidan escorted Laura to her room after the session. 'I need to ask you a favour,' I said. 'Come and sit over here.'

She joined me, sitting gingerly on the pink sofa where Laura usually sat. I noticed her glance up at the black orb of the camera and wondered if she was worried about overstepping her remit. If she was, then she was unlikely to agree to what I was about to ask her.

'What is it, love?' she said, fiddling with the scrubby ponytail where her hair was tied above her undercut.

The kindness in her voice made me swallow back tears. I desperately needed a friend. I needed someone to confide in, but I couldn't risk sharing what was going on in my head until I had some tangible proof. 'I'm concerned I'm not getting as far with Laura as I'd like. We only have this afternoon's session and one more tomorrow morning.' The pressure on my chest felt like hands pushing down, compressing my lungs. 'If I haven't been able to help Laura access her memories by the end of that, I'm worried she'll never be able to recall what happened. Someone might have died, and we may never know where to find them. She might go on trial for a murder she didn't commit.' I made my eyes widen in an earnest expression. 'I'm racking my brains for anything I can do to stop that from happening.'

Julie glanced at the camera again. 'I'm not a psychologist,' she said. 'I'm not even in the room when you're doing the therapy. I don't know how I can help.' She jutted out her lower lip and blew, lifting the stray hairs on her forehead momentarily. I fought off the guilt at making her nervous.

'Please don't feel obliged.' I didn't know why I said that. I needed her to feel obliged. 'But it's practical help I'm after.'

'Oh,' she said. 'What exactly?'

'Do you know where Laura's room is?'

She shifted her bottom on the seat, the trousers of her scrubs rustling on the synthetic fabric. 'Erm, yes. It's along the corridor from us.'

My skin tingled with the raising of tiny hairs. 'She's in the old barracks?'

Julie nodded. 'Didn't Melanie tell you they sometimes house patients over that side when there's an overspill?'

I had a dim memory of Melanie saying something about it, but the fact Laura had been that close to me when I was sleeping still brought a bitter taste to my mouth. 'Where exactly?'

'It's the last room before the walkway.'

Sweat stung my armpits. I'd passed her room every time I'd crossed from one building to the other and I hadn't had a clue. I leaned forward and lowered my voice to a whisper. 'Do you have a key fob that gives you access to all the patients' rooms?'

'All of them?'

I had to stop pussyfooting around. 'I need to get into Laura's room. Can you help me?'

A shout came from outside in the corridor. Julie jumped to her feet and rushed to the door. She put her face close to the glass, her hand on her fob as another shout rang out. A banging started, making me jump. My nerves already frayed, the shrieks that followed pierced my eardrums and sliced into my brain. Julie unlocked the door and looked like she was about to march out when the hammering abruptly stopped. Someone screamed again, but the noise became muffled, as though the mouth of the screamer was covered over. I had to stop my mind from conjuring a hand over my mouth.

I gasped for air, my inhalations too shallow to satisfy my need for oxygen. I tried to yawn to catch a full breath, but the bottom of my lungs felt squeezed. Light-headed, I watched Julie nod to someone I couldn't see and step back inside the room. The lock slid back into place and relief made my head spin. That struck me as disturbing, since I couldn't wait to get out of this awful place.

'I thought every team had to stick to their own patient?' I said, remembering other times Aidan and Julie hadn't intervened in what sounded like major incidents.

'Since we're on our own in here, I needed to make sure you were safe,' she said. 'That's my job.'

I smiled. 'Thank you.' I wanted to add that I felt more

threatened by Laura than the screaming people outside the room, but couldn't say as much. 'I really do appreciate your help.'

'No problemo.'

'So, could you get me into Laura's room?' I asked as she sat back down.

Julie frowned. 'I don't think—'

'It's important,' I interrupted. 'For her treatment. In cases like this, the patient can sometimes be lying to themselves as much as they're lying—'

'You think Laura is lying?'

I could have kicked myself for my clumsy phrasing. Forming coherent sentences was becoming a stretch, but I forced my brain to focus. 'Not lying, no, sorry. What I meant was, somewhere, perhaps deep down in her subconscious, she knows what happened that night. She knows where that blood came from, and she knows who it came from.' A sudden image of Connor's stricken face, blood pouring from a wound in his chest, made me wince. 'The reason I've been brought here is to open up her subconscious so that she can access those memories. But I'm running out of time. I don't think I could live with myself if I hadn't done everything I could to make sure I found out the truth. Could you?'

Julie shook her head, but from the way the left side of her mouth curled, I could see she wasn't convinced. 'How does getting into her room help with that?'

Good question. I dredged up a reply. 'Because, often, when someone is suffering from trauma but isn't processing it consciously, or verbally, their brain finds other ways to excise it.'

'Okay . . .' Her nose wrinkled and I knew I had to try harder.

'So, it's possible that Laura is using some other medium to deal with what's happened to her.' *Or what she has done*, I added, silently. 'She might have drawn something, for example, or written notes, perhaps a journal, or . . .'

Julie's eyebrows lifted. 'So, you want to get into her room to see if there's any evidence?'

'Not evidence,' I said, desperate to sound convincing. 'Anything that might help the therapeutic process. Because of the time constraints, it's pretty urgent, you see?'

'Right.' Julie nodded. 'That makes sense.'

'Great.'

'But I don't have a key.'

'Oh.' My heart sank. I'd allowed myself a moment of rising hope and now it was falling steeply away.

'But I could try to get one.'

I could have kissed her. I spoke quietly and quickly, 'Would you have to ask Melanie . . . It's just that . . . It's not standard practice, I mean, it's not unethical or anything, but you know what this place is like for protocol, and we have so little time left. If we have to go through all the processes to search a room . . .'

'It's not a search though, is it?'

I exhaled. 'Exactly. I just want to have a quick look around to see if there's anything that might help me to help Laura.'

Julie screwed her lips together, like she was giving it some thought. My pulse quickened. Eventually she said, 'If I just tell reception Melanie said I need access to the whole corridor, they might do it without all the box-ticking.'

'It would really help,' I said. 'Will you give it a go?'

'No harm in trying, I suppose. I can't promise anything, though. I'll drop you at your room, then pop down and see. If I can sort it, you could go in while she's having lunch. Would that work?'

'That would be great. You're an angel,' I said, smiling at her. That's what I needed right now, a guardian angel to save me from the devil, and the hell of Heaton Place.

Chapter Forty-One

I was feeling marginally brighter when Julie and I arrived at my room; less impotent now I had a plan of action. 'Thanks for agreeing to get the key,' I said. 'I really appreciate it.'

Her lips pinched. Fine lines pointed in towards her thin mouth. 'I've been thinking about it on the way up here,' she said, 'and, I'm sorry, I know I said I would, but I'm not sure I can risk going behind Melanie's back like that.'

A stone dropped in my stomach. 'It's not going behind her back, it's . . . helping Laura.'

'I'm just not sure the bosses would see it like that. Sorry, Emma. I want to help you, but I need this job,' she said. 'My Marnie's training to be an electrician. We're living on my salary while she's at college, so both of us would be stuffed if . . . I can't risk going against the rules.'

Aidan's door opened, and he stepped out, stretching his arms behind his head, peacocking his muscles. 'All right?'

I looked at Julie imploringly, but she gave me an apologetic smile and pressed her fob against the lock and opened my door. 'I'm sorry, love.' She opened her own door and hovered on the threshold. 'Maybe Aidan can help?'

'With what?' Aidan came towards me, dropping his arms, then weaving his fingers together and clicking his knuckles. He'd clearly seen too many gangster films. He stank of cigarettes and I wondered where he found to smoke in Heaton Place. If it was in his room, then he wasn't a stickler for rules and that could work in my favour.

'Come in,' I said, keen to get away from the corridor, where other people might pass by and overhear.

He glanced left and right before stepping inside my room with me and closing the door behind him. He moved towards the window, his strides confident, as if it was his own space. The cold air felt like an unwelcome hand touching my skin and I began to feel like perhaps I'd made a mistake inviting this man into my room. His broad frame blocked out most of the light from the window. He kept his back to me in what seemed like a deliberately dismissive act. He made small movements, tensing his muscles to demonstrate how his shoulders filled out his scrubs, his triceps and biceps lifting beneath the short sleeves. The skull tattoo peeked at me from his side. Its key mouth seemed to smirk as Aidan clenched his fist.

He turned his head, eyeing me slyly. 'What was it you needed help with?'

I was tempted to pretend it was nothing. My instincts told me I didn't want this man anywhere near me. But I needed to get into Laura's room. 'I was hoping you might be able to get me a key,' I said, annoyed that I couldn't make my voice sound authoritative. I was a lead psychologist. I was in charge here. His eyes were moving up and down my body. I'd had enough of his overt male posturing. 'Do you know what?' I said, my increased pulse telling me I could be in actual danger. 'Don't worry. I'll go down to reception and sort it out myself.'

He turned fully towards me. 'Whose room do you want to get into?'

I didn't feel safe. Adrenaline vibrated through me, making me shake. I wanted him out of my room. 'Seriously, it's fine.'

He stepped towards me, and it took all my strength to stand my ground. 'They won't give you any keys,' he said, his voice low, deliberately slow. 'You're not permanent staff.'

'They might when I explain what I want it for.' I didn't believe it myself, and the way his eyes turned to slits of ice suggested he knew that.

'Whose room?' His rank breath wafted into my face.

I raised my chin. I was inches taller than this man and I was his superior. Despite knowing that, I moved one foot backwards, nearer the door. 'I want to see if Laura is leaving any clues to what's going on in her subconscious. For that, I need to see inside her room.'

'I could help you with that,' said Aidan, moving closer. 'I can get hold of a key.'

I moved back, aware of the door just inches behind me. 'Great,' I said. 'Can you get it by the time Laura goes for lunch?' My voice faltered, giving away how uncomfortable he made me.

He moved so close that I could smell his stale odour,

vaguely masked by a peppery body spray. 'What do I get in return?'

'What?' I reached for the door handle, pressing down hard, but the door didn't move. 'Back off,' I said. 'Move away from me, now.' There was a sudden pressure in my bladder. I visualised a dark stain spreading between my legs. 'There's a camera above the door,' I said.

His eyes flicked up, then back at my face. 'Doesn't work,' he said. 'Anyway, all I want is a favour for a favour.'

I pressed down on the door handle again, grabbing for my lanyard and trying to yank it from my neck to get the key fob near the lock.

'Oh, come on,' he said. 'Don't be like that. I'm just saying we can help each other out.' He lifted his hand to my face and I froze, paralysed with fear, as he put his index finger on my bottom lip, pressing down to open my mouth, then pushing it inside, moving it in and out. 'See that's nice, isn't it?'

I couldn't move. I was so aware of the feel of his rough finger in my mouth, his nail rubbing against my tongue, that I almost didn't register his other hand undoing the button of my jeans. I was utterly rigid with fear and shock when I understood that his hand was inside the waistband of my trousers. I still couldn't move. His finger left my mouth, one hand covering the lower half of my face as his gaze fell to his other hand. His mouth twisted into an ugly grin as I heard my zip open and his fingers began to creep into my underwear.

I thought of Sarah. I saw her face as that bastard put

his hands on her. As if suddenly jolted back to life, I bit down hard on the fleshy part of his palm. He yelped and pulled away.

'Get the fuck off me,' I screamed.

'Mad bitch,' he snarled. 'Fucking psycho.'

I dragged at the door handle, pushing my lanyard against the lock desperately. 'Stay away from me,' I roared, hoping someone in the corridor would hear. 'Seriously, stay away. I'm going to report you. You won't get away with this.'

I yanked the handle, but the door didn't budge. I was crying now, my chest heaving with great, heavy sobs. I pulled at the door, then hammered my fist against the wood. I slammed my palm so hard against the door it stung like it had been whipped, but I carried on: slam, smash, bang.

Nobody came. I hit the door so violently I thought the bones in my hand might break. My pulse thundered in my ears, as I sensed the heat of him getting closer and closer.

Chapter Forty-Two

Suddenly the door shifted inwards, pushing me off balance. I staggered backwards, then felt Aidan's hands on my upper arms. I wrenched myself free. 'Get your hands off me.'

'What the hell was that noise?' Julie asked from the doorway.

I'd never been so happy to see anyone in my life. 'Call Security,' I said, between heavy breaths. I turned to Aidan. 'Get out of my room, now.'

'What's going on?' Julie looked at both of us in turn, a deep 'V' between her eyebrows.

'He attacked me,' I said. 'I need to report a serious sexual assault.' I don't know what I was expecting from Aidan, but it certainly wasn't the short, nasty laugh he let out. I spun to face him. He looked relaxed. Not at all like someone who would soon be arrested, who at the very least would lose their job and their reputation as soon as I reported him. 'I said, get out.'

He raised his hands and walked towards the door, shaking his head. 'All right, but we both know that's not what happened.' He reached Julie and turned back to the room. 'Offering sexual favours in exchange for keys to a patient's room isn't going to look great on your CV, is it?'

I gasped. 'What?'

He shrugged. 'Just saying. If it gets out that you were trying to find a way into Laura's room and thought you could bribe me like that . . .' He sucked in air through his teeth. 'Doesn't look good.'

I turned to Julie. 'That's not what happened. He attacked me.' My voice was desperate. I needed to keep control, handle this more professionally. A woman who appeared hysterical was less likely to be believed. I hated that word, hated what it implied and stood for, but knew it would be levelled at me, even in an institution like this. 'I need to see a senior manager, now. I need to call the police.' My jeans were still undone. 'See,' I said, waving my hand in front of the open zip, my cheeks burning at the sight of my black cotton knickers. 'He did this.'

Julie just stood there, scowling and looking between us. I moved towards the corridor, but they didn't budge. I steeled myself to push through them. If she wouldn't raise the alarm and get Aidan arrested, then I would do it myself.

'Julie,' said Aidan, a peculiar softness in his voice. 'Come on, you know me. I wouldn't do anything like that. I'm not that man. You know me.'

'Just a minute.' Julie put her arm across the door to stop me from leaving. 'Let's talk about this.'

I couldn't believe she was barring my way. 'Please move your arm.' My voice was still shaking. I stared at her pale, freckled arm, willing her to lower it. I wasn't sure how much fight I had left in me.

'You know I wouldn't do that to her,' Aidan's voice was crooning, as though he was talking to a lover, not a colleague. 'I don't need to, do I?'

'Don't need to?' I spat his words back at him. 'The defence of fucking rapists everywhere. *I can get sex any time I want, so why would I force a woman?*' I felt stronger then. I could use my knowledge of abusers to defend myself. 'Sexual assault isn't only about sex, is it? It's about power and control. You don't like being the little man in here, do you?' I stared down at Aidan. The hatred in his eyes showed me I was right. 'You don't like all these women being in positions of control.'

'You think you're in control?' He raised himself up to his full height. There was a wild look in his ice-blue eyes that brought my fear back to the surface.

'Aidan.' Julie's voice was sharp. 'No.'

'I can't have her saying stuff like that,' he said, flicking his fingers as if shaking off an insult. 'You want Marnie to have to see me in the dock for something I haven't done?'

Marnie? I watched indecision on Julie's face.

Aidan spoke again, his voice low. 'Everything would come out then, wouldn't it? If they investigate me, I'd have to tell them everything.' He waited a beat while Julie's eyes dropped to the floor. 'How would she feel about that, eh, knowing her mum was screwing her boyfriend?' He took a step towards her and she shrank away. 'How would she feel if she knew that you drop your knickers and bend over

269

for me every time she's at college? That you can't wait to get your pussy out for me to lick?' He'd moved close to her and was whispering now, but intentionally loud enough for me to hear. 'What would she do if she saw me fingering you by the lockers downstairs here, or knew you were sucking me off in the toilets?'

Bile flooded my mouth. I couldn't believe I hadn't sensed this dynamic between them. He clearly had all the power in their relationship. He was having sex with both her and her daughter and, by the look on her face, she was both ashamed and turned on. Electricity thrummed in the air between them. I suspected if he asked her to give him a blow job now, in the corridor, in front of me, she would.

Sex and control. The two went hand in hand and I was seeing the terrifying interplay now. 'Julie,' I said. 'This can stop. We can make this stop now.'

Julie raised her head and looked at me with an expression I couldn't read at first, then it turned into a sneer that sent cold needles up my spine. 'What if I don't want it to stop?' she said.

Chapter Forty-Three

The tip of Aidan's tongue showed between his teeth as he grinned at Julie. 'You know it, you dirty bitch,' he said.

'Julie.' I aimed for the calm voice I used in therapy, despite feeling anything but calm. 'This isn't a healthy dynamic, surely you can see that?'

She turned to me. 'Don't tell me what's healthy,' she said, all the motherliness gone from her. 'I had what you'd call a healthy relationship with Marnie's dad for years, and you know what? He bored me to fucking tears.' She looked me up and down, her chin tucked into her neck. 'I feel sorry for you middle-class types with your degrees, your pious, judgemental morality and your *healthy relationships*.' She let her eyes rest on Aidan's biceps. 'You can keep your missionary position with the lights out.' She turned back to me. 'Have you ever been screwed by someone you shouldn't? Do you know what it's like to be taken from behind by a man twenty years younger, somewhere you could be caught?' There was a wicked spark in her eyes. 'It's delicious.'

'The thrill, I get it,' I said. 'But he's blackmailing you.'

'He's no saint,' she said. 'I know that. But I work here a week on, a week off, and the boredom used to make my brain ache. Now . . .' She shrugged. 'Now I get a buzz.'

'A buzz?' I looked between the two of them. I wanted to smash my fist into Aidan's smug face so hard that the tip of his slimy tongue was severed.

'I can see why you wanted a piece of me,' said Aidan, running his hand through his slicked-back hair as he smirked at me. 'But, as you can see, I've got my hands full.' He moved behind Julie, and I stood, frozen in incredulity, as he snaked his hands under the top of her scrubs, lifting the material so I could see the soft, pale flesh of her stomach, then the lace of her bra. He looked over her shoulder at me as he cupped her breasts and squeezed, then slipped his fingers inside and rubbed her nipples.

I turned away, my insides heaving at the disturbing show, and stepped back into my room. I pushed the door, the slam bringing me back to my senses. What the hell did I do now? There was no way Aidan was going to admit that he'd assaulted me, and if I told Melanie about the attack, and his messed-up relationship with Julie, they'd deny it and it would be two against one. I had no phone to call the police. I was trapped, with no one to help me.

There was a sound like the door unlocking and, when I turned my head, my stomach lurched to see it inch slowly open. They had access to my room. They could get in whenever they wanted. 'Get out,' I screamed. 'Leave me alone.'

'Oh, come on,' said Aidan, filling the doorway. 'Don't be like that.'

I ran to the door and pushed him as hard as I could in the chest. He stood firm and grinned. 'You'll have to try harder than that.'

Julie leaned on the wall opposite. 'Julie, please,' I said. 'Don't do this.' A realisation dawned on me. 'It was you, wasn't it?'

'What was?'

'You . . .' All the energy left me. 'I thought it was Laura who was messing with me, but it was you who took my lanyard, wasn't it? Did you take the phone Melanie gave me too?'

'What?' Aidan glanced back at Julie. 'We didn't take no phone.'

Their faces looked confused, but I didn't believe them for a second. 'Why?' I said. 'What could you possibly have to gain from making me think I was going mad?'

Julie stepped forward. 'You've got it wrong. We're not messing with you. We just want to be left alone to do our thing.'

'Yeah,' said Aidan. 'I don't know anything about a lanyard or a phone.'

'I don't believe you,' I said, my brain stinging with a thousand tiny electric shocks. They clearly had access to my room and were always at the therapy room, so could have taken my phone, but it was the things Laura had said that disturbed me the most. 'You're all in it together,' I said.

'I don't know what you're talking about. I'm no thief,' said Aidan, as though that accusation was deeply insulting, never mind his assault on me, or the sex show I'd been forced to witness minutes before.

'Prove it,' I said. If I could get into Laura's room and find the evidence I needed, then I could go to Melanie and explain all the messed-up stuff that was going on and demand answers from Laura. When I was back home safely, I could involve the police, find out what had really happened to Connor and expose the mind-blowingly awful things going on at Heaton Place. 'Get me into Laura's room and then I can see if she has my phone.'

'I can't be bothered with this,' Aidan said, yawning and stepping away.

'They might not believe you assaulted me,' I said, 'but if I accuse you of theft, they'll have no choice but to search your rooms. Are you sure there's nothing in there you'd rather the police didn't see?' It was a long shot, but now I'd seen Aidan's true colours, and how enthralled Julie was with him, I suspected they both had more to hide.

Aidan glanced at Julie. She nodded, and he stepped back into the corridor. 'Wait here,' she said. 'We'll go and get the key. But only because we don't need any of this shit, not because we've got anything to hide.'

'Understood,' I said, instead of *fucking liars*. I unfurled my fists when they both turned and headed towards the walkway, hardly noticing the sting of the semicircular indentations my nails had made in my palms.

Chapter Forty-Four

I pushed the desk chair against the door handle, my hands still trembling. The two people who were meant to be in charge of my safety in here were colluding with the enemy. I was sure of it. Even if they weren't working with Laura, one was a sex offender, and the other was complicit. I'd gone from just being desperate to get out of Heaton Place to feeling I was in immediate peril if I stayed another night.

It was outrageous that these doors didn't have a double lock that could be used from the inside. I didn't care that they were sometimes used for patients; the staff should feel safe. Christ, I was at risk from everyone in this place. I'd been right to feel vulnerable in this room, I thought, as I wedged the chair tightly in place. I'd been sleeping next door to an abuser and a woman completely in his control, and down the corridor from a patient intent on harming me.

When I was sure the door was as secure as I could make it, I paced the room, feeling more alone than I ever had in my life. Sarah appeared in my mind's eye. She was falling from the bridge, her face frozen in a scream, mouth wide, eyes semicircles filled with terror. I couldn't stop myself from imagining how desperate she must've been to end her own life. I wasn't there to save her. And there was nobody I could turn to now. I walked to the window and looked across the courtyard. The side of the opposite barracks I'd been able to see before was now rubble, and beyond that was flat, featureless scrubland with the narrow road snaking away. It was hard to believe I was on that road yesterday. I'd been home, and then, inexplicable as it seemed now, I'd allowed myself to return to Heaton Place. How had I let myself be brought back here? I'd volunteered to descend back into hell.

The door handle rattled. I turned to see the chair's legs snag on the carpet as someone tried to get in. 'Emma.' It was Julie's voice. 'Let me in.'

Rage flared inside me. 'For God's sake,' I snarled. 'Stop unlocking my door without my permission. *Never* do that again, any of you.' As soon as I'd been into Laura's room and found the evidence I was sure I'd find there, I would insist on being released from this case today and get away from Heaton Place for good. I wouldn't spend another night in a facility where terrible people had access to my room whenever they wanted. This place was barbaric.

The chair stilled. 'I've got the key you wanted.'

'Is Aidan there?' I didn't want to see his face again, unless it was in a police custody suite.

I heard whispering, then a door opening and closing. 'It's just me now.'

Hesitantly, I lifted the chair away and opened the door.

Julie was standing outside, a key fob in her hand. She held it out, her eyes avoiding mine. I took it from her and marched ahead towards the glass walkway, stopping at the last door on the corridor. 'Is this the one?'

She nodded.

'And you're sure she's not in there?'

'No, she's having lunch.'

I didn't trust her to tell me the truth any more, but I held the fob against the metal panel and waited for the lock to click back, because I didn't know what else I could do to help myself. Nervously, I pushed the handle down, aware of the hypocrisy of my thoughts scant minutes ago. But it wasn't barbaric to have access to a person's space when they were already being investigated for a serious crime. That was logical, a necessary evil.

Julie was close behind me. I turned and held up my hand. 'Stay there,' I said.

She stepped back, still avoiding my gaze. 'Suit yourself.'

The motherliness from before had vanished. Had it ever been there, or had I conjured it up because it was what I desperately needed? I thought of how her face had lit up when she first mentioned Marnie. No, I hadn't imagined it, it just coexisted with the side of her that craved stimulation and attention and was willing to betray her own daughter for sexual gratification. People could be more than one thing at once. I knew that well enough, living with Connor. He was the charming, caring, attentive man I'd fallen in love with. He was also the man who ... I swallowed back the memories. Whatever had happened between us, I needed to stay present, to discover where he was now. The rest could wait.

The smell of a cloying perfume was the first thing I noticed. It occurred to me then that I had smelled it before, during my sessions with Laura, but I hadn't given it much thought. It was strong now, as though it had been sprayed seconds before I entered the room. The red, heart-shaped bottle with a black lid sat on the unit beside the bed. Poison.

I froze, hearing footsteps outside in the corridor. Someone greeted Julie and I stood, every muscle tensed, waiting for Laura and Melanie to throw open the door and find me trespassing. Seconds passed and the door remained closed. I had no idea how long Laura would be, and adrenaline spurred me to move quickly. I opened the cupboard to find grey sweatshirts stacked on one shelf and two pairs of jeans on another. I lifted one pair of jeans and shoved my hands in the front pockets, then the back. Nothing. I did the same with the others then hastily folded them and laid them back on the shelf.

I shook out the sweatshirts, but there was nothing inside or beneath them. I checked the corners, then closed the cupboard and went to the bedside unit. I expected to find the lower part locked, but it came open when I pulled. My heart pounded in my chest as I peered inside, but all I could see was a hairbrush and a few black hairbands scattered beside it. I pushed the brush aside, frustrated that the phone wasn't there.

The room was as sparse as mine. There were no immediately apparent hiding places other than the cupboard and the unit. I dropped on to my hands and knees on the carpet tiles and looked under the bed. The navy expanse was unbroken all the way to the wall at the other side of the room.

I stood and crossed to the window. From there I could see what remained of the barracks, the wrecking ball hanging beside it like a threat. The clocktower appeared to sway, or perhaps that was me. My legs felt like the stalks of a parched flower, no longer strong enough to hold up the heavy head. Shards of sunlight appeared from behind the tower, like bright eyes peeking out from a lair. I turned away, fingers twitching to uncover something that told me I wasn't going mad. There was nowhere to conceal anything in this room. If I didn't find any evidence, then how could I prove what Laura was doing to me, what she'd done to Connor? I marched to the bathroom, flinging back the shower curtain, but inside were the same mildewed tiles as in the room I stayed in. The shower tray was cracked near the wall. A dark hair curled towards the stained plughole, but there was nothing else.

Turning to the toilet, I remembered a film where a mobile phone had been stored in a plastic bag in the cistern. There was a scraping noise as I lifted the porcelain lid, then a clank as it dislodged. Water gurgled and I heaved as my fingers touched something slimy. I looked under the lid, inside the cistern, but there was nothing but brown watermarks and the metal and plastic of the flushing mechanism. I let it drop, not caring if I broke it. I was running out of time.

I wiped my hands on my jeans, frantically searching the

room for any other hiding place, but there was nothing but a sink with a toothbrush and toothpaste balanced on the side. Back in the bedroom, I approached the bed. My last hope. I grabbed the pillow and ran my fingers along its edges, desperate to find something rectangular and hard. It was soft, but I tore off the pillowcase anyway and searched inside. Nothing.

Air billowed against my face as I threw back the duvet, then lifted and shook it with my back to sun, which shone through the window like a searchlight. Nothing. I ran my hand along the mattress. It was as thin as the one on my bed, and I knew that the phone would be clearly visible if it was there, but I was desperate and shoved the mattress across the slatted base of the frame, pushing it until it slumped on the floor on the other side of the room.

But there was no phone. I stood, my breath ragged from the exertion and the seeping away of hope. I stepped to the side to assess the damage I'd wreaked, and something small on one of the pale wooden slats caught my eye. As I moved, the sun glinted on the edge of whatever it was and it sparked with light. It looked like a silver ring.

I leaned in and picked it up. It was cold in my fingers. I turned towards the window, holding the circular metal ring on my palm. My pulse charged when I recognised it was a wedding band, one side stained with something dark. Stepping close to the light, jaw tight with fear, I took it between my thumb and index finger to look at the inscription I already knew would be inside.

The drumming of my heartbeat deafening, I read the engraving inside the platinum band; EB & CB.

Emma Best and Connor Best. This was my husband's wedding ring. And the stain on the side was blood.

Chapter Forty-Five

I stood, nerve endings sparking under my skin, holding the ring between my thumb and finger. The sun glinted on the platinum band until I turned it to look again at the inscription inside, then the dull brown-red stain stole the shine. My mouth dropped open, but no sound came out, as it dawned on me exactly what finding Connor's wedding ring meant.

My mind presented the image of the last time I had held this ring between my fingers. My breath came in fast sobs at the memory of slipping it on to the third finger of his left hand in the registry office on the day of our wedding. Connor had persuaded me that the most romantic thing to do was to marry in secret, and I had gone along with it, suppressing the knowledge that Mum would be hurt at the exclusion, loving the excitement on the faces of the two passing students who we asked to be witnesses. And loving Connor, even though I already knew he was flawed. Aren't we all? I'd thought then. Nobody's perfect.

As far as I was aware, he hadn't taken this ring off since,

but now it was here, in this hellish facility, hidden under Laura's mattress. Why? My mind raced. I thought back to what I'd read in the file about how Laura was found. None of it made sense. If Laura had killed Connor and moved his body, surely she would have cleaned up the blood? Why would she want to be found when she knew where it would lead? Once again, any possible motive eluded me.

I turned to the door, desperately wishing Julie was the woman I thought she was the day before. I needed to tell someone all the extraordinary things going on in my head. Most of all, I needed to call the police. I couldn't imagine how Laura had managed to hide the ring from them. Surely they must've searched her when they found her? There was no point thinking about that now. Harrowing as it was, this was the evidence I needed to prove that Laura had hurt Connor. Surely now the police would have to force her to tell them where he was?

In trembling fingers, I held the ring carefully, trying not to touch the blood. My brain was moving too quickly, so I closed my eyes and tried to harness one thought at once. Now I had the evidence, I could take it to Laura and get her to confess. That's what I would do. There was no doubt in my mind that her amnesia was a ruse. I was more certain than ever she remembered everything that happened that night.

I rushed to the door and pulled it open. 'I need to see Laura, now.'

Julie looked astonished at the vehemence of my words. 'She's having—'

'I don't care what she's doing, I need to see her right now.'

Julie peered behind me at the devastated room. Her brow furrowed. 'What have you done in there?'

I was already marching past her, towards the glass walkway. My cortisol was so high, I thought I could fly through the tunnel, but no; the swelling of nausea started in my stomach and pushed up my throat after a couple of steps. A sickening dizziness made me stop.

I felt Julie's hand on my back. 'You all right, love?'

I lurched away from her. I wasn't her 'love'. Her touch disgusted me. I opened my eyes to find I was directly in front of the glass, facing the clocktower. I watched, queasily, as the wrecking ball swung and made impact. The crashing sound of metal on stone reverberated around my head as the tower tottered, then crumpled to the ground. I stepped forward, my face pressed to the cold glass, as plumes of grey dust rose like a scene from a nuclear explosion, then settled. I gasped, unable to bear the horror of what was on the ground below. The tower had fallen across the only road out of Heaton Place. If I hadn't been trapped here before, by Laura's lies, and my incomprehension, I was now by this collapsed heap of stone. I would confront Laura, then I would scale that pile of rubble if I had to. I would move every last stone with bloodied hands if it meant I could escape this hell on earth.

Dragging my eyes away, I lifted my foot and forced it to move, but the heaving in my stomach pushed harder up my gullet and I leaned over, letting yellow liquid splash on the frosted glass.

'For God's sake,' said Julie.

I ignored her and stumbled forward, keeping my eyes on the solid white wall ahead. I was sick again before my feet reached the carpet tiles, but I kept moving and soon I was staggering towards the stairs.

'Where's the patients' canteen?' I said, wiping bile from my mouth with the back of my hand, taking care not to get any on the ring.

'Don't you think you'd better—'

I spun around. 'Take me to Laura this second, or I swear, I won't be responsible for my actions.'

She shrank back, fear in her eyes. 'All right. This way.'

She walked ahead of me, unlocking the doors, the key fob shaking in her fingers. I was glad she was scared. It was the first time I'd felt in control since I'd arrived at Heaton Place. I followed her down the steps, feeling the strength return to my legs, my spine straightening with every stride.

At the next door, I was confused. Julie had brought us to the usual canteen. When the door opened and the room came into view, all heads turned to me. Conversations hushed and knives and forks stalled on the way to open mouths. I supposed I must look wild. I didn't care. I avoided eye contact with anyone but Julie. 'Where is she?'

Julie pointed to the small anteroom which had been allocated for our team. I narrowed my eyes, wondering why on earth a patient was eating with the staff. Nothing at Heaton Place made sense. At least now I was one step closer to getting out of there for good. I strode forward, the metal of the ring now warm between my fingers. This

was it. I was going to confront Laura and make her confess.
This ended here.

I stood in the doorway of the room and crossed my arms,
as three pairs of eyes turned in my direction.

Chapter Forty-Six

'I know who you are and what you've done,' I said to Laura, my voice cracking. It was a release to say it. The beginning of the end of this nightmare. The canteen was suddenly unbearably hot and all the energy I'd felt on the way here seeped out with my sweat.

Laura stared back at me from the space at the table where I usually sat. Why was she in my seat? She looked calm. Poised, almost.

I wiped my top lip dry. 'I know you were using the Bray case to destabilise me and I know you were having an affair with my husband.' Her face remained impassive. Why the hell wasn't she responding? I lifted the ring. 'I found this under your mattress, so don't try to deny anything. This is solid evidence.' I was finding it hard to talk. My breath was short and ragged. I gulped in air. 'It's time to come clean, Laura. You don't have amnesia at all, do you? You didn't have a psychotic break. You remember everything that happened that night, and you brought me here intentionally.'

All eyes were on me, but nobody spoke. Julie stood beside

me, legs wide, arms crossed. I glanced over my shoulder. Everyone in the outer room was still, watching. Turning back to the table, my heart battered my chest. Why wasn't anyone speaking? 'Admit it,' I said, glaring at Laura. Her serenity was bewildering. I didn't understand why Melanie and Aidan weren't on their feet, looking at Laura with the same horror I was. They just sat at the table, as though they were observing a scene in some kind of obscure street theatre.

Laura took a slow breath. 'What is it that you want me to admit to, Emma?' Her voice sounded all wrong. It was level and measured. Didn't she understand how serious this was? Her game was up. This was over.

I dropped Connor's ring into my palm and thrust it forward. 'I found Connor's wedding ring under your mattress. This is evidence,' I said. 'Proof.'

'Of what?' She dropped her head to the side, and that's when I noticed she was wearing a blue lanyard, like mine.

I shifted my gaze to Melanie, looking at her imploringly, but her eyes flitted between me and Laura, an audience member, not the supervising psychologist whose patient had been lying throughout her treatment and had now been exposed as a killer. Aidan was staring at me, a smirk at the corner of his mouth. More bile rose in my throat. 'Of murder,' I said.

Instead of the shock I anticipated, Laura sat back in her seat and nodded. My nerve endings prickled on the surface of my skin. What was happening? Panic squeezed the air from my lungs. I scanned the faces around the table, their calm more alarming than the bloodied ring in my hand. 'What's going on?' I whispered.

Laura turned her head to Melanie and nodded once more.

As if taking that as an instruction, Melanie stood. 'I agree,' she said to Laura, then turned to me. 'I think it's time.'

Chapter Forty-Seven

'Time for what?' I reached my hand to the wall to steady myself, the plaster cold against my trembling fingers.

Laura looked at me, and I saw something approaching sympathy in her eyes. She should save her sympathy for herself. Her life as she knew it was over. 'To tell you the truth,' she said.

'I know the truth,' I said, my voice too high. 'You hurt Connor, you . . .'

Laura shook her head slowly. 'I didn't kill your husband, Emma. You did.'

The sound of Connor's wedding ring clattering on the linoleum as it dropped from my hand sounded like a far-off echo. 'What?' I half-laughed. 'That's absurd.' I blinked fast, trying to refocus this incomprehensible situation. 'You're delusional,' I said, looking from Melanie to Laura, bewildered as to why Melanie's dark eyes were trained on me, not her. 'Melanie,' I said, forcing my voice lower. 'Laura is clearly having a psychotic episode. Maybe it's time to consider medication. I think she needs a psychiatrist more than a therapist now. I've done all I can, but it's clear she's a dangerous woman and we need to get the police here as a matter of urgency.' I tried and failed to sound authoritative. 'Please.' I didn't know why I said that. What was I pleading for? Somebody to make all of this make sense?

Nobody moved. The dizziness returned and my knees were trembling so hard I had to move to the table and sit.

'I know this is difficult to hear, Emma, but I need you to listen to me.' Laura's voice was gentle. She leaned towards me. I could smell her sickly perfume. Poison.

Why wasn't anyone coming forward to restrain her? I glanced at Aidan, but he was sitting back, thick arms crossed, an inexplicable look of amusement on his face. 'I don't know what you think is going on here,' I said to Laura, still failing to harness control over my voice, 'but you are a patient in this facility and I have proof you've committed a serious crime, so the last thing I need to do is listen to you.'

'Emma—' Melanie started.

'No.' I raised my hand to stop her. 'I should have spoken to you about this days ago. I wish I had, then you'd have a clearer picture. You don't understand what's happening here.' I pushed my hands against the table to sit upright. 'Connor's wedding ring proves . . .' The ring was no longer in my hand. 'Where's the ring?' I stood, scanning the floor. I couldn't see it. I fell to my hands and knees, scouring the dirty lino for the only solid evidence I had. I ran my fingers up to the skirting board, panic rising. Where was the ring?

'Emma, there's no need to—' Laura's voice was sweet, like her perfume. That made me feel sick too.

'Don't,' I said, pausing my search. 'Don't try to pretend you're innocent. You hurt Connor and you brought me here intentionally.' Julie's Crocs shifted out of the way as I crawled around her feet, desperately looking for my proof. 'You were having an affair with my husband,' I said, getting more frantic. 'And you killed him, and you asked for me to come here so you could play some twisted little game.' I shoved at a chair leg, ready to crawl under the table.

'Emma, stop.' Melanie's voice pierced the membrane of terror that shrouded me.

I stilled, understanding the meaning of what Laura had said to me for the first time. I sat back on my haunches and looked up at Laura. 'And now you're saying I killed Connor? Me?' All three of them stood, looking over me. Laura's lanyard dangled from her neck. I peered at the laminated ID badge and read the words 'Laura Winters, Senior Psychologist'.

Fear gripped my throat. I wrapped my arms around my knees and hugged them close. 'I don't understand,' I said.

'It's okay, Emma,' crooned Laura, taking a step towards me. 'Don't worry. I'm going to explain everything.'

Chapter Forty-Eight

They took me to the therapy room, and somehow I found myself sitting back on the sofa opposite the desk. Laura sat on the sofa to my right and Melanie was behind the desk with her pen poised. Through tear-filled eyes, I saw Aidan's ear through the glass panel in the door. Everything had returned to order.

But that wasn't true. Nothing was as it should be. Laura was leaning forward, elbows balanced on her knees, her blue lanyard swinging from her neck, taunting me, and my arms were wrapped tightly around my knees and my cheeks were wet from crying. Laura's hair was loose around her shoulders. Mine was tied back in a heavy ponytail, making the back of my neck burn with heat. I didn't remember putting my hair up.

'I need you to understand what's going on, Emma,' Laura said. Her voice was kind, and that frightened me.

I shook my head and buried it between my knees. It was too much. It was a nightmare. With my eyes scrunched tight, I told myself I would wake up in my own bed in a minute,

Connor beside me. Heaton Place, Melanie, Aidan and Julie, and especially Laura, would all just be the unruly creations of my brain, a vivid, hallucinatory, terrible nightmare.

'You know the term "therapeutic lying", don't you, Emma? It's sometimes called therapeutic fibbing.'

I did know the term, but I didn't respond. I was still fantasising about waking up, pushing away the understanding that I never would.

She waited a beat then continued. 'When you were brought to Heaton Place, we quickly realised that, at that time, you did not share the same reality as us.'

That's because none of this is real, I thought to myself. It can't be. If this was reality, I didn't want to share it. I wanted to go home.

She paused again, then continued in her slow, careful voice. 'After much deliberation, we decided to try a new method of treatment in the hope it would help you to regain the memories you lost during your psychotic break.'

I raised my head. That was ridiculous. She was taking this charade too far. 'No,' I said. 'This doesn't make sense. I am a psychologist and I was brought here to treat you. That's why I'm here.'

'I know that's what you've been led to believe, but, I'm sorry, Emma, that's not why you're here. We have been deliberately deceiving you for reasons we think are in your best interest.'

'No, I don't believe you.' I wiped my face with the sleeve of my sweatshirt then forced myself to look her in the eye. 'I am the psychologist, and you are lying to me now.' I gestured to Melanie then towards the door. 'I don't know how you've managed to get this lot on side, but you will be found out. You have to know that? Surely you can't imagine you can keep this up? Are you doing this because I made a mistake? I was vindicated by the inquiry. It wasn't my fault.'

'I don't know what you mean by that, Emma. What mistake?'

I shook my head. 'You do know. I know you do. Is Jimmy Bray making you do this?'

'I'm sorry, Emma, but I don't know who Jimmy Bray is.'

'You're lying,' I shrieked.

Laura pursed her lips. 'Okay, let's try looking at this another way. How did you get here, Emma?' Laura said, sitting back, hands relaxed on her thighs. I noticed her perfectly manicured nails again. I glanced at mine, and saw an uneven mess with cuticles bitten and bloody.

'What do you mean?'

'How did you arrive at Heaton Place?'

I searched my memory but, other than coming back in the car with Melanie yesterday, I couldn't exactly grasp how I first got here. 'I can't remember, but that's because I'm tired. I haven't slept well since I arrived. I know I left my phone in reception, but I don't remember . . .' I swallowed down the mucus gathered in my throat. 'I've been busy, working hard. Working on your case.'

'Haven't things seemed a little off since you arrived?'

'Yes,' I spat. 'Because you've been playing some kind of perverted game with me. That's why I'm exhausted. That and the fact I'm worried sick about my missing husband.

I think that's enough to explain why I haven't been able to sleep and my memory is hazy.'

Laura tipped her head to the side, unfazed by my outburst. 'Your lanyard, for example,' she said. 'Did the key fob ever work?'

I glanced down at the blue lanyard hanging limply around my neck. I noticed now that the photograph was different to both Melanie's and Laura's. Mine was still ghoul-like. Like Melanie's, the picture on Laura's was glorious Technicolor. She was smiling and wearing a silky blue shirt. I'd only ever seen her in the same grey sweatshirt and jeans I'd been wearing since I arrived. 'When you stole it,' I said, 'you could have deactivated it. Anyway, that list of rules in my room said the new system was glitching.'

Laura's head tipped slightly. 'Didn't that strike you as odd? In a high-security mental health unit like this, would it ever be acceptable to have an unreliable key system?'

'There's a lot about this place that seems *off*,' I said. 'I was planning to get to the bottom of whatever ... this is, and then have a meeting with the managers about all kinds of things.' I glanced at the door again, the sight of Aidan's ear adding to my rising fury. I would have him arrested the minute this situation was back in my control.

'Have you ever seen the managers?' Laura asked.

'No,' I said. 'This case was shrouded in secrecy. Melanie told me about a potential media circus.' I turned to Melanie, desperate for her to confirm what I was saying, but she looked down at the desk.

'Ok-a-y,' said Laura, drawing out the end of the word, as though considering her next move. 'And your possessions. Where are they?'

'I . . .' I thought of my phone, my keys. I tried to remember when I'd last carried a bag that wasn't a Heaton Place tote. I couldn't grasp a memory. I couldn't argue my points because everything was confused in my head. Hot, frustrated tears fell on my cheeks. 'Gail's got my phone. She's been on holiday.'

'I'm sorry, Emma,' said Laura. 'Truly I am. There is no one called Gail working here. Your phone was taken when you were admitted. You need to understand that the therapeutic lying was all aimed at helping you, but I understand it must be incredibly difficult for you to hear and accept it now.'

I shook my head. 'I don't accept it.' I couldn't accept it. If I did, that would mean I wasn't here professionally, I was a patient and, worse than that . . . 'I did not hurt my husband. I couldn't.'

Laura shuffled forward on the seat and took a small plastic bag from the back pocket of her jeans. 'Can you remember, though, Emma?' she said, holding out the bag for me to take. 'Can you try to remember when you last saw this outside these walls?'

Connor's ring glinted at the bottom of the bag. I reached for it. The bag was slippery in my fingers and suddenly an image appeared in my head. It was my hands, wet and slippery with blood. I gasped. In my mind's eye, I saw Connor's hand lying still on the tiles of our kitchen floor, the ring glinting in the light from the window. A dark liquid was creeping towards his fingers, and I heard myself screaming as loudly as I was now.

Chapter Forty-Nine

'No!' I screamed. I leapt from the sofa and rushed towards the door, the image of Connor, lifeless and bleeding, seared on to my retinas. I had to get out, get away from Laura and the macabre image she had tricked me into conjuring. This was her doing. She made me imagine it.

The door opened when I turned the handle. Aidan jumped in front of me and flung his arms to the side.

'Get away from me,' I shouted. 'Don't you dare touch me.'

'Let her go,' said Laura's voice behind me.

Aidan's hands dropped to his sides and I elbowed past him towards the stairs. I could hear their feet on the carpet, following me, but I kept charging forward to the door at the foot of the stairs. With shaking fingers, I tried my key fob. Nothing happened.

'Open all the doors for her,' ordered Laura. The fact that she was clearly in charge now made my scalp tighten with fear. I had a flashback to when I was in Melanie's car and saw the three figures looking down at me from the glass bridge. Laura was following behind Julie and Aidan, not being watched by them. I'd sensed something was wrong then. Why hadn't I listened to my instincts and stayed at home when I had the chance?

Julie stepped in front of me and pushed her fob against the pad. I saw the stubble of her undercut, her attempt to appear young and still relevant, and felt a fresh hatred for this woman who betrayed other women.

The familiar click of the lock drawing back made my stomach turn over. I marched ahead, resisting the temptation to slam my foot back into Julie's face as I ran up ahead of her. I visualised her falling backwards, taking out Aidan, him falling on to Melanie, then Laura, leaving her as a heap of broken bones at the bottom of the toxic pile. The image was comforting, not just because it meant the end of Laura tormenting me, but if I could imagine that, the vivid picture of Connor's body could have been a figment of my imagination too.

I took a deep breath when I reached the glass walkway. A small man in overalls stood halfway along, holding a mop over a bucket. He stepped aside when he saw me and my entourage, a look of trepidation in his eyes. I forged on, the smell of bleach burning my nostrils, the undertones of my vomit still detectable in the air. My foot slid on the wet glass and I almost fell. I imagined my head smashing against the frosted floor and the spiderweb pattern of the glass shattering, the cracks spreading until it completely gave way and we all fell to our deaths.

See, I thought, I have an overactive visual imagination.

That happened to me all the time. I saw things in my head. The picture I'd seen of Connor did not make me a murderer.

The door to Laura's room was still open. The mattress flopped on the floor, the corner curled up towards the base, like a body clinging to a life raft. The sting of finding Connor's ring penetrated me again. I charged on, finding my door open too. I stopped outside, trying to catch my breath. I looked back at the figures slowing to a stop behind me, then stepped over the threshold.

Once inside, I observed the room properly for the first time. I saw the window with its secured glazing, no handle to open it. The single bed, the unit by its side and the narrow cupboard looked, I realised, like hospital furniture. My heart plummeted. I opened the cupboard door. It was empty apart from a clean sweatshirt, a pair of jeans exactly the same as the ones I was wearing and some plain cotton underwear. I moved to the desk and chair. There was nothing of mine there. I stepped into the bathroom and flung back the shower curtain. Soap and a small bottle of shampoo with no label on the side sat on the soap tray attached to the shower rail. They were not the brand I used at home.

Turning to the sink, a plastic cup held a squat toothbrush. Where was my electric toothbrush, the one that stood next to Connor's in our bathroom at home? I wasn't the kind of person who forgot their toothbrush when I went away overnight. I looked up at the mirror and saw it was made of reflective metal, and the pale, distorted face staring back at me was barely recognisable as mine.

A trembling began in my core and radiated through my body. I desperately tried to remember the call or the email asking me to come to Heaton Place to treat Laura. I couldn't recall anything. The first memory I had was of sitting in the treatment room, reading through Laura's notes. Or what I had been told were Laura's notes.

I stumbled back into the bedroom. Laura was standing in the doorway, Melanie, Aidan and Julie in the corridor behind her. 'This isn't the staff quarters, is it?'

Slowly, she shook her head.

'It's a cell,' I said, the horror descending.

'It's a patient bedroom,' said Laura, her voice gentle.

'And I am the patient?'

'That's right, Emma. Aidan and Julie were stationed either side of you for security reasons. That's why you were never alone when you left this room. You are being held at Heaton Place on suspicion of murdering your husband. When you came here, three weeks ago, you were too unwell to stand trial.'

'I've been here for three weeks?'

'Yes,' said Laura. 'The staff tried various methods to help restore your memory before I suggested trialling this method. I've done a lot of work with dementia patients before. I put together this team to try the therapeutic lying technique. We planned to highlight elements of your life which might trigger memories of what happened that night. We were given six days to work with you before the trust was forced to admit your memories were gone for good and the legal process took over. But they're not gone, are they, Emma? You remember now, don't you?'

The image of Connor lying on our kitchen floor slammed back into my brain, but this time I could smell the iron tang of blood, and it wasn't like the imaginings I'd had before. This was visceral. This wasn't an invented image at all. It was a memory, solid and hideously real. My mouth went slack with disbelief. I struggled to form the words: 'I killed Connor.'

Laura took a step towards me. 'I'm sorry, Emma. Could you say that again?'

'It's true, isn't it?' I said, through horrified sobs. 'I killed him. I murdered Connor.' Memories of him towering over me, the feeling of his fingers gripping the top of my arms, of his spit landing on my cheeks as he snarled at me, appeared in my head. The unremitting fear I had lived with for years stole my breath. The knowledge that I must've snapped and retaliated brought me to my knees. 'What have I done? I'm sorry, I'm so, so sorry.'

Laura took a phone from her pocket and tapped the screen. She spoke over my sobs. 'DCI Okoro? Yes. It's time. Emma is lucid. She knows what she did.'

Chapter Fifty
Saturday

I sat at the desk in the police interview room, opposite DCI Okoro and a woman police officer he introduced but whose name I'd already forgotten. A duty solicitor sat to my right, and to my left was Laura. They'd explained to me that she would stay throughout the interview, acting as my appropriate adult. I was glad she was there. Funny how quickly things can change. I could smell her perfume. I found it reassuring now.

DCI Okoro explained the format of the interview, but his baritone voice had an underwater quality that washed through me, then away. As he spoke, I watched the way his jaw moved. The harsh light highlighted pockmarks in his skin and I wondered if he'd suffered from teenage acne. Maybe that's why he'd grown that goatee. An ingrown hair bulged at the edge of the beard, a white head contrasting with his dark skin.

'Do you understand, Emma?' he said through swishing waves of noise.

'Sorry?'

'Do you understand what I explained just now?'

I nodded. It wasn't that his words didn't make sense, it was more that they didn't penetrate my tired brain. I was even more exhausted than before. I suspected it was the tablets Laura had given to me when I broke down at Heaton Place. She'd been kind. She'd been trying to help me all along; I could see that now. We both knew she wasn't officially allowed to prescribe medication, but she saw I was in emotional agony and secretly gave me a mild sedative before the police car came, and another one before this interview. Although, it didn't feel mild. More like I was being held in liquid, like I was floating in a bubble and everything from the outside had to work its way through something viscous to get to me.

'For the tape, Emma, could you confirm you have heard and understood?'

'I understand.'

'Thank you. I know this is hard for you, Emma, but I need you to tell me about Connor, so I can get a picture of your relationship before the evening in question. Can you do that for me, Emma?'

I covered my mouth as sobs heaved out. Since the moment I'd realised the image of Connor's body was real, other scenes kept appearing in my head. Awful memories, of me cowering in the corner of our sitting room as he hurled obscenities at me, of him gripping my wrists and shaking me.

'You seem upset, Emma,' said DCI Okoro. 'Can you tell me what's making you feel like that?'

I moved my hand from my mouth, a string of saliva

attached to my palm stretching then snapping. 'Connor was abusive,' I said, my voice sounding loud in my head. 'He was coercive and sometimes violent. He controlled every-where I went, who I saw, he intentionally and methodically distanced me from my friends and family. He intimidated and degraded me, and I lived in constant fear ...' The understanding of how Connor had infiltrated my mind and infected me with his own voice broke through the fug of exhaustion and medication and shattered my sense of self into a million pieces ... 'And I didn't realise ... not prop-erly ... until ...' The next words stalled in my mouth. I still couldn't believe what I'd done.

DCI Okoro rubbed his hand across his mouth, his beard making a scratching sound. 'You're saying you were obliv-ious to this abuse?'

I nodded. I understood the incredulity in his voice. If I was him, I'd find it hard to believe too.

'Can you remind me of your line of work, Emma?'

'No,' Laura barked. 'Don't do that. You don't get to do that.' I turned to see her face flushed and angry. 'This is what's wrong with the police service in this country,' she said. 'If you had the first idea about how insidious perpe-trators of abuse can be, if you had any real concept of how they drip-feed their language, even their thoughts, into the minds of their victims, then you wouldn't use that tone.' She huffed and crossed her arms. 'If I had my way, every single police officer would have to read Emma's papers on intimate abuse before they were allowed to go on the beat. Maybe Connor Best might not have—'

'As you point out, Emma is an expert in the field of domestic abuse, so you can see—'

'You can see how skilled these men are,' Laura finished for him. 'If Emma can be targeted, despite all her knowledge and expertise, then God help mere mortals. I'm not surprised she snapped when she realised what was happening to her. Are you?'

DCI Okoro turned back to me. 'Is that what happened, Emma? Did you snap that night?'

I looked at Laura through my tears. I was so grateful for her intervention, but I knew she couldn't help me now. She wasn't there that night. I was. 'The memories are still fragmented,' I said, 'but I do remember kneeling over Connor ... Connor's body. I know he was bleeding and that the front of my shirt was covered in blood.'

DCI Okoro reached into a Perspex box by the side of his chair. He drew out a plastic bag with a knife inside and laid it on the table between us. 'Have you seen this knife before?'

I stared in horror at the dark red on the serrated blade. I nodded.

'For the tape, please, Emma.'

'Yes,' I said. My pulse pounded in my ears; the feeling of being underwater returned. 'It's one of the knives from the block in our kitchen.'

'And can you tell me what you did with this knife after you snapped?'

I shook my head. 'I don't know. I don't remember.'

'I think you do,' said DCI Okoro, softly.

'I don't,' I said. 'I promise I don't. I would tell you if I did. I just want this to be over, but I don't remember.'

DCI Okoro sighed. 'I'd like to believe you, Emma, but you seem to have rather a selective memory.'

I looked up, confused.

'I'm referring to the night I came to your room at Heaton Place,' he said. 'I was there that evening because I'd learned you'd been taken out without my permission.' He glanced accusingly at Laura, then back to me. 'I asked if you'd been at the facility all day. You said you had. When I asked if you were certain' – he took a notebook from inside his jacket pocket – 'you replied, "I think I'd remember."' He closed the notebook and pursed his lips. 'Sounds ... selective to me.'

'That wasn't ...' I floundered. 'I was lying because I didn't want Melanie to get in trouble.'

'Do you remember wiping your prints from the handle of the knife?'

'What?' I was swimming against a riptide, being dragged in a direction I couldn't control. I couldn't breathe. 'No, I don't remember ...' I gasped for air. I was drowning.

'You don't remember that, then?' His voice was cold. 'I'm sorry, but that seems a little convenient to me. I could understand if someone was so traumatised after something as harrowing as stabbing their abusive husband they immediately lost their memory, but' – his lips pursed for a moment – 'to pause long enough before that psychotic break to clean their prints off the murder weapon?' He ran his hand over his face again. 'Nah, doesn't ring true, does it?'

'I don't remember,' I said, looking from Laura to the

solicitor. The sympathy on their faces told me they couldn't help me. Looking back at the knife coated in Connor's blood, I understood I didn't deserve help. I had taken a life. I was worse than Sarah's abuser. The agony of that thought made me want to smash my head to pulp against the interview-room wall. I turned back to DCI Okoro. 'But I must've done. I must've stabbed Connor, then wiped my prints from the knife. It's the only explanation. I don't remember, but I admit it. I confess.'

Through the pulse in my ears and the sea of medication, I heard DCI Okoro's voice saying, 'Emma Best, I am arresting you for the murder of Connor Best,' before the sound crashing in my head became too loud and I disappeared under the waves.

Chapter Fifty-One

Two Weeks Later

A rapping sound nearby jolted me awake. Slowly, I turned my head towards the open door, where someone was knocking on the frame. I lifted my weighted lids and directed the muscles in my neck to move my heavy skull. I was rewarded for the enormous effort of focusing by the sight of someone familiar. Her knuckles stilled against the wood. I stumbled through the fog of my brain to find her name: Melanie.

'Emma,' she said. There was a hesitation in her voice that suggested a question. Was she checking it was really me sitting in this wipe-clean chair? I could understand that. When I looked in the mirror earlier in the day, I didn't recognise my sunken face either. I instructed my cheeks to pull back the edges of my mouth in a smile.

'She's not really engaging,' said a wiry man who was standing behind Melanie. 'Don't expect too much.'

I felt a prickle of indignation. If they had any idea the effort it took to breathe, to swallow, to fight the bloodied images of my dead husband that had surged into my head when Laura told me the truth, and had tortured me every second since, then they might stop expecting me to find the strength to speak.

Melanie gingerly stepped into the room. It was so like her nervous entrance into the therapy room the first time we met I could have wailed. How deluded I'd been. How ill. I could see now that I'd been struggling long before that awful night. Harvey had tried to help me, suggesting Connor and I might benefit from relationship counselling. I couldn't bear to face up to what my life had become, so I cancelled my supervision sessions. When Harvey came to visit me last week, he said he was sorry he hadn't done more. But what could he have done? I was too entrenched. I was no longer my own person; I was Connor's puppet.

I licked my dry lips, realising I probably looked more sick now with my unwashed hair and drooping eyes, but at least I knew who I was, where I was. I was a murderer, in a prison psychiatric hospital, where I belonged.

'Okay if I sit here?' Melanie said, her hand fluttering over the bed. When I didn't reply, she perched on the edge of the mattress. Her eyes flicked around the room and I wondered what she thought of my new world. It wasn't much different to my room at Heaton Place with its narrow single bed and almost empty wardrobe. The bedside unit even had a plastic cup of water on top. Here though, nurses and orderlies buzzed in and out constantly, and the noise was like a hive of bees.

'I came to . . .' She paused. I waited. 'I wanted to explain why we did what we did. I suppose I wanted you to know it never sat right with me.' She ran her index finger over the rough skin at the side of her thumbnail. 'I mean, it was a means to an end, but ... the process ...' She lifted her thumb to her mouth and tugged at the skin with her teeth.

'Tell me about the process.' My voice crackled with lack of use. She looked at me, mouth slightly open, as though a dog had just spoken. To be honest, I'd surprised myself. It was the most I'd said since I was brought here, but an unfamiliar alertness rose in me when I saw her in the doorway of my room and I was trying to harness the first hint of sharpness my gelatinous brain had offered in days.

'Okay, right.' She wiped her thumb on her jeans. 'Well, you know how you'd been at Heaton Place for three weeks and none of the treatment was working?'

I nodded. The effort of moving my head made me want to close my eyes and sleep. I grabbed at a fully formed thought. It told me I needed to be wholly awake to hear what Melanie was saying.

'That's when Laura approached us with the idea of therapeutic fibbing.' She scrutinised my face, as though trying to work out whether I was following what she said. I forced myself to nod again. 'She was new to the facility. She'd previously worked in geriatric care, and used that method a lot before. When she heard about your case, she arranged a meeting with the management and suggested we try kick-starting your recall by bringing in elements of your life before to ... to sort of stimulate your memory.'

She ran her hand over the white bedsheet, smoothing out the creases. We both watched her hand move back and forth. 'I didn't feel entirely comfortable with it, to be honest. I suppose that's why I'm here, to try to explain it to you. Or maybe to justify it to myself. I don't know.' Her hand slowed to a stop. She didn't lift her eyes from it. 'In geriatric care, therapeutic lying is more like bending the truth to stop a patient becoming agitated because they either can't remember or believe something different. What Laura proposed we tried with you was far beyond that. It was creating an alternate reality. From the research I've done, the treatment isn't meant to be about deceiving the patient, it's supposed to make them feel safe and secure.'

My mind went back to Heaton Place. The last thing I'd felt was safe and secure.

'Anyway, the police wanted answers, so the managers agreed to let Laura work with you for a week. She put the team together and told us the plan. I was glad she offered to pretend to be the patient. I wouldn't have felt comfortable with that.' She glanced up at me, then back at her hand. 'But, in the end, I felt like I had to do more lying than she did. I started to question whether it was ethical . . . It came to a head just before I took you back to your house. Me and Laura argued, but she persuaded me it was for your own good, so I went along with it.'

The memory of her sitting in Connor's chair while I begged her to call the hospitals brought tears to my eyes. I let them fall.

When Melanie looked at me, her face crumpled. She went into the small en suite and brought out a wad of toilet roll, handing it to me without meeting my eyes. 'I'm sorry,

Emma. I probably shouldn't say this, but I didn't think it was right to take you back to where it ...' She shook her head. 'But Laura said DCI Okoro had sanctioned it, and she was my superior ...' She sighed. 'Now, I know he hadn't okayed it. I should have known – I mean, it was a crime scene. Apparently, your mum was allowed to have the place cleaned after Forensics had finished. I'm not even sure Laura had checked that. Imagine if ...' She shook her head. 'Sorry. I suppose it would all have come out if there was a court case, and Laura would have got in trouble, but since you've confessed ...'

I held the rough tissue in my lap but let the tears fall on to the back of my hand. They settled on the skin momentarily, then rolled in uneven tracks on to my jogging bottoms and soaked in.

'God, I'm sorry. That was insensitive,' she said. 'I don't really know why I'm here.' She rubbed her nose with her palm, then clasped her hands together in her lap. Her movements were familiar; comforting almost. I realised she was the nearest thing I had to a friend. 'I'm so sorry if I was part of something unethical.' Her voice cracked. 'I've left Heaton Place now,' she said. 'I got the job at Bethlem.' She looked me in the eye briefly. 'I wanted you to know.' She looked around the room again. 'Is there anything I can do? Can I get you anything to make you more comfortable?'

I sensed she had said what she needed to, and her desperation to leave brought more tears tumbling on to my cheeks. I shook my head and forced the words to come. 'No. But thank you.'

The soles of her boots clattered on the floor when she stood. She paused, looking down at me, her face earnest. 'I hoped it would end differently.' She swallowed. 'When we were in your kitchen, I was willing you to remember what happened. All the time we were there, I was waiting for something to click, for everything to come flooding back, for you to remember seeing someone slipping out . . . or . . .' She laid a warm hand on my shoulder. 'I'm sorry you went through what you did, Emma. I'm sorry it ended like this.'

I sat, frozen in the chair, the noise of her retreating footsteps muffled by the sound of my heart suddenly slamming against my ribs. Click. She was waiting for something to *click*. I was back there, in my house on that night. It was as clear as if it was happening in that moment. I'd just opened my front door, and everything was quiet. I could feel the key in my fingers and sense that the air was too still. I heard the thud on the hall floor as I dropped my bag and shouted Connor's name. There was no reply.

That's when I heard it: the sound of the back door clicking closed. I vividly remembered now that it occurred to me that Connor must've taken the rubbish out. I recall thinking *miracles do happen*, because he never voluntarily put the rubbish out.

I definitely heard the click of the back door. But it wasn't Connor. It couldn't have been, because when I went into the kitchen he was lying on the tiles in a pool of blood. I remembered it all so clearly, my shriek of anguish, the sting of pain when I dropped to my knees, the feel of his still-warm skin under my fingers when I searched for a pulse.

The click of the back door closing.

'Melanie!' I leapt from the chair. 'Melanie, I've remembered something.' I ran into the corridor, bolting past open doors. 'Melanie,' I shouted, rushing past hands trying to catch me. 'There was someone else there,' I yelled, as fingers grabbed my shoulders. 'It wasn't me.' I wrenched myself free, but more hands gripped me. It was harder to shout over the noise, and the arms around my middle constricted my lungs. 'I didn't kill him!' I screamed. 'It wasn't me.' The noise around me was too loud. I gasped at a sharp sting in my arm. Then the world faded to black.

Epilogue

Laura

If I'd walked away when I'd discovered Connor was married, then none of this would have happened. But I didn't, and I can't change that. You have no idea how much I wish I could.

I'm writing this account to get it out of my head, like a confessional, I suppose, although I don't expect to be forgiven. Some things are unforgivable, aren't they? I'll burn it afterwards, but I hope that getting it down on paper might help me move on.

The first thing I need to say is that Connor insisted his marriage was over ... but it was complicated. He swore he and I were meant to be together for the rest of our lives and, as soon as he could extricate himself from his difficult wife, we would be. Fool that I am, I believed him.

I'm ashamed now that I didn't recognise the warning signs after the first time I met him in that wine bar. There were clear red flags: love bombing, vigilant attentiveness, the sharing of vulnerabilities. I even fell for the bullshit about his abusive father. Bastard hooked me and reeled me in. It's like he wrote the textbook on how to make a woman emotionally captive. Perhaps he took one of those Andrew Tate courses I read about in the news.

When I realised what kind of man he really was, my first thought was that he must've suffered some childhood trauma to have turned out like he did. But I was falling into the age-old trap, as if I didn't know any better. I shouldn't blame his childhood. The simple truth is that it was arrogance and inflated entitlement that made Connor into the self-aggrandised, abusive prick he was. It was entirely his choice to behave as if his needs and desires had priority over anyone else's. His working-class Scouse parents didn't fit with the image he had of himself as a high-flying counter-terrorism officer, so they were discarded, along with any other truths which didn't fit the idea of who he was, or how he deserved to be treated.

I feel dreadful that Emma's paper, which was published shortly before the *incident*, was what made me realise that the minor changes in his behaviour were, in fact, clues about his true personality. When I read her take on how intimate abusers groom their targets, I realised *I* was Connor's new target. He'd already suckered me into feeling like I couldn't live without him. I'd even got to the stage where I was justifying his actions to myself using *his* language, believing I was responsible for the temperature of our relationship, that if anything went wrong, it was up to me to apologise and put it right.

It's so unjust that Emma woke me up to the dysfunctional relationship I was having with her husband, despite still sleepwalking through her abusive marriage herself. He'd worked so hard on her that she didn't have a clue that he had inveigled his way into her head years ago and had been controlling her like a fucked-up puppet-master ever since. She knows now. It's tragic she can't use what she's learned to help other women any more. When she's recovered, I hope she does write that book she's been planning.

The day it dawned on me that I was being manipulated, I looked back over my relationship with Connor and understood he'd been grooming me as clearly as if I was watching it happen to someone else. That evening I went to his house to tell him the game was up. I absolutely did not plan to kill him. I swear on my life I just wanted to regain some power. I wanted him to feel exposed, to know that somebody saw past his carefully constructed veneer. I wanted him to know he'd lost control for once. What happened to Connor was a terrible mistake, unlike everything he did. If anyone was premeditated, it was him.

I wanted to throw him off balance before I confronted him, so I sneaked around the back of his house and tapped on the kitchen window. He was sitting at the table, scrolling through his phone. His face was incredulous when he saw me, then it turned dark, but he opened the back door and I marched in and said everything I'd planned to. He never was one to accept culpability, so he tried to smarm his way out of it, telling me I'd misinterpreted him, then, when I didn't listen, he started yelling and flinging insults. I should have been prepared for that. I wasn't.

I made the mistake of screaming back. That's when he

grabbed my shirt. He dragged me so close to him that I could feel the heat of his breath on my face. I remember his spit landing on my lips as he snarled at me and threatened me. I was terrified. I feared for my life.

When he let me go, I fell backwards, hitting my spine on the corner of the sink. The rest is a bit of a blur. I feel a connection with Emma in that. I know I must've grabbed a knife from the block on the worktop, but I don't remember anything else clearly until I heard Emma's key in the front door.

I was in shock myself, after . . . what happened. I quickly wiped my prints from the knife and dropped it at the sound of her key in the lock. Then I let myself out of the back door as she was shouting hello from the hall, making sure the latch clicked locked behind me. It sounded as loud as gunfire to me and I was terrified she'd heard it, but by the time the police arrived I was long gone, and they had no reason to look for anyone else. They had a body, a suspect, a murder weapon. And the only living witness couldn't remember a thing.

When I heard Emma had suffered a psychotic break and had been admitted to the unit where I'd recently taken a job in the hope she could be made well enough to stand trial, I panicked. If she remembered she was innocent, an investigation would uncover my relationship with Connor. I had to think on my feet. That's when I came up with the therapeutic lying plan. I had no idea if it would work, but I couldn't see any other way out for myself. I had a good reputation for the therapy I'd done with geriatric patients, and nothing else they tried had worked, so I persuaded the management it could help to reinstate her memory. All the while I was desperately planning how to recreate memories which would condemn her. I know how callous that sounds. I truly wish there'd been another option. Other than the obvious, I mean.

When I explained that the method was generally used to ease the lives of dementia sufferers and hadn't been trialled with patients experiencing amnesia through trauma, I also promised to let the top dogs take credit if it worked. As I predicted, that was enough for them to give me carte blanche. It makes me sick to my stomach when I think about those puffed-up morons in Management slapping each other on the back while Emma languishes on a psychiatric ward.

When I got the go-ahead, the deceptions started to pile so high I thought they might crush me. I put the small team together: my junior psychologist, Melanie, and orderlies Julie and Aidan. I felt as uncomfortable about the lying as they did, so I offered to act the part of patient myself, to save Melanie having to compromise herself any more than necessary. I didn't let them know I'd be using actual events from Emma's life that I'd learned through Connor. They thought I'd just done a lot of diligence. I was diligent. I had to be. There was a lot at stake for both of us.

I almost came clean the day Emma and Melanie left the facility to go to Emma's house. I lied about it being sanctioned by the police, but I was running out of time and the pressure was unbearable. When Melanie said she wasn't comfortable ringing me instead of Connor's office at the Met, I tried hard to persuade her it wasn't unethical. We both knew it was. A low point was casually mentioning I'd be the one writing her reference for the new job at Bethlem. After that conversation, I was so revolted with myself I actually vomited. I essentially blackmailed a colleague. I don't recognise myself.

Melanie is a good person, but Julie has a dark side. It only took me hinting I knew about her unseemly relationship with that creep Aidan to get her to follow my instructions without question. I could no longer sleep by this point. I spent every night awake, simultaneously hating myself and plotting what I had to do next. I realised Julie being in the next room to Emma was convenient because she could hear when she was in the shower and slip in to take the lanyard. I felt awful about making Emma second-guess herself, but it was the only way I could see of making her think she might have done something as horrific as ... as stabbing someone. Connor had told her she was mad enough times for her to believe it when inexplicable things happened to her. Of course, despite my denial, I knew all about the Bray case and presumed making a mistake like that would have knocked her confidence even more. I used that knowledge to add another layer of confusion and self-doubt.

Leaving the wedding ring under the mattress was another low point. I pretended to struggle with the morality of planting evidence, but allowed Julie to persuade me it was simply an aide-memoire, or words to that effect. I suspect that, when Emma accused Aidan of assault, Julie would have done anything to discredit her and get her out of the way. I knew DCI Okoro wouldn't give us Connor's actual wedding ring but, to my eternal shame, Connor had always taken it off before we had sex, and I'd once examined it when he was asleep and seen the engraving inside. It had made my insides shrivel with envy back then. Now, I'd swap this guilt for that feeling in a heartbeat. I bought a cheap silver band, had it engraved with their initials and coated it in fake blood. Julie never questioned how I knew about the inscription.

When things die down, I'll make sure that Emma's complaint against Aidan is properly investigated. She didn't deserve to be targeted by that creep. She didn't deserve any of this. But then, neither did I.

The weird thing is, I wish I could talk to Emma about what happened. In different circumstances, this would make a brilliant case study: examining how two psychologists were taken in by one man, and the aftermath.

Melanie's started her new job now, and I'm thinking of moving on myself. My experience might be of some use helping the victims of domestic abuse. If I carry on Emma's good work, that might make some small reparation. It's a tragedy that her promising career was cut short. If I take over where she left off, it will be my silent tribute to her.

And I could help a lot of women. Victims who have been targeted by abusive men. Victims like us.

Acknowledgements

My first thanks go to my exceptional editor, Lucy Dauman whose vision, masterful insight and enthusiasm for *The Woman in Ward 9* spurred me on to make it the very best book it could be. Thank you to brilliant editor, Sophie Wilson, for pushing it over the finish line with the lovely and ever-helpful Isabel Martin. You three, along with the wonderful team at Headline, have made publishing this book a hugely enjoyable adventure.

To my agent Laura Williams, thank you for the rounds and rounds of early edits, and for making sure I am always in the room. You listen, advise and act, and knowing you always have my back makes everything about this rollercoaster ride easier. There's no one I'd rather drink Old Fashioneds with.

My early readers, Emma Warburton, Heather Moore, Suzy Oldfield, Hannah Maynard-Slade, and Aine Loughrey, I don't know what I'd do without your wisdom and guidance. Thank you.

I'm eternally grateful to Suki Greaves for answering

my questions about some of the mental health conditions addressed in the book, and to Bev Thomas for helping me thrash out tricky plot points.

Readers and book bloggers make the online book community a wonderful place to hang out. My special thanks go to the admins of The Bookload, The Fiction Café Book Club, and Fiction Addicts (SDBC) for their generous support.

To my parents and the old friends who are always there for the highs and the lows, Jodi, Julie, Tracy, Katherine, Claire, Sam and Si, thank you for being my foundations. My brilliant writing buddies have become the walls of my house; endlessly supportive and always there to help me with the buffeting when things get stormy.

Since I've started this metaphor, I'll end it with my family, John, Eva and Isla. They keep the rain off and the warmth in. They are my home.

I hope you enjoyed *The Woman in Ward 9*. If so, please consider leaving a short review. I read and appreciate each one, and reviews can help other readers discover new authors, for which we are always grateful!

Credits

*Naomi Williams would like to thank everyone involved
in the production of* The Woman in Ward 9

Editorial
Lucy Dauman
Sophie Wilson
Isabel Martin

Copy editor
Sarah Day

Proof reading
Kate Truman

Audio
Ellie Wheeldon

Design
Alice Clark

Production
Victoria Lord

Marketing
Ana Carter

Publicity
Lily Birch

Sales
Becky Bader
Sinead White

Rights
Grace McCrum
Ruth Case-Green

Contracts
Helen Windrath